Spark of Destiny

A Jake Desmet Adventure Book Two

Gail Z. Martin

Larry N. Martin

e-book ISBN 978-1-64795-056-9
Paperback ISBN 978-1-64795-057-6

Spark of Destiny Copyright © 2023 Gail Z. Martin and Larry N. Martin
Cover art by Lou Harper

The right of the author to be identified as the author of this work has been asserted in accordance with the Copyright, Designs and Patents Act 1988.

All rights reserved. No part of this book may be reproduced in any form or by any electronic or mechanical means, including information storage and retrieval systems, without written permission from the author, except for the use of brief quotations in a book review.

This is a work of fiction. Any resemblance to actual persons (living or dead), locales, and incidents are either coincidental or used fictitiously. Any trademarks used belong to their owners. No infringement is intended.

SOL Publishing, an imprint of DreamSpinner Communications, LLC

SPARK of DESTINY

A Jake Desmet Adventure

GAIL Z. MARTIN
LARRY N. MARTIN

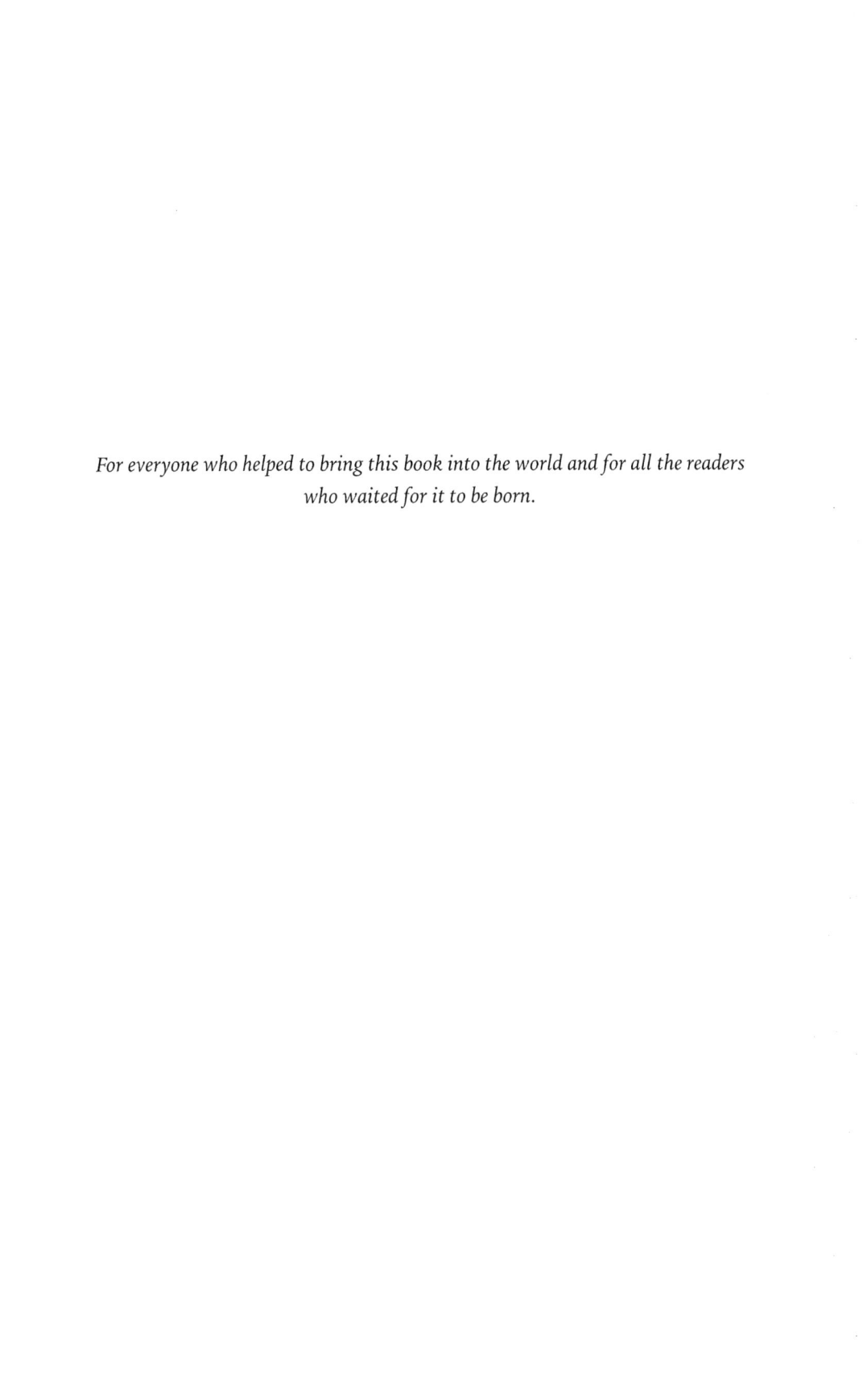

For everyone who helped to bring this book into the world and for all the readers who waited for it to be born.

Chapter One

1898

"And for heaven's sake, be *careful*," Catherine Desmet admonished as Jake grabbed his briefcase.

"I'll do the best I can, Mother." Jake leaned in and kissed Catherine on the cheek. "You know how these things go."

"Exactly. Henry is still in a snit over the last time," Catherine reminded him.

Jake managed not to roll his eyes, although he knew his mother privately shared the opinion that his elder brother was overly dramatic. "Henry is *always* in a snit."

"And it wasn't our fault about the shootout in front of the house," his cousin, Veronique LeClercq, added helpfully as she clutched a small carpetbag. "We didn't know they were going to try to blow us up."

Catherine closed her eyes as if counting to ten. "No, it wasn't our fault. We did what we had to do. But Henry doesn't really understand these things." She sighed. "And neither do the neighbors. I haven't been invited to tea nearly as often since then."

"All part of saving New Pittsburgh and the world," Jake said, which was not an exaggeration. Unfortunately, the full story behind the danger had to remain a secret, even—or maybe especially—from Jake's temperamental brother.

"He's still upset that your father named you in his will as the managing partner instead of him. I tried to explain more than once that primogeniture is out of fashion, but you know your brother."

Unfortunately, all too well.

"Hey, Jake! Are you coming? The carriage is waiting." Rick Brand, Jake's best friend and business partner, stood in the doorway. "Wilfred has the luggage loaded."

"Do try not to cause an international incident," Catherine said. "I still have a few social club memberships remaining, and it would be a pity to get dropped from my Bridge group."

"We've got to go," Jake said apologetically, silently grateful for the opportunity to escape. "I'll send you a telegram from Key West."

Jake gave Nicki his arm as they descended the steps to the driveway, where the carriage waited.

"You know Aunt Catherine worries about you, for good reason," Nicki murmured.

"I understand. But she also knows it goes with the job as it did for Father."

Nicki met his gaze. "I think that's *exactly* what she's afraid of."

Jake winced. His father, Thomas, had been killed by a dark witch's curse.

"Point taken." Jake kept his voice low. "But unless we give up the company entirely, risk is part of the business."

"Cady promised me she'd drop by as often as possible while we're gone," Nicki reassured him. "She and your mother love playing Whist and working jigsaw puzzles. Plus, they read most of the same potboilers, so there's always something to talk about."

Cady McDaniel was a friend of Nicki's and the head librarian at the Pennsylvania College for Women. "She sent her apologies for not being here to see us off." Nicki dropped her voice. "You know she fancies you."

Jake squirmed. "We're friends." He left unsaid that he was quite taken with Cady in return, but circumstances hadn't lent themselves to acting on that attraction.

"Are you two done arguing?" Rick teased.

Wilfred, the Desmet family's butler, took the small bags from them and stowed them away. "I hope your trip is successful and extremely boring," he said with his usual dry humor. When put to the challenge, Wilfred was an excellent sharpshooter and fiercely loyal to the Desmet family.

"Maybe we can bring back some fresh citrus as a peace offering." Jake gave Nicki his hand to climb into the carriage amid her full skirts. Rick was already inside and helped to pull her the rest of the way.

"Bribery can be very effective." Wilfred winked. "Especially since your mother is quite fond of fresh orange juice."

"Keep an eye on her," Jake told Wilfred.

"Always."

Jake swung up to the running board and looked to their driver. "Ready, Charles?"

Their coachman nodded in assent, he was a *werkman*, one of Adam Farber's more advanced mechanical men, and a longtime employee of the Desmets. Charles was average in height and build and dressed as befitted his station, with a billed cap that hid the lack of hair. Unless someone were to look closely, they wouldn't notice he wasn't human. He often served as their coachman and was strong and fast enough to provide extra security.

"I believe we still need Mr. Kovach," Charles replied in a mechanical monotone.

"I'm here." Mark—Miska—Kovach hopped onboard. "Wilfred already stowed my bags. I had to go back to get a couple more guns." He pulled back his jacket to reveal a shoulder holster in addition to the sidearms Jake knew his friend had at the small of his back and in his belt. "Can't be too careful."

"Looks like the gang's all here," Jake said. "Take us to the Aspinwall train station, Charles."

Wilfred remained standing on the carriageway with his hands folded in front of him as they pulled away. Jake thought he glimpsed his mother watching from the parlor window.

"Maybe this trip will be quiet and peaceful." Jake Desmet leaned back in his seat as the carriage pulled onto the road. "For a change."

Nicki gave a decidedly unladylike snort. "Sure. We're heading to the southernmost point in the United States during a naval war just offshore. What could possibly go wrong?"

Rick chuckled. "I like to think I'm as optimistic as the next fellow, but things never go that smoothly for us. Although I'm hoping for a bit less shooting this time around."

"I bet there will be explosions." Nicki sounded far too excited about the prospect. "Those always seem to happen."

"We're going to try to go two whole weeks without explosions or being shot at." Jake stared out the window.

"Let's hope so," Rick said with uncharacteristic fervor. "The bloody Spanish Navy is only ninety miles offshore."

Jake stretched out his long legs. He was just under six feet, with a lean, athletic build. His angular features and intense blue eyes took after his late father. Recent losses showed in those eyes, making him appear older than his twenty-six years. Even here in his family's carriage with its protective modifications, he wore a shoulder holster with his favorite Colt Peacemaker.

"We are definitely not going there to get involved in any of that." The direct look Jake gave Nicki would have made most people avert their gaze. Nicki just smiled, a glint of excitement in her eyes.

"Now where's the fun in that?" she teased. "And aren't we involved—indirectly—by virtue of Brand and Desmet spiriting sensitive cargo out of Cuba at the eleventh hour for a secretive group of collectors?"

Nicki adjusted her skirt and crossed her booted feet at the ankle beneath the voluminous petticoats that hid her Derringer pistol. Slender with violet eyes and dark, ringlet curls, Nicki had demonstrated her spitfire personality and strength of will more than once when the chips were down.

"Jesus, Nicki, you make it sound like some tawdry spy novel," Rick chided in a fond tone. "Don't be spinning up adventures for us. We've barely had time to recover from the last time."

Brand and Desmet handled delicate, expensive, and sometimes questionable cargo for its very rich, very privacy-hungry, and occasionally supernatural clients. They moved art and antiquities for the Fricks and Carnegies of the world and quietly helped long-lived or immortal vampires and warlocks re-acquire cherished possessions that had been lost through the centuries.

Often the objects they handled were cursed, haunted, or magical, requiring specialized skills. In the regrettably not infrequent cases where original ownership was hotly debated, a successful run depended on a fast airship or an excellent brace of carriage horses.

Jake and Rick had recently stepped into the company's day-to-day management following the death of Jake's father and the semi-retirement of Rick's dad, who had founded the firm together.

"With luck, nothing about this will drag us into saving the world—or even Florida." Jake hoped with all his might that would be true. Their last big job led to his father's murder and a series of dangerous encounters with mad scientists and dark warlocks, as well as nearly unleashing an ancient evil on the world.

"Except for the top-secret cargo on a sunken ship that's either magic or alien, I couldn't agree with you more." Nicki kept a straight face except for a twitch of a smile that touched her lips.

"Except for that." Rick's heavy sigh conveyed his ambivalence about this run. Jake couldn't fault his best friend for being wary.

Rick's father favored a European education for his son. And despite his fondness for cricket, Rick had hurried back to the United States as soon as he graduated, picking up the friendship with Jake that had started in childhood. Rick was the same age as Jake but blond with light blue eyes, a few inches taller and leaner, and he carried a Remington revolver as his gun of choice.

"Sorry I was running late." Kovach matched Jake's height and had a soldier's build, dark brown hair, black eyes, and a perpetual five o'clock shadow. Kovach was the head of Brand and Desmet security as well as being a close friend.

"Problems?" Jake asked.

"I hope not." Kovach kept his gaze fixed out the window, constantly on guard. "I've got four men in place at the station to make sure nothing goes awry with boarding the train. I wish we could have gotten on at the Shadyside station."

"They don't have room for the Pullman cars," Jake replied. "Trust me; Henry pitched a fit over the 'inconvenience' of having to go all the way to the other side of the river. We were lucky that Mr. Flagler decided to speed up his construction timetable. Otherwise, the line to Key West wouldn't have been done for years."

Brand and Desmet's business required frequent travel. Sometimes Jake and the others traveled in the company's airships, but the nature of this trip was better suited to making the journey by train. The private Pullman cars, as well as specialized cargo cars, had already been hitched to an engine the company contracted for the trip.

"I'll feel safer when we're aboard the train," Kovach muttered.

"Really, Miska. The carriage has steel-reinforced sides, bullet-proof glass, and a built-in Gatling gun, and our coachman is perfectly capable of holding his own in a fight," Rick said. "You worry too much."

"Worrying is what I do best," Kovach grumbled.

"I thought that was brooding," Rick teased.

"That's second-best." Kovach's smile made it clear he enjoyed the banter.

"I'd have felt better if Renate hadn't had a premonition about 'darkness ahead,'" Nicki fretted. Renate Thalberg, a powerful absinthe witch, had passed along a warning that morning. Unfortunately, her divination didn't supply details on the meaning of the cryptic phrase.

"We'll figure it out." Jake didn't want to admit that the prediction made him jumpier than usual. "We always do."

They crossed over the Allegheny River into an area that was less thickly settled than the city proper. Large open spaces with trees had

Spark of Destiny

not yet been filled with houses and shops. Traffic thinned, leaving them one of the only carriages on the road.

Kovach shifted, trying to see more from his window.

"Is there a problem?" Rick asked.

"Gut feeling," Kovach admitted. "Something's not right."

Charles thumped three times, his signal that they had pursuers. The four travelers in the carriage pulled their guns.

"Get down!" Kovach ordered just before a hail of bullets pinged against the steel plates in the carriage doors and struck but didn't shatter the special glass in the windows.

Charles pushed the horses to a gallop, forcing Jake and the others to hang on as the carriage bounced and jostled.

Rick and Kovach crouched and opened the compartment above their bench, revealing a specially-mounted Gatling gun that rose above the roofline, a different location than in their other carriage. Jake and Nicki moved to see what they could from the windows without making themselves targets. Jake flipped a latch in the corner, and the gun's controls and a periscope activated, descending to give Jake a full view of what was going on outside.

"Five gunmen on horseback," he reported. "We're ahead of them, but they're gaining."

They crouched on the floor since the metal panels only went as high as the windows. Bullets dug into the upper section, splintering wood. Getting into position with a full carriage to fire the swivel-mounted gun made for a tight fit.

"Any civilians?" Kovach maneuvered to get a better look.

"None in sight. I'm opening fire. Brace yourselves." Jake worked the controls, spraying the road with gunfire. "Two down, three to go," he reported, jaw tight.

Shots tore into the top of the carriage, blasting a hole.

"More shooting, faster please." Rick tried to angle his body to protect Nicki, who worked to fire her Derringer out of the hole.

Jake swiveled the gun again, raking the road from side to side. One more pursuer fell, and the other two fled. "That's it." He watched until he felt sure no more attackers were waiting to ambush them.

"Nice shooting," Kovach remarked.

"We're going to have to file a report about the damage," Rick lamented.

"Next time, I want to fire the gun," Nicki sulked.

"Everyone okay in there?" Charles shouted.

"Peachy," Jake replied. "How about you?"

"I am well, sir. No damage taken," Charles said.

"How close are we to the station?" Jake asked.

"Another mile. I don't observe anything out of the ordinary ahead, but you should take cover, just in case," Charles replied.

Nicki bumped Rick and jostled him to move. "You're standing on my skirt."

Jake and Kovach kept an eye out for another ambush, but the last mile passed without incident. They pulled up to the train station, where four of Kovach's armed guards ran to surround the carriage.

Charles jumped down and wrenched the carriage door open. Wood splintered, and the damaged glass cracked but did not shatter.

"Everybody on the train," Kovach ordered.

Flanked by the security guards, Jake and the others hurried to board.

"Any idea who sent the bully boys?" Kovach asked as they climbed the steps to the waiting private Pullman car.

"More running, less talking!" Nicki gathered her skirts as they piled into the car, slamming the door behind them and locking it.

Kovach went to the speaking tube that connected to the engine compartment. "Everyone's onboard. Let's go."

They tumbled into the car's parlor and collapsed into the armchairs as the train pulled out of the station.

"I've got no idea," Jake belatedly answered Kovach's question. "But it's got to be connected with what's going on in Key West. I just don't know who—or how."

Jake and the others found their sleeping rooms and took some time to freshen up and calm down. Their private rooms were small but well-appointed. Each boasted a lofted bed with an armchair and writing desk beneath, as well as a sink, commode, and closet. On a secure shelf near the chair, Jake found that a bottle of his favorite whiskey had already been stocked together with crystal tumblers.

Splashing cold water on his face cleared his mind. Jake ran a comb through his hair and straightened his tie, trying not to look like he'd been in a shoot-out worthy of the Wild West.

He poured himself a drink and sat for a while, puzzling over the attack. Business in the New Pittsburgh area had been quiet of late, and the matter that took them to Key West was the only notable situation.

We helped our Havana clients airlift art and antiques to Key West for the duration of the war. Nothing military. Not even any "special acquisitions" for our immortal customers. Nothing in the airlift was supposed to be dangerously magical or haunted. There shouldn't have been any disputed ownership issues.

So why were people shooting at us? And who sent them?

Because the odds are good that whoever targeted us will do it again.

He finished his drink and closed his eyes, enjoying the rocking motion of the train for a few minutes. All too soon, he left the comfort of his armchair and stretched, knowing the others would be gathering in the parlor prior to dinner.

Rick and Nicki looked up from playing cards as he walked in.

"Where are Miska and Adam?" Jake asked. Adam Farber, a friend and genius inventor, was also along for the trip.

Rick played his hand before answering. "Miska went to check on his security detail and ensure their arrangements were in order. Adam is holed up in his room working on who knows what."

Jake took a seat near them but waved off an attempt to have him join the game. He still felt jittery and lacked the concentration for cards. Instead, he paged through a magazine, focused more on the pictures than the articles.

The long trip had been timed to make the most of traveling overnight. When arrangements were made, Jake hadn't thought much about that, but after the attack he worried if they had made themselves more vulnerable by moving in the dark.

Too late to change things now, although I'll bet Miska has switched up plans with the security guards over what happened.

Jake availed himself of the pot of tea and tray of light snacks set out to tide them over until the meal. He saw that Rick and Nicki had done so as well. Under normal circumstances, using the Pullman cars was Jake's favorite way to travel because it was much like being in a private hotel on wheels.

Jake lost track of time and was surprised when an older, distinguished man stepped into the doorway and cleared his throat quietly to gain their attention. He wore a black waistcoat and trousers, with an immaculate starched white shirt.

"Welcome aboard. Dinner is served. If you would be so kind as to move to the dining room," Edward, their butler, announced.

Jake, Nicki, and Rick followed Edward and found a thin young man with sandy-brown hair and silver-rimmed spectacles waiting for them.

"You're up early, Adam," Jake teased about the odd hours the wunderkind inventor tended to keep.

"I loaded my stuff into the cargo cars this afternoon, and I don't have much to tinker with away from the lab," Adam Farber replied as they all took their seats at the table. "Mostly, it's working out equations in my notes. I'll need to make progress on some of my projects at Tesla-Westinghouse when we get back to New Pittsburgh, so I don't want to fall behind."

Jake doubted that the brilliant inventor would lose time due to accompanying them. Adam seemed to subsist entirely on coffee, half-eaten sandwiches, and nervous energy.

"I see you brought a friend." Rick nodded toward the gleaming metal man who stood silently in one corner.

"I didn't like leaving Ben in my room alone." Adam sounded unconcerned that his mechanical assistant was not human.

Jake and the others were used to Adam's eccentricities. His clockwork creations, called *"werkmen,"* had saved their lives more than once. Ben was the newest of Adam's prototypes, similar to Charles and Lars but specifically altered for their mission.

"It's been a busy day, and we're just getting started," Kovach said. As head of Brand and Desmet security, Kovach rarely seemed to sit still. But where Adam's twitchiness reminded Jake of a squirrel,

Spark of Destiny

Kovach moved like a wolf, restless and lethal, which made it easy to remember he had gained his experience as an Army sharpshooter.

"Problems?" Rick asked.

Kovach shook his head. "No—just busy keeping it that way."

They gathered around the table set with monogrammed silver and China place settings bearing the "B&D" company insignia. Edward's assistant poured water and a round of wine while Edward served a chilled cucumber soup.

"My boys asked me to pass on their compliments for the meals," Kovach told Edward. "Good food and plenty of it is definitely the key to their hearts."

Edward remained stoic, although Jake saw his pleasure at the remark from the twinkle in his eye. "Thank you. I'll relay that to the cook."

The primary Pullman car had six bedrooms as well as a sitting room, dining room, and galley kitchen. Jake, Rick, Nicki, Adam, Kovach, and Edward slept in the main car. The kitchen staff and security detail had bunk cabins and their own seating area on a second car. Behind that was a warded cargo car specially created to contain objects with supernatural energies, as well as a car with some of Adam's larger inventions.

The lead car was as well-appointed. Its comfortable parlor had dark wood paneling, sapphire blue carpet, upholstery, velvet draperies, and brass accents. It served as secure transportation when Jake or Rick needed to travel on business, as well as providing visible evidence of the company's success. The fact that the windows were bulletproof and the siding and undercarriage had been reinforced to withstand Gatling gun fire went unmentioned.

Everyone remarked on the refreshing soup. A salad of fresh greens in a vinaigrette dressing and hot yeast rolls came next. During the first courses, the conversation remained light, focused on headlines from the newspapers that Edward had picked up that morning at one of the train stations, studiously avoiding the matter for which they were hurtling toward the farthest point in the country.

Jake knew the polite fiction of light conversation was doomed to end sooner rather than later.

"Nelson has been monitoring the telegraph chatter since we left New Pittsburgh," Kovach said as the main course was served—roasted chicken with root vegetables in a fig sauce. "Diego helps with any Spanish transmissions we pick up."

"Hear anything important?" Jake was less interested in his food than Kovach's update.

"It looks likely that the skirmishes between the US and Spanish navies are going to escalate." Kovach paused for another bite. "I won't be surprised if we're not in a full shooting war very soon."

Nicki murmured a curse in French. "Is it unavoidable?"

Kovach grimaced. "All wars are 'avoidable' if the people on high wish it. I get the feeling that the US and Spain are spoiling for trouble. I doubt Cuba's much in favor given that they'll be smack dab in the line of fire, but no one's asking them."

"All because of the *Maine*?" Rick looked guilty for talking with a mouthful of yeast roll.

The *USS Maine* had exploded under questionable circumstances a few months before, providing a perfect excuse for the US to gin up backing for a war.

"They're all saying it's because of the *Maine*, but my money's on the *Vincente's* cargo," Kovach told them. "I'll give the details after dinner. With Adam's help, I think we stand a good chance of getting to the prize first—although we might have to fight for it."

Jake and Rick exchanged a glance. *Here we go again.*

The assistant returned to take their dinner plates while Edward served slices of freshly baked lemon chess pie and hot coffee. When they returned to the parlor, decanters of scotch and gin, together with crystal tumblers, were on a side table. Edward had also set out a fresh pot of coffee and cups with a plate of sliced fruit and cheese.

Kovach and Adam opted for coffee, although Adam's right leg already jittered, and he fidgeted endlessly with a pencil. Jake and Rick chose scotch while Nicki poured herself a gin and tonic water. Ben followed them from the dining room and took up his post in the corner of the parlor.

"Thanks to Farber's clockwork turtles—" Kovach began.

"Techno turtles," Adam interrupted. "Like my mecha-pigeon."

Kovach looked amused. "Techno turtles," he repeated. "Anyhow—thanks to Farber's mechanical sea creatures, we'll be able to 'see' more of the area around the wreck of the *Vincente*, which will give us and our team of wreckers an advantage over anyone else out there who might be interested."

Jake remained in awe of Adam's creations, many of which were top-secret or licensed by Tesla-Westinghouse. But with Brand and Desmet's patronage, and the lab built to replace the one lost in a recent explosion, Adam always saved his best creations for them.

"Do the…techno turtles…feed signals to a *werkman*?" Rick leaned forward.

Jake knew engineering entranced his business partner, who liked to hang around Adam's lab and help as much as the inventor genius would permit.

Adam nodded. "Yes, the signal distance is limited—I'm working on that. But with a *werkman* on the same frequency and in a boat over where the techno turtle is swimming, we get a decent view of what's below."

"We're lucky that the *Vincente* isn't in one of the deepest areas, but it's still a challenge for human divers," Kovach continued. The photograph on the corkboard behind him showed a non-descript freighter that was the unfortunate ship.

"Who else is looking for the *Vincente*?" Nicki proved she had been paying close attention in contrast to her studied ennui.

"We're not sure," Kovach admitted. "We know that whatever unusual cargo it carried, the ship was chartered by an experimental laboratory in Spain heading to a secret facility in Havana. A false manifest and travel plan were filed with port authorities. It left at night without fanfare. The ship belongs to the private fleet of a Spanish financier, who also employs the crews."

"Convenient," Rick muttered. "Sure cuts down on dockside gossip."

"I'm certain that was part of the plan," Jake acknowledged. "These wreckers we're working with on Calusa Key…how do we know we can trust them?"

Kovach gave a predatory smile. "Andreas Thalberg vouched for them. He said they are descendants of a family he's worked with for lifetimes. I got the feeling that one of his long-ago wives might have been related."

Andreas Thalberg, a powerful vampire warlock, was one of their allies in New Pittsburgh. His connections and occult knowledge, forged over centuries, had aided them on several occasions.

Jake turned to Adam. "Have you been able to figure out more details about what this super-secret cargo is?"

Adam looked to Kovach, who nodded for him to go on. "Tesla-Westinghouse keeps tabs on competitors and so does the Department of Supernatural Investigation. When they hear rumors of some new shiny invention, they show up in my lab wanting me to copy it for them."

The inventor sighed. "It's like chasing ghosts. Actually—ghosts are easier to find. All the spies usually have are rumors, which have probably been exaggerated because agents are always one-upping each other. They describe something that might not even exist and expect me to whip one up from scratch."

"So we don't know what was in the cargo?" Rick's skepticism had a sharp edge.

Adam shot him a look. "We don't have all the details, and what we know is rumor and speculation. There are reportedly two main items. One is a tourmaquartz converter to adapt anything that runs on steam to work on the mineral instead. And the other is a magical relic. There doesn't seem to be any agreement over what the relic does. I've heard several theories, but the most likely is the ability to command sea monsters—or their ghosts."

"*Mon Dieu*," Nicki murmured. "Those would change the game."

Kovach nodded. "Not just the game—the balance of nations. I

wouldn't be surprised to find that shady secret players in our country have been trying to invent the same things, but it looks like Sombra—the company that is linked to the cargo ship—might have done it, or at least stole it, first."

"Sombra…that means 'shadow' in Spanish," Nicki mused. "Not disconcerting at all."

"Sombra stays in the shadows," Kovach confirmed. "But there are rumors that it's got links to some really bad players. Drogo Veles's name came up, as well as some of the witch dynasty families who rule the Caribbean."

"Why do I get the feeling you've been chatting with Mitch Storm and Jacob Drangosavich?" Jake fixed Kovach with a look.

"Mitch and Jacob have a soft spot for Farber and want him to stay alive," Kovach replied. "They're the only government agents I'd even partially trust. As soon as they heard about the *Vincente* wreck and got wind of Brand and Desmet's Havana airlift, they sent over some useful information—knowing it would go right to you." He glanced from Jake to Rick.

"The airlift? That wasn't supposed to be in the government's sights," Rick protested. "Private business—helping some of Brand and Desmet's established clients safeguard their treasures when war broke out."

Nicki cleared her throat. "You mean running a secret emergency evacuation of objects that could be priceless, haunted, or magical for a group of very wealthy, very private individuals to avoid having their treasures confiscated?" Airships had ferried precious cargo from Havana to Key West, managing to evade both pirates and official channels.

"I think I just said that," Rick sparred but without heat behind the words.

Nicki sniffed in mock annoyance. "I said it better."

"The Havana airlift isn't all that different from what Brand and Desmet does every other day," Jake protested. "It's not the first time we've needed to spirit irreplaceable occult items out of unstable areas."

"True," Nicki replied. "And there's nothing that says government agents didn't know about those trips too."

Jake didn't like the implication, but had to admit Nicki was probably right. "What about Veles? Do you think he's involved?" That might explain who was behind the ruffians who chased their carriage. For all his magic, Veles tended to favor intimidation and violence to warn off involvement in anything he considered to be his affairs.

"Possibly. We're looking into that," Kovach replied. "As for the airlift, it's a bigger haul for more players than usual. That raises government interest right there. Brand and Desmet didn't do anything illegal, and as far as we know, the cargo owners were just safeguarding their own stuff. But really rich people tend to have their fingers in a lot of pies. There's a reason the government folks keep tabs on that sort."

"Go back to the witch dynasties for a minute," Rick interrupted. "Why are they involved?"

"If the *Vincente's* cargo is magical, they're going to want it for themselves," Jake replied. "And if it's technology that might let mere mortals compete better with witches, they'll want to stop it."

"There's a rumor that they might already be involved—or at least that some of them are sniffing around to see if throwing in their lot could give them an advantage," Kovach said. "I don't want to see either Spain or Veles come out ahead."

Ten witch families dominated the magical community of the Caribbean. Spread among the islands were five "major" and five "minor" families who vied for control from their bases. Jake felt sure it was no coincidence that their locations could be traced into a pentagram on a map.

"Can they beat us to the cargo?" Rick asked.

Kovach shrugged. "I don't know. One of the wreckers we'll be working with is a water witch, so I'd have to think that Caribbean based witch families would have people who could also influence the weather and the tides. I would bet we have better technology, but I don't know if they could use magic to locate the cargo."

"Then it's a race." Nicki's bright eyes and the flush of excitement

Spark of Destiny

confirmed Jake's suspicion that his cousin had joined their expedition, in part, for the thrill of the chase.

"A very expensive, potentially deadly one," Kovach pointed out. "From the information Mitch and Jacob passed along, the witch dynasties aren't the only contenders. Drogo Veles has been making the rounds of the Eastern European countries which stand to benefit from political instability on the Continent."

Kovach sighed. "Spain will claim the cargo is theirs, although it belonged to a private company—with questionable connections. And of course, there's the current 'unpleasantness' between Spain and the United States—with the wreck site on the edge of what might become a war zone."

"I'm just glad we have backup with some experienced wreckers," Adam said. "I've got my submersible and a diving suit, and Ben can function underwater. Plus, the techno turtles. But I'd rather not have a shooting match going on over our heads."

"Will Cullan be bringing the airship? I'm happy to run the Gatling guns again." Nicki grinned, likely still basking in her role helping to stop a nearly world-ending situation.

"I sincerely hope that won't be necessary," Jake said. "We want to avoid precipitating a war between major powers."

"Pish posh." Nicki dismissed the concern with a wave of her hand. "Where's your sense of adventure?"

"I thought you stowed away on this trip because you wanted to visit an old friend from boarding school?" Rick teased.

"I most certainly did not 'stow away,'" Nicki corrected with mock outrage. "I brought far too much luggage to go unnoticed. And while I came along to visit Liliana, I would generously give up some of my free time for gunnery duty." Her eyes gleamed with the long-standing game of wits.

"And besides, Lili is a spirit medium. She's got real ability," Nicki added. "So if we need to talk to ghosts, I'm sure she'd help. Her husband has some magic as well, if I remember correctly."

"A medium? That might come in handy." Jake's eyes narrowed.

"The *Vincente* went down with all hands aboard. No survivors. I wonder if any of the crew would respond if she tried to reach them?"

Rick fixed him with a look. "Do you know how many shipwrecks are in this area? That would be like raising an army of the dead." He shivered. "No thanks. I really hope it doesn't come to that."

The train shuddered, making them grab for something to hang onto. Jake and Rick exchanged worried looks.

"That can't be good." Jake sprinted to the speaking tube that connected to the train's engine room. "What's going on?"

"We've got a situation," Daren McCarthy, the engineer replied. "There's a crossing coming up, but the light signals say the switch is thrown wrong. Best case, we go the wrong direction. Worst case—there's another train heading our way. I'm going to try to slow us down, but you'd better hold on tight."

Their private train had four cars. While that didn't compare to the length or weight of a freight train, Jake knew that stopping a locomotive wasn't like pulling the reins on a carriage horse.

"Miska and I are going to see what's going on. Rick, telegraph the next station and see if they can get someone to the switch and make sure it's thrown. The rest of you, stay seated and cross your fingers." Jake and Kovach sprinted toward the exit, pausing only long enough for Jake to grab binoculars and Kovach to get his rifle.

"You know we can't get to the cab," Kovach said.

"Yep. So we're going to have to go up," Jake replied.

"Do you realize how crazy that is?" Kovach's grin belied the warning in his words.

"Probably not. But there could be hired guns out there. McCarthy's got his hands full trying to make sure we don't wreck. Let's scout and see if we need your sharpshooters."

Jake and Kovach wrestled the door open. Although McCarthy had already slowed the train somewhat, the wind felt fierce.

"I'm going first." Kovach shouldered ahead of Jake and started climbing the ladder on the back of the car.

Jake steeled his nerves and followed. He made it to the top just as the car rocked, straining his grip. One foot slipped from a rung and Kovach reached down and grabbed his wrist, anchoring him.

"It's the side-to-side motion that'll get you," Kovach warned as Jake hauled himself on top of the car beside him.

Smoke billowed from the engine, stinging Jake's eyes and throat. A stray cinder burned his arm. He and Kovach scanned the moonlit area around the track ahead of them, looking for obstacles or robbers.

"There." Jake pointed up ahead where a group of men on horseback waited not far from the track. A makeshift barrier of wood piled on the track was probably intended to force the locomotive to slow even more.

"Go back down—carefully," Kovach said. "Send my boys up with their guns. Have the others watch out for anyone coming up from behind. They might try to sandwich us."

Jake nodded and started to wriggle backward, keeping a death grip on the grating so he didn't tumble off. The train rounded a curve and he rolled, losing his hold with one hand and splaying his legs to slow himself so he could regain his grasp.

His heart thudded as he started down the ladder. Rick was waiting to help him inside, looking anxious. Jake held up a hand to forestall questions until he reached the nearest speaking tube.

"Security—Kovach wants you on the roof of the cars with your rifles—now!" Jake ordered. "McCarthy—we've got trouble ahead; looks like armed robbers on horseback and junk on the rails."

"I see them. You got a plan?"

"Putting snipers on the roof right now," Jake replied. "We'll handle watching the back. Will the mess on the tracks derail us?"

"Shouldn't. We're still going fast enough to plow through—and to give someone on horseback a run for their money," McCarthy assured him.

"Talk to me. What about the switch?"

"It should be green. It's red—which means the switch is turned the wrong way. If we run over a switch that's set wrong, we could derail—or run into another train coming from the opposite direction…"

"Who sets the switches?"

"There's supposed to be an operator on duty at all times. Since we're a private train and not a regularly scheduled passenger or cargo train, we had to file a route plan. That means the operator should be expecting us—and should have already worked out how to avoid another train being in our way."

"Can you get us stopped in time?" The scenery flashed by and the wheels rumbled beneath the cab, giving Jake a visceral feel for just how fast they were moving.

"Trying to," McCarthy replied. "I've managed to slow us some, but this train takes at least a mile to stop, and the switch is just a few miles farther. It's going to be close—and the bandits are between us and the station. Unfortunately, it's all or nothing."

"Maybe Ben can help." Jake turned to Adam, who had joined him. Ben stayed back a few paces. "We saw what Lars could do when he saved us. He's strong and fast, and you've made improvements with Ben, right?"

"Faster than a train?" Rick questioned.

"Maybe. What've we got to lose?" Adam responded, taking the challenge.

"I'm all for not wrecking, so if Ben can help, let's see what he can do." Jake turned to Rick. "Miska and his boys are on the roof. I need you, Nicki, and Edward to watch from the back vestibule and shoot anyone who tries to catch us, just in case they come at us from both sides."

"You know she's going to be way too excited about another shoot-out," Rick said over his shoulder as he headed toward the parlor. Jake looked back to Adam.

"Can your *werkman* jump and not be destroyed?" Jake's skepticism was clear in his voice.

Adam nodded. "I did the calculations—it should be possible. He'll have some scratches and dents, but he should be able to withstand the impact."

"And he knows what to do?" If their lives weren't on the line, Jake would be fascinated. Right now, with his stomach tight with fear, he could only think of survival.

"I've given him instructions." Adam looked like a proud and worried papa.

Jake opened the sliding door. The wind whipped around them, and Ben's metal feet clanked as he lowered himself onto the step. Then without looking back, he loosed his grip on the handle and tumbled from the train.

Adam lurched forward to see how his clockwork progeny fared, yanked backward by Jake before he risked falling as well.

Jake's heart caught in his throat, doubting that anything could survive that fall. Adam's jubilant shout pulled Jake from his thoughts in time to see a gray streak racing with the train.

"Go, Ben!" Adam cheered.

"He's got to beat us there, or it's not going to do any good." Jake slid the door shut to keep Adam from leaning out to watch.

"He will. I believe in him," Adam replied stoutly.

"Can he keep up his speed that long?" Jake focused on technicalities to avoid worrying about an impending crash.

"Theoretically, yes. I've never had to test it in field conditions—"

"So...*maybe?*" Jake felt less than comforted by Adam's response.

"Definitely, maybe." Adam didn't seem to understand why his companions were upset.

"Go where you can brace yourselves," McCarthy yelled through the speaking tube. "This'll be rough no matter how it goes."

Jake and Adam returned to the parlor, each keeping a hand against the wall as they walked to steady themselves.

They found Edward and Nicki firing out the windows at pursuers who had appeared behind them, bracing themselves on the furniture.

"I have an idea." Adam disappeared into his room and emerged with one of his mechanical turtles. He punched some buttons and withdrew a control box from his pocket.

"What are you doing?"

"Adding reinforcements." Adam gave an enigmatic smile. He went to the door with Jake right behind him, grabbing his belt as Adam set the turtle on the ladder for the roof.

"What's that going to—" Jake stopped mid-sentence when the

turtle climbed to the top and sent a fiery blast at the riders closing on them from behind.

"Good boy," Adam whispered.

The train shuddered and steel wheels shrieked. Kovach's guards traded gunfire with the ruffians ahead while Jake and the others—including the techno turtle—blasted the toughs coming from behind. That complicated matters because the train had to slow to avoid disaster with the thrown switch, but reducing speed before the attackers were driven off played into their hands.

Which was probably their plan.

Jake felt the train slowing but feared it wouldn't be in time and wondered if they would derail or slam into a northbound engine. Neither scenario was good, but one might be survivable.

"Any luck with the telegram?" Jake asked Rick in between shots. Firing from a moving vehicle at galloping targets in the dark was harder than he imagined.

"Sent it. Don't know if anyone received it or if they can get there fast enough."

"Ben will get there in time," Adam promised, loyal to his creation. "Just wait and see."

"Traveling with you is always exciting." Jake could see the fear in Nicki's eyes despite her chipper tone.

"I want a word with whoever is operating the signal station," Jake grumbled. "They had damn well better not have gone out for a smoke and forgotten to set the switch." But he feared the reality might be bloodier—the attendant kidnapped or dead. Maybe just paid to look the other way. He felt certain, deep in his bones, that this was deliberate—meant as an attack or warning. Maybe intended to keep them from reaching Key West altogether, stopping the salvage effort cold.

"C'mon, Ben," Adam muttered over and over.

Rick swore under his breath.

Bullets pinged off the train's reinforced sides. The windows were also special glass, but opening them enough to return fire meant weak spots. Nicki swore fluently in French when a bullet nearly parted her hair and lodged in the woodwork on the other side of the car.

"Watch yourself!" Rick snapped.

Nicki bobbed back up, fired several rounds, and faced Rick with a smirk. "Got him!"

Adam's turtle took care of another pursuer, and their steady volley of fire made the last two fall back.

The train rocked on its rails, and the overtaxed brakes screamed like the damned.

Neither Jake nor Rick was particularly religious, but Jake spared a prayer in case anyone on high might be listening. Nicki's dark curls looked storm-tossed, and despite her grit, she had gone pale as they hurtled toward their fate. Edward, always implacable, now looked seriously rattled, and that disturbed Jake.

The train lurched, signaling they'd run out of time. Jake shut his eyes, held on with all his strength, and wondered if his mother would survive losing him and his father within a few months of each other.

He felt the swerve and waited for the car to careen from its rails and slam to the ground. Jake realized he was holding his breath.

"He did it," Adam whispered, awestruck.

"We're stopping." Rick sounded like he had witnessed a miracle, and maybe they had.

Jake stayed braced, fearing their reprieve was too good to be true. He heard the *clickity-clack* of the steel wheels slow and then go silent. Only then did he open his eyes and dare to believe their good fortune.

Kovach and his men poured back into the car. One of the guard's arms was bleeding. Edward, looking impeccable as always, hurried to get medical supplies.

"The attackers up front are either dead or wounded," Kovach reported. "But a couple of our folks have minor injuries. Could have been a lot worse. Nice work back here. Was that a *turtle* doing some of the shooting?"

"One of mine," Adam replied proudly.

Jake helped Nicki to her feet. Her hands shook as she smoothed her skirts and pushed her curls back from her face. "I'd say that was something to write home about, but we're definitely *not* mentioning it to your mother."

"No kidding," Jake agreed.

A deafening whistle sounded seconds before they felt the car sway as another train roared past them on a parallel track.

That's how close we came to dying. A few seconds longer, and they'd have hit us head-on.

As the others returned to the parlor, Jake went to the speaking tube. "Good job. Thank you for not letting us die."

"Hey, Adam. Come take a look." Kovach yelled from the door.

Adam and Jake climbed down to the tracks. They stopped just past the signal station. Ben stood next to the small wood and glass enclosure. In the glow of the lantern inside, Jake saw blood spattered on the windows and caught his breath, fearing the worst.

"What do you make of that?" Kovach pointed to the long lever that threw the manual switch for the tracks, holding a lantern for Adam to see better.

Adam hunkered down next to the mechanism and studied it in silence for a few minutes. "It looks like someone tried to jam it."

"Damn right," Kovach huffed. "Probably the same someone who killed the switchman. Shot in the chest."

"Shit," Jake muttered. "Definitely not an accident or an oversight."

"Someone's got us in the crosshairs—again," Kovach fumed. "And we've got no idea who or why."

They looked up at the clatter of hooves, and Jake and Kovach pulled their guns. A carriage thundered toward them at top speed until the driver pulled up sharply in front of them.

A man in a railroad uniform jumped down from the driver's seat and his gaze went immediately to their undamaged train beneath the electric lights of the station. "Oh, thank God." He sagged with relief.

It took him a moment to realize that two men faced him with drawn weapons. "I think there's been a misunderstanding," he stammered. "I'm from the next station. We got a distress call about a stuck switch—"

Jake and Kovach exchanged a look and then holstered their weapons. "Sorry. We're just rattled," Jake said.

"Someone tampered with the switch and killed the switchman," Kovach snapped. "This is *not* the way to run a railroad."

"Tampered? *Killed?*" The railroad man paled, and his eyes widened. When he spotted the bloody glass of the switch house, he looked like he might faint.

"What is that metal man? Is he responsible?"

Too late, Jake realized that Ben still stood in plain view. "He's a top-secret government prototype, and he's the only reason we're still alive. He managed to throw the switch—which had been jammed—but got here too late to save the switchman."

"*Top secret*," Kovach repeated. "You'll want to forget you ever saw him."

The railroad man nodded fervently. "Don't worry. No one would believe me. But the switch—"

"You need to get someone out here for a repair and reroute traffic," Jake said. "Whatever the saboteur did to the mechanism, it's dangerous to send any other trains over the switch until it's replaced."

"The switchman—"

"When you get to the station, please contact the police and send them out. Someone killed one man and tried to derail our train."

"Sure. Yeah. Need to send the Railroad Police." The man sounded traumatized. "Are you okay?"

"A little shaken, but no one's hurt," Jake assured him. "We'll be heading on our way as soon as our engineer says it's safe. We put the brakes on pretty hard."

"Thank you for coming out to help." Jake guided the man back to his wagon. "And for taking care of things."

They sent the man on his way. Jake glanced back at their train and saw Nicki and Rick in the windows.

"Nothing else to do here. Let's hope the train's not damaged," Jake said.

"It would be very nice if we weren't here when the cops arrive," Kovach warned. "Adam, Ben—get back onboard."

Jake lagged behind, keeping pace with Kovach. "Did you take a look at the body?"

Kovach grimaced. "Very carefully, from a distance. Single bullet to the chest. Guy probably never saw it coming. Looked pretty recent, which would make sense. Whoever jammed the switch, probably the same guys waiting on the tracks, wouldn't have wanted to do it too far before our train came through."

"They knew our itinerary and came out just ahead of us to wreck the train," Jake concluded in a grim tone. "We're not even in Key West yet, and there's already trouble."

"Did you really think there wouldn't be?" Kovach asked as they climbed back aboard the train.

"No—but I nurture a few hopes now and then."

"Highly overrated." Kovach's lopsided smile took the bite from his words.

They traveled through the night, keeping a moderate speed in case they had another need for an emergency slow-down. When they reached the Key West station without further incident, Jake let out a sigh of relief.

"Mr. Desmet?" the station master greeted him. Jake nodded. "There's someone here to see you."

Jake frowned. "I'm not expecting anyone." Rick and Kovach took a step closer on either side.

"She's been here since first thing this morning," the stationmaster said. "Refused to leave. I asked if I could pass the message along and she said she needed to talk to you in person."

Jake glanced at Rick and Kovach, who shook their heads, clearly as surprised as Jake.

"Okay—let's see what's so important," Jake replied, and they followed him inside the small station.

An older woman sat alone, fingers flying with her knitting. She looked up when they entered.

"Mr. Desmet?"

Jake nodded. "I'm told you wanted to see me."

She set her knitting aside and stood, barely coming up to Jake's chin. "I'm Netty Carmichael, from Cassadaga." When Jake didn't react, a faint smile touched her lips. "Cassadaga is like Lily Dale in New York. A town of psychics. I had a vision, and I came here to give you the message."

Jake had worked with several people who were gifted, so he didn't doubt that psychic abilities were real. Whether this stranger could be trusted remained to be seen.

"What did you see?"

"I saw a man under the water in a metal suit, and a bad storm on the surface. Green lightning strikes, and ghosts arise. I don't know what it means except that you're in great danger." Carmichael's tone indicated she was clearly worried. "I know some people don't believe in psychics, but what I see comes true. That's why I made the trip to warn you."

Jake wasn't sure what to make of the vision, but noted the woman's sincerity in her eyes. "Thank you. I appreciate the effort."

She took both his hands in hers. "Remember—the dead are on your side." With that, she gathered her knitting and walked away.

"What was that all about?" Rick looked as perplexed as Jake felt.

"I'm not sure. That's the problem with psychic visions—they make more sense in hindsight than they do upfront."

"I'm all for staying clear of dead people." Kovach scanned the train station for threats. "Let's get to the compound. We can figure out what the hell is going on once we're safe."

Jake and Rick followed him from the station, but as they presided over loading what they needed into wagons for the short trip to the Brand and Desmet compound, Jake wondered if there was anywhere they could truly feel secure.

Chapter Two

I'd forgotten how large this place is. Been a while since I visited," Rick mused when the carriage stopped inside the company compound.

"It's hot, humid, and the bugs are big," Jake grumbled. "I can't say I've missed it."

"There are palm trees." Nicki looked around with wonder. "Not something you see in New Pittsburgh—or Paris."

Kovach had gone on ahead to check the compound security and connect with the captain of the guards. Adam lagged behind, fussing over unloading his inventions from the wagons. McCarthy and his crew stayed with the train for repairs. Rick suddenly felt out of his element.

"Mr. Brand. Mr. Desmet. And Miss LeClercq. Welcome." Eli Conroy, the compound manager, hurried to greet them. Rick knew that Conroy had been with the company for decades, and that both his father and Jake's considered the man to be a friend as well as a valued manager. He was in his early fifties with thinning blond hair, a yellow bowtie, and a blue and white seersucker suit. His square-jawed face gave him a military look despite his welcoming smile.

Amid the handshakes, Rick thought Conroy looked worried. "Is something wrong?"

"Every day's an adventure." Conroy's laugh seemed forced. "We have a lot of catching up to do—and I'd sure appreciate a briefing on what brings you down to the Keys. But first, let's get you settled. I'll have your bags brought up, and I can show you to your rooms so you can freshen up."

Rick refrained from commenting that they had traveled from New Pittsburgh in high style aboard the Pullman, so they arrived in better shape than if they had taken a regular sleeper train.

A two-story yellow conch-style house awaited them, with a wide porch on each floor and a gabled roof with a widow's walk at the summit. Piers raised the house off the ground to prevent flooding in bad weather. White trim and large windows added charm.

Rick remembered that Conroy lived in the house, a perk of being the compound's caretaker. The building doubled as an office and provided guest quarters for visitors like themselves. A dormitory housed the rest of the workers.

A huge warehouse and an equally large airship hanger dominated the view, along with a barn for horses and wagons. Rick didn't recall how many acres the compound covered, but the high fence and sturdy entrance gates hadn't gone unnoticed. The Brand and Desmet Key West installation had high security, protecting the valuable items that passed through it as well as the people who worked there.

A warm ocean breeze stirred, and Nicki sighed in contentment. "I think I could get to like it here."

"New Pittsburgh gets snow, but it doesn't get hurricanes," Jake reminded her. "I think I'd rather face a blizzard than a tropical storm."

The inside of the house welcomed them with high ceilings, pastel blue walls, white wooden trim, and furniture that mixed Caribbean carved mahogany, bamboo, and wicker. Woven rattan mats covered the wooden plank floors. Linen curtains and swagged sheers replaced the heavy velvet popular in northern homes. The combined effect made the house feel light and open.

Conroy showed them to their rooms—Rick and Jake on one side of

Spark of Destiny

the hallway, and Nicki on the other. Kovach and Adam were at the end of the corridor, while Conroy had a private suite on the first floor. Edward also had a room, while the rest of the Pullman crew stayed with the train.

"While you catch your breath, I'll make sure there's hot coffee and tea with refreshments," Conroy told them. "Dinner won't be for a while yet, but traveling makes a body hungry. Come join me in the parlor when you're ready."

Rick found the guest room as he remembered it, with a four-poster bed of carved mahogany draped with mosquito netting, a writing desk and chair, and a small armchair. Electricity powered the lights and an overhead fan. French doors looked out onto the upstairs wrap-around porch. The shared bathroom connected his room with Jake's. Rick suspected that Miska and Adam also shared, but that Nicki had a private bath.

The house was pleasant and airy, but Rick couldn't shake the sense that something was "off." He doubted the house was haunted—they knew people who could take care of that. Rick decided to ask the others if they also got a strange feeling, although compared to everything else going on, something "creepy" was a minor annoyance.

Although he had showered and shaved that morning aboard the train, the humidity made him look longingly at the bathtub. With a sigh, he resigned himself to splashing water on his face and combing his hair. Once his bags were delivered and unpacked, he could avail himself of a fresh shirt for dinner.

Rick glanced at his reflection, and while not up to his usual sartorial standards, it would do. He was used to winter in New Pittsburgh and back in England, where layering on more clothes was always possible. With the heat, one could only strip down so far and even less in polite company. Pretty as the locale appeared, Rick didn't think he'd be moving south.

When he came downstairs, he found Nicki and Jake already sipping iced tea and nibbling canapés. Rick took the glass offered by the kitchen server and helped himself to a chilled shrimp from the platter.

"Iced tea will cool you off, but there's also fresh coffee to wake you up," Conroy told him.

"Adam and Miska are still getting all the equipment stowed to their liking, and Adam's setting up his lab space," Jake explained. "They'll be along."

They settled into comfortable chairs on the broad deck near a serving table set with a pitcher of tea, a pot of coffee, and a large platter of vegetables, shrimp, and fruit. Rick poured a cup of coffee to go with his tea, hoping it would revive him after a sleepless night.

"Nicki and I were just catching Conroy up on our exciting train trip." Sarcasm laced Jake's voice.

"Definitely something I won't be forgetting any time soon," Rick agreed, and Nicki muttered something in French under her breath that he couldn't translate.

"We didn't publicize that we were coming to Florida for obvious reasons," Jake told Conroy. "But the mishap with the switch was clearly no accident. So that makes me wonder—who's trying to kill us this time? New enemies or old ones?"

"Aren't you just cheery." Nicki gave him a look, but despite the admonishment fondness glinted in her eyes.

Rick leaned back in his chair. "Not that I think Drogo Veles has forgotten us, but even the Department of Supernatural Investigation thinks he's still out of the country, somewhere in Eastern Europe. That doesn't mean he couldn't have minions doing his dirty work, but he's an immortal vampire witch. His attacks are usually flashier than a stuck railway switch or gunmen waiting in ambush."

"But the armed riders could be his idea of warning us off," Jake pointed out. "He's always viewed his minions as disposable."

Nicki nodded. "Veles might have an interest in the *Vincente's* cargo, but causing an accident isn't his style. And he'd want us to know it was him."

Veles had been one of the masterminds behind an illicit tourmaquartz mining operation that had raised dark entities from the depths of the earth and nearly destroyed New Pittsburgh. Rick and his companions—with the help of allies—had bested Veles and his supporters, but not all of them had been captured.

"I agree." Jake's finger traced the condensation on his glass. "But if it's not Veles, then who? And why? If it's about who salvages the *Vincente's* cargo, it seems like our mysterious attacker would do better focused on reaching the wreck rather than crashing our train."

"We keep our ear to the ground here, and I've got contacts with the Coast Guard and the shipping authorities," Conroy told them. "Sombra, the Spanish company that owned the *Vincente* is claiming salvage rights, but given the impending war with Spain, US authorities aren't of a mind to cooperate. Javier Cortez is their representative in Florida. I'd trust a starving gator before I'd turn my back on that man."

"Good to know," Jake replied. "What else?"

"The Keys have a very active wrecker tradition—legal and less so," Conroy replied. "We've contracted with the group that was recommended, and we did some checking on our own. The Boyers are a trustworthy team specializing in supernatural acquisitions, and we've got people watching the wreck area. But to some folks, every sunken ship is a galleon stuffed with gold doubloons. I'll be shocked if we don't encounter competition."

"Okay," Rick allowed. "We've got security for that, and Adam's equipment should give us a leg up on regular wreckers. Is anyone slinging magic?"

"We have a relationship with a Cuban witch who now lives in Key West," Conroy replied. "We've worked with him for other situations. He's reliable—and talented. I figured we'd bring him in on the recovery efforts, if not before."

"Before?" Jake raised an eyebrow.

"There have been…problems…with the cargo in the warehouse," Conroy admitted. "I'm not surprised that some items are haunted or that others possess supernatural energy—might even be cursed. But put them all together in one place, and it's like they're feeding off each other. It's getting worse."

"Tell us what's going on." Rick leaned forward, ignoring his coffee.

Conroy rubbed a hand through his thinning hair. "We've had reports about strange things happening in and around the building—from guards who aren't known for having wild imaginations. Dramatic temperature changes. Footsteps when there's no one else around. Smells that are out of place—perfume, tobacco, limes."

He cleared his throat as if worried they wouldn't believe him. "Scarier stuff too. The guards reported a tall shadowy figure who disappears when they get close and gives off a feeling of dread. They won't patrol alone around the building."

"Has anyone been threatened or injured?" Jake frowned.

"No—thank God. At least, not yet. But weird stuff keeps happening. Crates too heavy for a few men to shift, move in the middle of the night. Equipment turns on by itself or breaks in peculiar ways. No one wants to spend much time in the building because it makes them jittery, like they're being watched," Conroy confessed.

Rick and Jake exchanged a look. "I'm not surprised that the kind of art and artifacts our clients wanted to safeguard includes haunted and occult pieces," Rick said. "But precautions were supposed to be taken in the way items were packed to prevent…leakage."

"If the clients packed in a hurry because of the war, it would be easy to cut corners," Nicki pointed out. "Or if they had servants pack up who skipped special instructions."

Jake sighed. "Guess I need to figure out whose crates are causing the problems and get in touch with the owners. Tomorrow I'd like to have a look at the manifest and see what was declared for the shipment. The clients were supposed to note anything that could be potentially dangerous or magically active. We need to know—but we can't just go breaking into boxes without authorization—it would violate our contracts, and it might be dangerous."

"The friend I'll be visiting is a medium," Nicki reminded them. "She's the real thing. If we need someone who can see and talk to ghosts, she'd be a good pick. I'll find out if she's available."

"Thank you," Jake said. "That could be helpful."

"On the brighter side, I'm looking forward to finding out more about Mr. Farber's new inventions," Conroy added. "The two velocipede prototypes he left for us have come in handy. I trust he has some technology to help with the salvage operation?"

"I've only gotten glimpses so far." Rick's interest came through in his voice. "I can't wait to see what he's cooked up. Adam always exceeds my wildest dreams with his inventions."

In Rick's mind, the velocipedes were a great example of what their genius friend could create that was both practical and amazing. The steam bikes were fast, maneuverable, and powered by innovative secret technology that Adam remained cagy about describing. Rick suspected they used the very rare, very valuable tourmaquartz, but so far, Adam hadn't confirmed that suspicion.

They had polished off the snacks long before a server came out to call them to dinner. "Don't worry about changing clothes—here on Key West, we're quite a bit less formal," Conroy told them. "I'm afraid I'm ruined for ever going back to polite society."

To no one's surprise, Adam requested his meal be sent to the workshop, where he and Ben were busy reassembling equipment that had been broken down for transport. Kovach joined the group, giving his update on the compound's security.

"Fences and wardings are secure," he told them as they started the first course—chilled pineapple and mango soup. "I approve of the sky watchers you've got in place, but if someone does come after us with airships or armed remote mini-ships, we'd be vulnerable."

"We have guns that can shoot anything at low range out of the sky and a couple of Mr. Farber's energy ray machines capable of hitting an airship," Conroy replied. "Short of putting a roof over the place, we're pretty well defended."

"Nice," Kovach replied. "Makes my job easier."

They put aside heavier topics for the rest of dinner, enjoying the fresh fish, local fruit, and lime bars that made the most of local ingredients and recipes.

Conroy entertained them with stories about the birds, animals, and reptiles that frequented the compound and held their attention with a recount of battening down through the most recent hurricane.

"All the wonderful things here have a tradeoff for that awful weather—and those alligators," Nicki exclaimed when he ended his stories.

Conroy laughed. "The alligators aren't hard to avoid, and we've built storm shelters to get us through the hurricanes. But on the plus side, it never snows!"

After dinner, Nicki begged off on account of a "headache" that Rick privately believed meant she wanted to finish reading the penny dreadful that she had barely set aside for the entire train ride. Conroy excused himself to see to unfinished work in his office.

That left Rick, Jake, and Kovach, who took a bottle of bourbon with them to the screened porch. Electric lights hung like glowing fruit from the black cords overhead. Beyond the house, security lights on high poles punched holes in the darkness.

Rick sipped his bourbon and listened to the night sounds, so different from back in New Pittsburgh. He heard the buzz of insects and the hoots of owls, with the rush of the sea beneath it all.

"It's been a while since I've been down here," Jake said after a few moments. "I'd forgotten the charm of this place."

Kovach snorted. "It's too warm, they have big bugs and bigger snakes—not to mention alligators—and the ocean storms try to kill you several times a year. Leave me in New Pittsburgh. I'll take the snow any day."

"Do you think Adam will be ready to start the salvage work soon?" Rick asked Jake.

"I guess that depends on how putting all the pieces back together again goes," Jake replied. "He told me that taking his creations apart to fit into the cargo cars wouldn't hurt anything, but I doubt the parts just pop back into place. Adam makes it all look so effortless that we forget how insanely complex his machines really are."

"Knowing Adam, he'll be up all night," Kovach observed. "Assuming there's enough coffee in Key West."

Jake chuckled. "I wouldn't be surprised if he managed to get his own personal stash of coffee onboard the train, just to make sure he had what he needed."

"Even Adam can't go without sleep forever," Rick pointed out. "If he stays up all night tonight, he's not going to be in any condition to do a diving mission."

Jake held up his hands in a gesture of surrender. "Don't shoot the messenger. I agree with you. But winning Adam over to that idea is a whole different matter."

Rick, Jake, and Adam had become fast friends, patrons to the inventor, and occasional partners in crime. Kovach treated the quirky young genius with amused protectiveness, and they had become very close. For all his brilliance, Adam tended to ignore the impact of his inventions on the world outside his lab and the reasons why power-hungry people might covet his genius and his creations.

The sudden screech of alarms broke the evening silence. Lights flared at the warehouse, making Rick blink until his eyes adjusted.

"What the hell?" Kovach was out of his chair and running seconds later, gun drawn. Rick and Jake followed hard on his heels, weapons in hand.

"Someone's out there." Kovach pointed. Rick spotted the velocipedes and jumped onto the nearest one, twisting the key and gunning the engine to take off in pursuit.

Kovach muttered a string of curses in Hungarian and followed on the second motorized bike while Jake ran behind them, watching the shadows for movement.

By now, the compound's guards were streaming toward the warehouse, fanning out and surrounding the perimeter.

Rick spotted a dark figure between the warehouse and the house and veered to intercept. Kovach must have guessed his intent because he circled around, moving to cut off the stranger from the other side.

Rick caught a glimpse of the thief, dressed in black with a scarf covering his face. The man held a wrapped bundle in his arms and changed course when he saw the pursuers, zigzagging away from the house to escape the motorbikes.

"Put down the package and get on your knees," Kovach shouted above the din of the engines.

Instead, the thief jumped at Rick and tried to wrest away control of the velocipede. Rick hung on, kicking at his attacker while trying not to wreck the motorbike. The bike careened crazily as they fought. Rick veered sharply, timing his change of direction with a kick that sent his assailant sprawling.

Rick shifted to drive tight circles around where the man hunched in the dirt, joined a moment later by Kovach, who parked his bike and drew his gun. Rick stayed astride his velocipede but stopped circling, alert in case the thief made a break for it.

"Put the package on the ground and your hands in the air!" Kovach shouted. Footsteps pounded as Jake and the rest of the compound guards caught up.

The thief set the cloth-wrapped bundle on the ground. Part of the object inside slipped free, the glow of the security lights revealing what looked like a white porcelain clock.

"Don't touch the bundle!" Jake's voice rang out. "It's cursed!"

Jake, Kovach, and Rick held the thief at gunpoint while a guard cuffed the man and hauled him to his feet.

"Shit. Wilson—what in blazes were you doing?" the guard growled.

"You know him?" Rick glanced from the thief to the guard.

"Yeah—this piece of shit is one of the warehouse workers." To emphasize his disdain, the guard gave his prisoner a hard shake.

In the distance, Rick heard the rumble of an engine and saw a vehicle heading their way from the direction of the house.

Jake stepped forward, close enough to look the thief in the eyes. "Who sent you? You didn't just happen to pick that particular object out of everything in the warehouse."

"That there's Mr. Desmet," the guard supplied, shaking the man again hard enough to rattle teeth. "You'd better answer if you know what's good for you."

Rick wondered if the man could string two thoughts together after all that. He appeared to be in his mid-twenties, wide-eyed, and terrified, not exactly what Rick pictured as a high-end burglar.

"A man offered me money if I'd do a job for him," Wilson said. "Pa's been sick, and Ma's behind on the rent—I've been sending her nearly all my pay, but it's not enough."

He licked his lips nervously and then continued. "The fellow knew I worked here, and he seemed to know about Ma being in a bind. Offered me enough to pay her rent for a year and Pa's doctor bills too. Told me which box to go to in the warehouse and what to take out. I didn't bother anything else, I swear."

"Why were you heading for the house?" Kovach asked.

"He told me to put the clock in Mr. Desmet's room but not let anyone see me. Then I was supposed to meet him in the far corner of the compound, at the back gate, and he'd pass me the money. No need to go outside the fence."

Jake and Kovach exchanged a glance, and Kovach roared off on his velocipede in the direction of where the payoff was to take place. Rick doubted, with all the alarms and hullaballoo, that the mastermind would show up.

"Did you know the man who hired you?" Rick asked.

Wilson shook his head. "No. Once a week, we all go into town to do shopping, stop by the Post Office, and get a drink or two. I met him in the saloon. Never saw him before that, but he knew all about my folks. Didn't see him talking to no one else."

Conroy clattered up in a motorized wagon. On the bed was a large gray lump. Rick recognized it as a containment box, most likely made from lead and etched with powerful runes to contain the power inside and keep other magic out.

"Got here as fast as I could," Conroy said apologetically and glanced at the white clock on the ground.

"You working with anyone else?" the guard asked Wilson with another shake.

"No. Just me."

"Your call, Mr. Desmet, Mr. Brand," Conroy said. "What do you want done?"

Rick gave a nod, ceding the decision to Jake. "Lock him up and put a guard on him. I'll have more questions in the morning and get our witch friend to see what he can make of the curse. Don't take any chances with him." They watched as the guards dragged the man away.

"What about the item?" Conroy looked toward the clock that lay half-covered by a velvet bag.

"Don't let anyone touch it barehanded," Jake instructed. "I recognize it from a conversation I had with its owner—but it was supposed to stay in Cuba. Use an iron shovel to put it in the box. We'll need to contact the owner—and that witch of yours—and see if the curse can be broken."

"Do you know what kind of curse it held?" Rick asked, unable to help his curiosity.

"It's a rather nasty piece of work." Jake stood shoulder to shoulder with Rick as they watched Conroy carefully deposit the clock in the lead container. The other guards dispersed, sent on an extra perimeter check by their chief.

"If I recall correctly, it was a betrayal gift. The clock itself is very pretty, very expensive. But it puts a killing curse on the recipient once they accept the present. Whoever takes possession and touches the clock dies within a few days," Jake replied. "For obvious reasons, that sort of object was definitely *not* supposed to be part of the airlift shipment."

"So the thief—"

"He's out of luck unless our client or Conroy's witch knows how to undo the spell," Jake said.

"You think the person who sent him to fetch it knew that?" Rick suspected he already knew the answer.

"I'm sure of it. Saved him the payoff and eliminated the witness. As long as the guy who put him up to it didn't touch the merchandise, it would have been a slick crime."

Conroy walked over from the wagon. "How do you want the situation handled, sir?"

"Let's keep the cops out of it for now," Jake replied. "Nothing was removed from the property, and the item was recovered. If we can't break the curse, Wilson will be dead in a couple of days. If we can cure him, give him a choice between a job on one of our cargo ships or getting turned over to the police."

"Very well, sir," Conroy said.

"And since someone's obviously watching our people and looking for vulnerabilities, I'd like you to meet with each of the employees here—no matter what their level or position," Jake continued.

"Find out who has debts, sick family members, money problems. Offer a plan to fix them in exchange for their loyalty and continued employment. Someone could always offer a small fortune in exchange for dirty work, but the less desperate people are, hopefully, the less easy they are to tempt," Jake said.

"I'll set those meetings up tomorrow, sir. And I'll have the manifest for the airlift cargo on the breakfast table." Conroy climbed aboard the rattletrap wagon and chugged back toward the house.

The purr of the velocipede's engine was a stark contrast as Kovach rode up beside them.

"Anything?" Jake asked.

Kovach shook his head. "Nothing inside the fence, and nothing I could see outside it, either. Once they knew we were on to the thief, I'm sure they lit out of there."

"Thank you both for your quick action," Jake told Rick and Kovach. "You handled those bikes like pros."

Rick grinned. "No harm in having a little fun on the job. You want a ride back?"

Jake shook his head. "No thanks. I'd rather walk, clear my head. I'll meet you on the porch—there's still bourbon left."

Rick and Kovach raced each other back, not testing the bike's limits but competing to arrive first. They parked the velocipedes and retreated to the porch. Nicki had pulled up a chair and poured herself a drink.

"All that noise made it impossible to read," she mock-chided, taking a sip of bourbon. "So I decided to come down and see what all the fuss was about."

"Guy tried to sneak a cursed clock into Jake's room. Didn't go well." Rick shrugged and refilled his glass.

Kovach stared out into the darkness, and Rick guessed he was surreptitiously keeping an eye on Jake. "You think he's doing okay?"

"Jake?" Rick asked. "Reasonably so. Better than right after his father died. Why?"

Kovach shrugged, still on watch. "Just wondered. It's my job to worry. He's seemed a little…pensive."

"His dad died, Father stepped back from day-to-day management, and dropped running the business into our laps." Rick walked up to stand beside Kovach and hitched a foot into the railing. "It's been a douse of cold water for both of us. I think we've been getting used to the change."

"In other words, you both had to grow up," Nicki observed with a repressed smile. "Become respectable businessmen instead of vagabond rogues."

Rick nearly fell into her teasing trap to rebut the characterization but recalled too many occasions filled with gunfire and daredevil escapes and refrained, refusing to be egged on by Nicki's chuckle. "Maybe you're right."

Jake walked up the steps to the porch as Rick and Kovach returned to their seats.

"Here you go." Rick held out a freshened glass with a couple of fingers of whiskey. "It'll help you sleep."

Rick had traveled in close quarters with Jake often enough to know that both of them had nightmares, reminders of close calls. Alcohol didn't completely guarantee a good night's sleep, but it often bought a few untroubled hours.

Jake nodded his thanks and sat. The group fell silent for a few minutes, and Jake sipped the bourbon, staring beyond the screen into the night.

"Don't let it eat at you, Jake," Rick cautioned, worried about his friend's mood. "We'll figure out who was behind it, and with luck, the curse can be undone."

Jake nodded. "I expected trouble around the salvage operation. I'd been thinking of the airlift being business as usual. I feel like I left my guard down. Now we don't know who's after us—Veles, Cortez, or someone we might not even know is in the game."

"You trade in items that are rare, unusual, and precious," Nicki remonstrated in a gentle tone. "By definition, they're sought-after, usually by the wrong sorts. Even seers can't predict every possibility. Don't blame yourself."

Jake's grunt sounded unconvinced. "First the incident with the railroad switch and the attack on the train, now this. I can't help wondering—what's going to happen when we get to the dangerous part?"

Chapter Three

"There's something out there," Nicki called to her carriage driver. "Go!"

Nicki hurried to look out the rear window, where strange shadows stretched toward the coach. Shades without bodies, they elongated and bunched like a creature running at full speed, closing on the carriage.

Nicki thumped on the front to tell the driver to urge the horses even faster. The carriage jolted as he complied. They were outside the city, in a sparsely populated stretch.

Eerie howling intruded, more like what Nicki might expect in a dense forest than this sunny open land. She had heard wolves many times in the forests of Europe, but whatever bayed now was something different. *Dark magic. Revenants. Monsters.*

Nicki opened the secret compartment and took out a shotgun, loading it with rock salt. She opened the window, climbed halfway out, and fired.

The scatter of salt hit the shadows dead center, and they screeched in pain and anger but barely slowed their pace.

"Miss LeClercq! Please get back in the carriage!" the driver yelled. The wild pace meant they felt every bump in the road. Nicki grabbed the doorframe to keep from tumbling out, but she squeezed off another shot before reloading.

She fell back onto the velvet seat cushions, shoving two new shells into place. She nearly got thrown across the carriage when they swerved. Nicki kept hold of the shotgun with one hand and crawled back to the window, popping up to fire two more shots with accuracy that should have felled a living pursuer.

"*Merde*! They're getting closer." Nicki reached for more shells. A sudden jolt sent the shells rolling across the seat and onto the floor. She scrambled after them, then lost her balance and landed hard on her ass. Cursing fluently in French and English, Nicki retrieved the shells and dragged herself back to the window.

A shadowy appendage grabbed for her. Nicki shrieked and pulled back, firing point-blank into the darkness. She didn't know whether it meant to pull her from the carriage or knock the gun from her hands. Another shadow rose in the window, and she blasted it, forcing a temporary retreat.

Nicki knew the horses couldn't go faster without tipping the carriage, but she doubted she could hold the shadow creatures off much longer. She spared a glimpse out of the front window and realized they were near the gates to Liliana's villa.

We'll never be able to get out to open the gates without those things swarming us.

Are they here to kill us or drag us off?

Did the same person send them who set up the attacks on the train? Or is this a new enemy?

"*Alto*! Stop!" A voice cut through the clatter of hoof beats, loud and commanding.

The driver reined in the horses, and Nicki braced to be overrun by the shadow creatures. She chanced a look out the window, and her eyes widened.

A gray contingent of ghosts surged forward from the elaborate wrought-iron gates, forcing the darkness back and forming a line between the twisting shadows and the carriage.

A hidden man began a chant in what Nicki guessed was Latin. The shades shrieked, a hellish sound that made her clap her hands over her ears. The horses didn't bolt, but their nervous shifting shuddered through the carriage.

The cacophony hit an ear-splitting crescendo, ending with a triumphant command and a final scream.

Everything fell frighteningly silent. Nicki popped the barrel of her shotgun above the sill before she raised her head.

The huge gates swung open and the carriage rolled past them. Nicki's heart pounded, and her breath came fast enough that she thought she might pass out. Fear made her palms sweat, and the barrel of the gun trembled.

"Nicki, darling? Are you all right? It's safe to come out," a familiar voice coaxed.

Nicki warily lowered the shotgun and scanned the lawn until she saw her friends Liliana and Elian standing near the driveway.

The driver opened her door. Nicki smoothed her hair and wiped her palms on her dress, hoping she didn't look too disheveled from their mad flight.

Liliana rushed to meet her. "Oh, Nicki! Are you hurt?" She threw her arms around Nicki and hugged her hard. Elian stepped closer, standing behind Liliana with a concerned expression.

Nicki found the presence of mind to return the embrace before stepping back to look at Liliana.

"What were those things? Why were they chasing us? And did you and Elian make them go away?"

Liliana slipped her arm through Nicki's and started toward the villa while her husband Elian went to talk with the driver.

"They were revenants, manifestations of dark energy. Clearly, they intended harm. As for who sent them, I have a good suspicion," Liliana said. "Let's get you inside and settled, then we can talk more."

Nicki let her friend lead her inside the elegantly appointed home and guide her to an upstairs guest bedroom.

"Go freshen up." Liliana gave her a concerned smile. "Take your time. Lie down if you need to. When you're ready, come downstairs. I'll have a bite to eat ready for us."

Nicki gave her arm a squeeze. "Thank you for saving us. I really thought we were goners. When I said I wanted us to catch up, I didn't have this in mind!"

The door clicked shut behind Liliana, and Nicki collapsed against the wall, feeling suddenly boneless as the adrenaline rush of the fight faded. It took a few more moments to collect her wits and make her way to the bathroom. She ran a cloth under cold water and dabbed at her face and neck as she tried to slow her breathing.

Little by little, her heart slowed to a normal rhythm, and she no longer felt light-headed. The pleasant smell of lemon and verbena soap helped to calm her, and the cold water cleared her mind. Nicki checked her reflection in the mirror, patting her hair back into place and straightening her dress.

She met her gaze in the reflection. "You're safe. Elian and Liliana aren't going to let anything bad get inside. Breathe," she told herself.

Nicki held her head high as she descended the steps and managed a mostly real smile.

Liliana looked up from where she had been reading in a chair and rose to greet her.

"You look better." Liliana swept her gaze from head to toe. "Let's go into the courtyard. There are treats waiting for us there."

She escorted Nicki into the walled center garden alive with brightly colored flowers, ferns, and tall, broad-leafed tropical plants. A café table with rattan chairs awaited them near a fountain. The table was set for two with a spread of pastries and cups for coffee.

"Come—sit down," Liliana invited. "Elian will stop by shortly to say hello. He went to get your driver and the horses settled, and then he'll take a look at the area outside the gate."

"Has there been trouble?" Nicki still wasn't completely over the earlier excitement. "I'm trying to figure out whether the shadows were sent after you—or me."

Liliana sighed. "Hard to say. These are dangerous times. Are you sure you're okay?"

Nicki nodded. "I should be used to things like this. They seem to happen often enough. I'm just a bit jangled."

Spark of Destiny

Liliana pushed a plate of cookies toward her and filled her cup with dark coffee. "Eat. Drink. We can discuss the *situation* when Elian returns."

Nicki bit into a cookie and let out a sigh of contentment. "Do you ever miss Paris?" She thought it was best to change the subject and give herself a moment to relax. She leaned back in the rattan chair and sipped the strong, thick Cuban coffee, holding the sweet flavor on her tongue.

"Sometimes, in the spring." Her hostess, Liliana Mariela Delgado Ruiz, smiled, and Nicki wondered if she was recalling their finishing school days.

"There are times when I miss the city, but I'm happier in America—much to Papa's distress," Nicki replied with a laugh.

"I understand," Liliana agreed. "Madrid and Paris will always be close to my heart, but I have come to love Havana and Key West in a different, special way."

Liliana's home recalled the best of Spanish and Cuban architecture, with light pink stucco walls, arched doorways, and a tiled roof. Elaborate cast iron railings decorated the balconies. In the central private courtyard, a fountain burbled amid a garden resplendent in the wild colors of tropical plants.

Nicki basked in the sense of peacefulness, a byproduct of both good décor and ample magic.

"You and Elian have done well for yourselves," she observed.

Liliana patted the updo that piled her long black hair atop her head, smoothing a stray dark strand into place. Elaborate gold earrings framed her jawline, setting off the warm tones of her skin, brown eyes, and red lipstick. She wore a dress made of lightweight linen, elegant in its simplicity and cool in the sub-tropic temperature. Nicki guessed that amid the decorative blind stitching were protective runes and sigils.

"We survive well," she replied. "Right now, we are estranged from both Havana and Madrid. I don't like sitting out this pointless war even in a very pleasant exile."

"It's not safe for you to go either place?"

49

"No. Our gifts would command a premium, and neither of us wish to be conscripted." Liliana's lips thinned with anger. "Yet we could not sit by idle. Which is why we have allied with your cousin."

Liliana's abilities as a psychic medium had been evident even when she and Nicki attended school together. Back then Liliana tried to hide her talents, fearing the censure of gossips and the priests. Her husband, Elian Diego Lopez Ortiz, drew from his Spanish, Cuban, and Taino heritage in his powerful magic, including deep knowledge of Voudon and Santeria. Nicki could well imagine that generals and politicians might want to weaponize their talents.

"I didn't realize that when I hopped their train to come for a visit, but I'm glad it gives us even more in common." Nicki set her fragile demitasse cup back on its saucer and leaned forward conspiratorially. "Jake, Rick, and I have had adventures that might turn your hair gray."

Liliana's laugh filled the courtyard. "Still the same Nicki after all these years! *Dios mio*, never change, my friend! Always the spitfire, I see."

"Much to Papa's chagrin, I fear," Nicki gave a smile that made it clear she felt no guilt. "He wants grandchildren. I told him to discuss that with my older sister. I want adventures."

Liliana shifted as if to tell a secret. "They say it's possible to have both. So I'm told. But I'm skeptical."

"Pish posh." Nicki made a dismissive gesture. "I don't believe it. I'll probably be one of those wealthy women living in a townhome or a country pied-à-terre in between fabulous travels with my loyal ladies' maid and several handsome dogs."

"My dear, I believe you and I already are very close to that, compared to the stories that I hear of our classmates." Liliana reached out to pat Risa, her papillon, on the head as it sat in her lap. She snuck a sliver of cookie to the dog, and it licked her fingers and favored her with a look of adoration.

"Good for them." Nicki finished off her drink with a gulp. "Lili—you absolutely must tell me how this coffee is made. It's delicious."

"Cubano secret," Liliana teased. "It's the special sugar. For you, I will tell all."

Nicki drew in a deep breath. Flowers perfumed the air, along with an undertone of cumin and sofrito from the kitchen. "Your home is beautiful. I love the garden and the courtyard. So peaceful."

"Thank you." Liliana inclined her head. "But once again, magic helps. Elian protects us well with all sorts of spells and sigils built into the bones of the home itself. Look closely at the patterns in the iron railings, the paving stones, and the colored tiles and you'll see. For my part, I have made sure that only friendly ghosts remain here and that any others have moved on. Nothing left to chance."

"And Luis? Is he here in Florida with you?" Nicki asked. Liliana's older brother had turned heads whenever her family came to visit at boarding school. Only a few years separated them by age, but at the time, he had seemed so worldly and sophisticated.

Liliana's expression darkened, and she looked down. "Luis isn't here."

"Is he still in Cuba? Or Spain?"

Liliana shook her head. "No—at least, I don't think so. The problem is, I don't know. Luis is missing."

"Oh, Lili!" Nicki caught her breath and reached out to take Liliana's hand. "*Mon Dieu*. I am so sorry. What happened?"

Liliana blinked and dabbed at the corner of her eye with a handkerchief. "We aren't entirely sure. Luis is an engineer, very clever. He's worked for Edison-Bell since he graduated from university."

"Was he working on something secret?"

Liliana shrugged. "I don't know. He didn't like to talk about specifics—maybe he couldn't—but sometimes he would get excited about a project, and I could see how happy it made him. He loved his job."

"Do you know what sorts of things he worked on?" Nicki couldn't help thinking that Luis's disappearance probably wasn't random.

"Whenever I'd ask, he would just say 'propulsion systems' and leave it at that. I gather it involves engines and fuels. Luis loved to design and build things. As a child, he tried to take things apart so he could 'improve' them when he put them back together again. Papa nearly lost his mind at finding everything in pieces," she recalled with a sad chuckle.

"Would Luis have any reason to run away or hide?" Edison-Bell was a competitor to Tesla-Westinghouse, the company that employed Adam Farber, their genius friend. The rivalry between the two companies, as with their founders, blazed fiercely as they tried to outdo each other.

"Luis is a pacifist," Liliana told her. "He refused to work on war machines. Needless to say, given his skills, there were many offers. I fear that he has either gone into hiding to avoid being conscripted into the war effort—for either side—or that he's been kidnapped to force him to do that."

"That's terrible," Nicki said, "How long has he been missing?"

"It's been a month since I've heard from him." Liliana's voice faltered. "Usually we connected every few days—a letter, a telegram, sometimes a phone call. He's never gone this long without being in touch." She swallowed hard. "I am afraid for him."

"Does Luis have any magic? I don't remember you ever saying." Nicki knew she was playing detective, but Brand and Desmet had allies and resources that might go beyond Liliana's personal reach.

"That's always been up for debate," Liliana replied. "He doesn't get visions or glimpse the future or talk to ghosts, and he can't move things with his mind. But when Luis is building something, working on the schematics, he seems to…transcend…the world around him. It's difficult to put into words, but I've always wondered if it was a different kind of magic. That's how it always seemed to me."

"What about your magic, and Elian's? Have they given you any clues?" Nicki tried to hope for the best but feared the worst.

"Elian scried when we lost contact. He saw Luis in a dark house, afraid. Elian didn't see anything to hint at the location. Luis seemed to be hiding, not imprisoned," Liliana confessed in a quiet voice. "When we didn't hear from him, I searched the spirits. Fortunately, Luis did not reply."

"Has Elian been able to learn anything more?"

"Elian's gift is not divination, although he has some ability with that. He tried locator spells and auguries, but he said something blocked him. At first, a neutral power," Liliana told her. "Later, something darker."

"If Luis was running away from someone, would he know enough about magic from you and Elian to get amulets or objects that might help him evade pursuit?" Nicki's fingers drummed on the tabletop as she thought.

"Luis always teased me and said that mathematics was the real magic," Liliana replied, smiling at the memory. "But yes, he saw enough of the practice around us to know what might be possible for protections and wardings."

"You said that there was a different energy more recently. What changed?" Nicki's heart went out to her friend. Now that she looked more closely, Liliana did not look like she had been sleeping well, and her always-thin frame seemed gaunt.

"A little over a week ago, I had a nightmare. It was a memory from childhood but horribly twisted. When Luis and I were little, we visited cousins who lived out in the countryside on a large estate. We were city children, and we could find our way around streets and large buildings, but we were hopeless out in nature." Liliana stared off into the distance as if remembering.

"We wandered away from the house and main garden, probably playing hide-and-seek. I remember that there were topiaries and tall plantings. Luis and I went into the boxwood maze late in the afternoon as the shadows lengthened. We got lost, and it started to get dark."

Liliana twisted a gold ring with a cabochon cut garnet as she spoke. "We thought we heard something in the maze. Probably a bird or a small animal, but by that time, we'd gotten ourselves worked up and properly terrified. Luis started to run, I ran after him. We got all turned around and couldn't find the way out. Then I lost him somewhere in the maze. When he realized he couldn't see me, he started screaming."

She sucked in a breath and continued. "Of course, that brought the groundskeeper and our frantic nanny. We weren't really lost and in no actual danger. Mama gave us a scolding about wandering off, but she also fed us hot chocolate and churros to make everything better." Liliana's hand shook as she reached for her coffee.

"In my dream, the maze closed in around us, and something bad chased us through the darkness. It reached for me but couldn't catch hold, but then a hand—or maybe a branch—grabbed Luis and pulled him inside the bushes. He screamed like he was hurt and afraid, and I couldn't get to him. That's when I woke up." Liliana downed the last of her drink with a gulp.

"You are certain Luis is in danger?" Nicki spoke just above a whisper.

Liliana nodded. "I think whatever he was running from found him and took him away. But with this crazy war, where do we even begin to look? The Spanish might want him for their weapons. The Americans might want him to build a better kind of engine. And there are always people during troubled times who play both sides against the middle—gunrunners, smugglers, pirates. If they had an inkling about what Luis could do, they might want to force him to help them."

A maid poured more coffee and brought a fresh plate of guava-filled sugar cookies. Stressed by Liliana's story, Nicki popped a cookie into her mouth and washed it down with a mouthful of strong coffee.

"Even for you, sometimes a dream might still just be a nightmare," Nicki consoled. "Has anyone else reported him missing? Did you receive a ransom note?"

Liliana shook her head. The light danced in the gold of her earrings. "No note, no ominous letters. Nothing like that. Luis worked on projects for Edison-Bell, but he had his own workshop and kept odd hours. Most of the time, he worked alone unless he needed help moving big equipment. So there was no one who was used to seeing him every day to notice when he wasn't there."

"What about a private investigator? When we had a situation in New Pittsburgh a while ago, Jake and Rick worked with an investigator who was very useful," Nicki suggested.

Unfortunately, the man who had helped them was far away in Pennsylvania, probably without any local contacts.

"That was something I planned to ask about when Elian and I came to the Brand and Desmet compound," Liliana replied. "I realize the facility here is more of a depot and not the headquarters, but perhaps one of their people will know someone who might help. I'm at wit's end. Luis and I have always been very close. To think of him afraid or a prisoner—I can barely stand it."

"I'll help you find out what's going on," Nicki pledged. "We'll bring him home."

Liliana enfolded Nicki's hand in both of hers. "Thank you. I have been mired in worry, but seeing you gives me hope."

Nicki squeezed Liliana's hands and prayed that she did not let her friend down.

"I didn't realize that you and Elian were working with Brand and Desmet," Nicki said after a moment, giving them a chance to shift the mood. "Jake and Rick mentioned working with a psychic and a witch, but I never put two and two together. How did that come about?"

Liliana paused to take another sip of coffee and nibble a cookie. "Mutual acquaintances, as all the best connections are." Her smile did not chase away the sadness in her eyes. "Renate Thalberg—I expect that you know each other?"

Nicki nodded. "Definitely. Her absinthe magic is impressive. We worked together in New Pittsburgh. I assume you know Andreas as well?"

Andreas Thalberg was a centuries-old vampire warlock and the master vampire of the city of New Pittsburgh. Renate posed as his sister, while in reality, she was his many times great-granddaughter. Both were staunch allies who had helped Jake, Rick, Nicki, and their friends defeat a monstrous threat.

"Oh, yes. He and Elian move in many of the same circles in the Craft, while Renate and I have also crossed paths along the way," Liliana replied. "So when she asked for our help, we were intrigued. Brand and Desmet's reputation precedes it."

"I can imagine how Elian's magic might come in handy trying to find the wreck of the *Vincente* and retrieve its cargo, but where do your gifts come in?" Nicki had been trying to figure out the connection since she had realized Elian's involvement.

"While my magic won't help locate a sunken ship or affect the waves, I have been working with *Los Ahogados* for many years," Liliana told her. "Now, it keeps me sane when all my leads on Luis have gone cold. I've expended all my options, and I am left depending on my contacts to find him."

Nicki frowned. "Forgive me—my Spanish is rusty."

"*Los Ahogados*. The 'drowned ones,'" Liliana translated. "They are the ghosts of the souls lost at sea. In a place like Key West, with the ocean so near, it is impossible for those with mediumship to ignore them. There are so many, and they have been storm-tossed for so long."

"How…what do you do?" Nicki asked, intrigued.

"For those who find their way to me, I offer rest," Liliana said. "I go down to the beach many mornings very early and listen for their voices. Some are still tangled in the tragedy of their deaths, even after centuries."

She patted her hair again, a nervous gesture Nicki suspected meant that Liliana was self-conscious talking about her magic. "Others have nearly faded away on their own. And of course, some of the shipwrecked dead never became ghosts at all. Their spirits found their way onward right away. But the remainder are the drowned ones. I attract them to my energy and open a door of sorts for them to move on and be at peace."

"There must be hundreds—thousands—of ghosts!" Nicki exclaimed. "These waters have been major shipping lanes for at least three hundred years, and the ocean near here is known for shipwrecks."

"*Tens* of thousands of spirits," Liliana corrected gently. "Many unknown and unmourned. All of them so far from home. Some had no choice about setting out to sea. They were conscripts or slaves—some of them kidnapped—and never saw land again. Their ghosts have the easiest time letting go once they find me. They never wanted to be here in the first place."

Spark of Destiny

"I can't imagine why any ghosts would want to stay," Nicki replied with a shiver.

Liliana's eyes held a shadow of shared pain. "Many who sailed these waters loved the sea with all their hearts. They were only ever at home aboard ship and their crew was their family. Some fear the afterlife. Others would gladly remain in the bosom of the waves for eternity. I don't bother them, and they don't endanger the living."

"You make it sound very peaceful." Nicki picked at her cookie.

Liliana shook her head. "Not always. There are restless and vengeful spirits who still rage over the unfairness of their deaths or who have unfinished business or grudges that run so deep they won't let go. They envy the living, and sometimes during the worst storms, they rise up to hasten the sinking of ships and add more ghosts to their number."

Nicki gasped. "I'm glad I didn't know that the last time I sailed on an ocean liner!"

"You may face storms on an ocean liner, but you are probably safe from ghosts. The vengeful spirits are much more likely here in the islands instead of in the middle of the Atlantic," Liliana said with a patient smile. "Maybe the cold lets them slumber. But I'm not the only medium who helps *Los Ahogados* find rest. It is a duty borne by a great many of us who are near the sea, and we regard it as a holy obligation."

Nicki frowned, putting the pieces together. "Have you contacted ghosts from the *Vincente*? Could they help with the salvage operation?"

"I've been casting my thoughts to seek them, but so far haven't heard any replies," Liliana said. "Closer to the time, perhaps Elian and I will see if we are more successful."

Elian entered the courtyard from the French doors of the home's breakfast room. His thick, dark hair had just begun to gray at the temples, with handsome, chiseled features and dark eyes.

"Nicki—so good to see you. I'm sorry your entrance was so… dramatic." Elian carried himself with all the confidence borne of his aristocratic heritage and his powerful witchcraft.

"I'm thrilled to be with both of you," Nicki replied. "Did you find anything outside the gates?"

Elian and Liliana exchanged a glance Nicki couldn't quite decipher, as if a silent conversation occurred in minutes. "I was able to confirm my suspicion that Javier Cortez's witch was behind the magic." Elian's voice took on a hard tone. "The traces of power that remained stank of his touch."

"I've heard of Cortez." Nicki thought of her conversation with Jake and the others the previous night. "He's with Sombra. And untrustworthy."

"In the extreme," Elian confirmed. "As for his reasons—I suspect he and his witch see Brand and Desmet as a threat."

"I'm guessing that's why Jake said you were both coming back with me to the compound?"

Elian nodded. "Yes. But not just yet. Enjoy your chat with Lili while your driver and the horses recover. We'll be well protected on our return."

Nicki and Liliana spent the next hour catching up on news and gossip, studiously avoiding heavier topics. Finally, Elian returned.

"My dear Lili—I'm sorry to interrupt your conversation, but our carriage is ready." He looked to Nicki. "And of course, you are more than welcome to travel with us. Your driver will follow, and I have guards who will accompany us, as well as a few spells I've tweaked in case those shadows turn up again."

Nicki felt certain that their carriage was also probably warded with more magic than the vehicle in which she had arrived. "Thank you. I would be glad to join you."

Liliana smiled and squeezed Nicki's hand. "You're going to be staying in Key West for a while, won't you? We'll have more mornings to talk. After all, we have a lot of catching up to do."

"I'd like that." Nicki was pleased to see Liliana's eyes alight.

A liveried driver awaited them. Elian offered a hand to help Nicki and Liliana into the vehicle. The carriage house was within the walls of the villa-style home, and a stablehand opened the wide wooden double doors to allow them to exit and closed the gateway behind them. Nicki's original carriage followed, and both vehicles had several discreetly armed bodyguards.

"Nicki and I were just discussing the *Vincente*," Liliana told her husband. "Now that Adam Farber and his inventions have arrived, I'm hoping the salvage can begin. Helping recover its cargo is like being a part of its history."

Elian smiled at Liliana, the warmth of their bond clear in his affection. "I suspect that it will get messy, which is the part history books always gloss over." His deep voice rumbled, and while his English—like Liliana's—was flawless, both carried the accents of their native Spain.

"I'm glad Jake and Rick asked you to look at the warehouse," Nicki said as they jostled along on a road paved with crushed shells. "The clients weren't supposed to include dangerous pieces in the airlift cargo, but it appears some of them didn't pay close attention."

"I can't say that I'm surprised people who collect arcane and occult objects might want to safeguard their valuables regardless of whether those items are cursed or haunted," Elian replied.

He folded his hands in his lap. "I don't doubt that the warehouse has safeguards, given the company's business. But those items came from dozens of private collections, each with their own wardings and security. Just having them close to each other could trigger energies that might not have manifested in their original locations."

JAKE AND RICK were waiting for them when their carriage pulled inside the compound. Handshakes all around and friendly greetings welcomed Elian and Liliana, who had apparently not visited the company's grounds before.

Nicki told them about the attack on her carriage and how Liliana and Elian used their abilities to protect her. Jake and Rick looked thunderous as she described the danger.

"I recognized the magic of Javier Cortez's witch," Elian said. "I am certain he was responsible."

"Thank you for getting Nicki back to us in one piece," Jake said. "We'll add extra precautions anytime someone leaves the compound."

They began to cross the yard. "Mr. Conroy, our location manager, went ahead to open the warehouse." Jake fell into step with Elian and Liliana as they walked toward the large building. Rick and Nicki were right behind them. Jake told them about the strange occurrences the staff had reported, including the ominous shadowy figure, moving crates, and broken equipment.

"Those all sound like manifestations of angry ghosts," Liliana said, and Elian nodded in agreement. "I am hopeful we can help."

"I've been going over the manifest of the items that were shipped for safekeeping," Jake told them, "and I've identified some crates that I'd like you to take a closer look at for magic or hauntings. But after an incident last night, I suspect that some extra pieces were tucked into shipments without being officially listed. If you sense something worrisome, be sure to point it out even if it's not on the list."

Nicki hadn't been inside the warehouse. The place made her mouth drop open.

The warehouse was about the size of a football field and held ten rows of crates stacked six feet high running the entire length of the building.

"That's a lot of artifacts." Nicki didn't have any magic or psychic abilities, but she sensed a shift in the energy inside the large building that she doubted was her imagination.

Rick sometimes saw ghosts, much to his chagrin—although nothing on the order of Liliana's talent as a medium.

Much as it fascinated her to hear about real magic and see what her friends with supernatural abilities could do, Nicki did not envy them their gifts or the responsibilities that came with them.

"This will work best if we split up," Elian suggested. "I'll start at one end of the building with someone to keep track of which boxes catch my attention. Let Liliana begin from the other end, with a helper to take notes as well. Once we've both made a full circuit, we can compare findings. Some items may trigger both of us, while others are likely to be noticed by one or the other, depending on what forces are in play."

Jake and Conroy went with Elian. Rick and Nicki headed to the other end of the building with Liliana. Over the course of many adventures with Jake and Rick, Nicki had witnessed powerful magic, malicious ghosts, and dangerous monsters. But the subtle feeling of dissonance and unease she sensed in the warehouse made her skin prickle.

Nicki had seen Liliana talk with ghosts one-on-one, and she'd been part of a couple of séances many years ago. Scanning the warehouse for dangerous ghosts was something on an entirely different scale. She felt certain that in the intervening years, Liliana's mastery of her gifts had grown, and she realized that she had no idea what her friend was capable of doing.

"How can I help?" Nicki asked, at a loss. "Do you need to shut your eyes? I can guide you."

Liliana chuckled. "Fortunately, I can keep my eyes open. I'll put myself in a waking trance, which will let me pay more attention to my inner senses than to what I see in the regular world. In addition to taking notes on any phenomena I notice, I'd be very grateful if you and Rick would watch my back. When I'm focused on the spirits, I can't pay full attention to what's going on around me."

"We've got you covered." That's when Nicki realized that in addition to carrying a copy of the inventory and a pen tucked into his shirt pocket, Rick held an iron fireplace poker, useful against ghosts. "Here you go, Nicki." Rick held out a long-handled wrought iron ladle. "I've also got a bag of salt in my pocket in case the spirits aren't friendly."

"You want me to sauce and season a ghost if it attacks me?" Nicki stared at the unlikely weapon, unsure whether to be offended or amused.

"Figured the ladle would be easier for you to swing than the other hearth tools," Rick admitted. "It's the touch of iron that dispels ghosts, not the shape of the object. But if you want the heavier one and don't mind sore shoulders tomorrow, I'll be glad to swap." His teasing grin dared her to take him up on it.

"That's very gentlemanly of you, but I'll keep the ladle," Nicki replied with a sniff, as if declaring the superiority of her weapon. "Thank you very much."

Liliana watched them with amusement. "You argue like siblings. Are you done yet, or shall we have a tug-of-war?"

"Ready when you are." Nicki gripped the big spoon's handle white-knuckled.

The walls were made from concrete block with a metal roof to withstand the storms that often buffeted the island. Nicki recognized many of the sigils painted on the walls as protective markings.

If it feels this creepy in here with the wardings, I hate to think what it would be like without them.

Liliana took a few deep breaths. Her features relaxed, and her whole body lost its tension. "I'm ready."

She stared straight ahead, but her eyes looked glazed and unfocused as she concentrated on seeing into the spirit world.

Nicki kept one hand on Liliana's elbow as they walked at a slow pace down the first long aisle. Rick hung back a few steps, ready in case of trouble but not wanting his iron poker to interfere with ghosts that might be helpful.

Gradually, Nicki realized that Liliana murmured comments from time to time. "Be at peace. You are free to go now. It's time for you to rest."

Nicki couldn't see who Liliana was talking to, but whatever spirits clung to the objects in the crates seemed to heed her quiet urging or else chose not to manifest. That was completely okay with Nicki, who decided that it was far better to hear a good ghost story than to live one.

Once Liliana began her trance, the air around them grew chilly, then cold—rare in southern Florida at this time of year. Nicki had spent time in haunted old homes back in France, and while she had rarely glimpsed any ghosts, she recognized the unsettling feeling of being watched.

The temperature dropped to freezing as the ghosts made themselves known to Liliana. Nicki heard the sound of footsteps down empty aisles. She shivered from the cold and picked up a faint smell of pipe tobacco and limes, although no one was nearby as the ghosts manifested.

Liliana takes it all in stride. How is Rick handling it? I never expected to be on ghost patrol!

Nicki glanced over her shoulder at Rick. He looked pale but resolute, fire poker in a two-handed grip like he wielded a cricket bat on the playing fields back in England.

Liliana stopped abruptly. Nicki opened her mouth to ask why and snapped it shut as the air in front of them wavered. The faded image of a beautiful woman appeared, dressed in the fashion of a socialite from the time of Napoleon. The ghost flickered, sometimes appearing lovely and undamaged, then bloodied in the slashed remnants of her gown.

"I see you." Liliana's voice quiet and calm. "What binds you to this place?"

The ghost's lips moved, but Nicki couldn't hear her answer. The bloodied revenant terrified Nicki, but she remained stalwart at Liliana's side. Rick sidled up closer, the poker held ready.

Liliana's voice took on a dreamy quality, and Nicki guessed she was relaying what the spirit said that only she could hear.

"I loved an artist who asked me to model for his paintings. He was unfaithful and killed me to make room for a new lover. My ghost remains with the last portrait he painted of me, which is spattered with my blood."

Nicki stifled a gasp, and Rick paled. Nicki quickly noted the number of the box so Jake could talk to the owner. Without an imminent threat, they couldn't just open a crate and destroy an object, although Nicki's heart went out to the sad revenant.

"I will do my best to free you." Liliana sounded like herself again. "For now, will you rest quietly and do no harm?"

The apparition flickered, nodded somberly, then vanished. Liliana let out a breath, and Nicki steadied her. "Is she gone?"

Liliana nodded. "For now. I don't think she intended to hurt anyone, but I could feel her misery, and I want to help her move on."

They continued their slow trek up and down the warehouse aisles. Sometimes Liliana murmured to the spirits, and Nicki felt a shift in air pressure, a change of temperature, or a slight breeze that she took to mean a spirit had appeared and been dispelled. On occasion, Liliana noted that she could sense magic strong enough to be a worry.

Each time, Nicki wrote down the number of the crate for Jake to discuss with the owner or for Elian to neutralize dangerous magic. As the list grew, she wondered how Jake and Rick would deal with quite so much haunted cargo.

Nicki thought it was a wonder that the original airlift didn't suffer from any ghostly interference.

Nearly halfway across the warehouse, Liliana stopped and held out an arm, warning them to stay back.

"What is it?" Nicki whispered.

Liliana's wary expression warned of danger. "That box holds trapped souls. I know Jake wants to honor his word to the owner, but imprisoning souls is an abomination and a great danger."

"Do we need to call for Elian?" Rick asked.

"I'm already here." Elian rounded the corner at the end of the row. "It seems we have met in the middle. What have you found?"

Liliana pointed at the problem crate. Jake and Conroy followed close behind Elian as the witch moved near enough to read the shipping marks on the wooden box. "Souls are bound to something inside. I sense dark magic, but I'm not sure how the binding was done."

Elian frowned and held out one hand, palm facing the offending container. He closed his eyes, and Nicki felt a frisson of energy that sent a chill down her back.

"Can you tell what's inside—and whether it's a danger?" Jake asked.

"I know you don't want to intrude on your client's privacy, and I would not ask you to do so if it wasn't important," Elian replied, "but this cannot wait. Whoever sent this on the airlift showed complete disrespect for everyone's safety. I might go so far as to suspect they bore you ill will."

"You think the owner included something malicious on purpose?"

Jake leaned forward to try to make out the labels and shipping marks. Nicki had already jotted down the crate number.

"I don't recognize the name offhand. Do you, Rick?" Jake didn't move closer, and Nicki wondered if he felt the same bad energy that she sensed.

"No. I thought I knew everyone who had cargo in the airlift. If other items were added that aren't on the manifest, we've got a whole different level of trouble," Rick agreed.

Jake met Elian's gaze. "Do what you need to do, please, to keep everyone safe. I'll take responsibility for dealing with the client."

"You brought salt and iron. Put down a circle on the floor large enough for the four of you, and stay inside it no matter what you see or hear. Keep your weapons ready, but pray you don't need them," Elian instructed. "Liliana and I will deal with the twisted energies inside."

Rick and Jake pooled their salt to make a large circle at a distance from the crate sufficient to give Elian and Liliana room to maneuver. They gathered inside, close but not crowded, and Nicki paid special attention to ensure her skirts didn't break the line.

Her heart pounded, half in fear of the danger and half from the thrill of adventure. Nicki had never seen Elian work magic or seen Liliana and him use their gifts in tandem. *I probably ought to be terrified right now that we're all going to die, but I'm more worried I won't have a good view of what's going on.*

Elian had come prepared to dispel dark magic. He had a leather messenger bag slung over one shoulder, from which he pulled three thick candles and a pottery bowl, all marked with symbols in red, black, and purple that Nicki didn't recognize. Liliana held the bowl as Elian dropped items inside—tobacco, dried chili peppers, coffee grounds, cowrie shells, and a couple of hard candy lozenges.

All the while, Elian chanted in a low voice. Nicki thought some of the words were in Spanish and others in Cajun, while some were not in a language she recognized.

"Look," she whispered to Rick, elbowing him in the ribs. A faint glow surrounded the crate holding the trapped spirits, like a translucent green-gold bubble of energy.

Elian took a flask from his bag and added a few drops that smelled like rum into the bowl. Liliana set a match to the mixture, and flames the same color as the protective bubble leapt high into the air.

He passed the bowl to Liliana as the fire died, sending fragrant smoke into the air. "Spirits of the box. Reveal your names," she commanded.

Nicki might not have magic, but something primal deep inside recognized the elemental energy radiating from the witch and the medium. Liliana spoke with authority, standing with her head tall and shoulders back, a force to be reckoned with. Elian's suave charm hardened into the look and manner of someone comfortable with wielding power and certain he would be obeyed.

"Jose. Felipe. Mateo," Liliana said in a much deeper tone than her usual speaking voice. Nicki suspected that meant she was speaking on behalf of the spirits, if not actually channeling them.

"Why are you bound?"

The box trembled within the protective bubble of energy. Nicki hadn't been able to hear the ghosts speak their names without Liliana as the go-between, but there was no missing the shrieks and wails that came from the crate.

Liliana's expression went blank, and Nicki guessed she was listening to the ghosts once more.

"Debt of honor, debt of money, debts of blood. For these you were imprisoned. Why were you not released when the term of your binding was completed?"

Once again screams and moans filled the air and the crate rocked violently as if trying to dash itself on the floor to burst apart at the seams. Elian's bubble of light flared brighter, but Nicki found that she had taken a half step back on pure instinct.

Liliana inclined her head as if listening to the ghosts. Elian's look of concentration never wavered, although Nicki saw him clench his jaw, suggesting strain.

"You were wronged, but you are not guiltless," Liliana announced.

"The binding served as much to stop your crimes as to punish you for your unpaid obligations and broken vows. Free or imprisoned, you cannot stay here. It is time for you to move on."

Nicki caught a whiff of pipe smoke and cologne. Out of the corner of her eye, she thought she saw a tall, thin man dressed in black standing in the shadows. Movement drew her attention, and she glimpsed an old man with a pipe and a cane, there and gone.

The wooden crate trembled. The crash of breaking glass echoed in the warehouse, and then the box exploded in a shower of splinters and boards. Elian's protective field contained the blast, something Nicki realized after she and the others had already crouched and thrown their arms up to protect themselves.

Three furious ghosts rose from the wreckage, strong enough to manifest and appear nearly solid. They hurled themselves at the barrier and shrieked curses, pounding with their fists against the curtain of light. It seemed as if the ghosts focused their attack on Jake and Rick, and Nicki wondered if they had been sent for that purpose.

Whoever these ghosts had been, only an echo of malevolence remained. Their crimes and remorselessness twisted their faces and bodies to be only remotely human. Nicki was not devoutly religious, but she imagined that such spirits might have spawned the legends about demons.

"If you will not go peacefully of your own accord, you will still leave this place and not return." Liliana confronted the ghosts stern-faced, without fear, her voice clear and commanding.

Nicki sensed that the two shadow figures had returned, but she kept her eyes focused straight ahead. Gut instinct told her that the living need not meddle with them.

"The door is open. The grave is dug. Be gone," Liliana ordered. The protective bubble flared blindingly bright, making Nicki look away. As she turned, she saw the ghosts drawn by an inescapable force toward the two shadowy figures. The spirits twisted and writhed, but they could not escape the grip that held them.

They swarmed past the old man, and the tall figure in black opened his arms to receive them, drawing their squirming, clawing essence to his embrace.

In a puff of pipe smoke, the two figures and the ghosts were gone.

"Stay where you are!" Elian warned.

Liliana handed back the pottery bowl, its fire now extinguished. She closed her eyes and drew several deep breaths as if cleansing herself of the stain of the malicious ghosts. Elian murmured his thanks and lifted the bowl to the quarters before covering it with a lid to hold its contents. He snuffed out the candle and intoned another incantation, then replaced everything in his bag.

"What…happened?" Rick asked, and Nicki didn't fault him for the quiver in his voice.

Elian turned toward them and smiled, no longer the fearsome figure he had appeared to be just moments before.

"My ancestors were Catholic, Spanish, Caribbean, and Taino," he replied. "Their blood and their magic run in my veins. I called on Papa Legba—whom some call Eshu Elegbara—to open the door to the afterlife. He rules the crossroads. Baron Samedi is a Ghede, a psychopomp who escorts the souls of the dead. They are revered in Voudon and Santeria. I am honored that they heard my prayer. Those ghosts will trouble us no more."

"That was impressive," Jake said, sounding only marginally more composed. "Thank you."

"You are most welcome," Elian replied. "It is good that they are gone before we work in earnest on the *Vincente*. Whoever included them in the shipment intended harm."

Jake's jaw tightened. "I'll be looking into the owners of the crates you and Liliana noted and seeing to how we can neutralize threats."

"What about that other box?" Conroy asked. "The empty, open one?"

Rick and Nicki turned to stare at Jake. "Is that where that cursed clock came from, or something different?" Rick questioned.

Jake shook his head. "No. We found that box too. The clock was packed with other items. But there is one crate—a fairly small one,

Spark of Destiny

shipping labels damaged and unreadable—that was empty. And the force that opened the crate appears to have come from *inside*."

"Well, that's just lovely," Rick muttered.

Liliana swayed, and Elian reached out to steady her. "I think we've all had a taxing morning. She needs to rest."

"Let's all go back to the house," Conroy suggested. "I'll have tea and cakes to refresh everyone and then see to lunch. There's room for a few people to ride back with me in the wagon, and I can send a carriage for the rest."

Nicki took Liliana's arm. "How about the two of us go in the wagon?" Her suggestion prompted a smile of gratitude from Liliana. "Let the men walk."

Back at the house, Nicki and Liliana made themselves comfortable in the parlor, and the others arrived shortly after. A servant brought hot tea and a plate of cookies. Everyone dug in like they were starving, except for Elian, who only took tea. He watched Liliana silently but with concern, and Nicki wondered how much working their gifts had cost them.

"I'm troubled that we had 'stowaway' objects on the airlift." Rick licked the crumbs from his lips. "I'd say that means we have a problem with our Havana base crew."

Jake nodded, looking worried and worn. "Clearly. Then again, with the war, I'm sure some of our long-time staff have relocated. It would only take one or two new hands to smuggle the items into the shipment. The same is true for the clients—pieces that were under wards for a reason might have been packed haphazardly by panicked servants who didn't know better."

Elian cleared his throat. "Don't be too quick to give the benefit of the doubt. That might account for some of the items with minor magic or benign ghosts. But the cursed clock you described and the bound ghosts Liliana and I dispelled could not have been overlooked so easily. I suspect that someone wanted to disrupt your operations here in Key West—interfere with the salvage of the *Vincente*, or perhaps seriously injure or kill you and your people."

Nicki muttered a decidedly unladylike curse under her breath. Liliana heard her and gave a conspiratorial smile in return.

"What's our best bet to contain the harmful items?" Jake asked. "Tracking down the owners could be tough—most of them probably are out of the country for the duration of the war."

"Do people need to go in and out of the warehouse on a daily basis?" Elian leaned back and held his cup with both hands. "If not, we could strengthen the magical protections to keep things *in* as well as keep intruders *out*. Such things work best if undisturbed, so it would be ideal if nobody else went inside after the new wards are set."

Jake looked to Conroy, who thought for a moment, then nodded. "We could do that. We're storing the items for clients, so there's nothing in that warehouse needed for the everyday running of the compound. The guards can patrol outside, but they don't need to go in."

"It's an imperfect solution—it won't last forever, and I can't guarantee that it will hold forever against any power or creature—but I believe it will hold for as long as necessary and will keep both the people and the objects safer."

"When can you do it?" Jake asked. "Just add it—and today's help—to our bill. We're grateful. You saved our bacon in there. Someone could have been badly hurt."

Liliana smiled at the praise, and Elian looked pleased. "We are happy to help. If our assistance can, in any even insignificant way, shorten this dreadful conflict, we are at your service."

Nicki touched Liliana's arm. "Are you feeling better?"

"Yes. Working with the spirits drains my energy, and when they are malevolent, it's even more taxing. Sugar, tea, and rest are the cure. I had hoped our search through the warehouse wouldn't provide any dangerous surprises, but I'm glad we were able to dispel the worst of it."

Conversation at lunch was lighthearted by design, skirting any mention of the warehouse, the *Vincente*, or the war. Afterward, Liliana begged off further socializing to rest. Their driver brought the warded carriage to the front door.

"Come again tomorrow for coffee, Nicki. We still have a lot of catching up to do." Liliana gave a smile that assured the invitation was meant to be fulfilled.

"I'll be there. For your scrumptious coffee as well as the conversation," Nicki promised.

When Elian and Liliana were gone, Nicki felt her energy droop now that the danger and excitement were past.

"I'm going to take a cue from Liliana and lie down," she informed them as the men moved to the parlor with coffee. "Someone wake me if I'm not back before supper."

She headed upstairs, still taking in the charming décor. Someone had made the effort to add artwork and knickknacks that made the house feel like a home and not just a business lodging.

Nicki noted the figurines, decorative lamps, leather-bound books, and nautical paintings that gave a warm, comfortable feel to the rooms. She smiled at the touches of whimsy that graced the occasional bookshelf or side table—figures of faeries or sprites, curious cats and dogs, even a doll tucked into a corner as if the house belonged to a real family.

She was even more grateful for the exceedingly comfortable bed and good linens that awaited her when she reached her room. Reluctantly, she stretched out on the chaise since she didn't intend to undress and arranged her position to do the least damage possible to her hair.

Just as Nicki drifted off, she heard the faint sound of a child's giggle in a house where there were no children.

Chapter Four

"Am I gonna die?" Tom Wilson, the thief who stole the cursed porcelain clock, looked from Conroy to Jake with wide, fearful eyes.

"Hopefully not." Elian's neutral tone didn't coddle. "But it's a good lesson in why you keep your hands off things that don't belong to you."

"I'm sorry. It won't happen again. Please, save me."

"Have you decided whether you're going to crew one of our cargo ships, or are we turning you over to the police?" Jake asked. "Cargo ship crew gets the same pay as here, and if you stay a year without any other problems, we'll forget about the clock."

Wilson looked haggard just in the day since the attempted theft. Even allowing for worry and fear, Jake suspected it was the curse at work, draining his life energy.

Conroy had confirmed that before the clock, Wilson had been long in their employ, in good standing. His parents' dire situation seemed to have pushed him into a desperate choice.

"I'll go on the ship." Wilson sounded defeated. "If I survive."

"We've taken care of your parents' problems," Conroy told him.

"And we'll keep an eye on them, so you won't be put in this situation again."

Wilson looked up, stunned. "Really? My God. Thank you. I promise I'll make it up to you." A wracking cough shuddered through his body and, together with the pallor of his skin, made it clear the curse took its toll.

"First, let's get you healed." Elian laid out the tools and materials needed for the counter spell. He bid Wilson sit quietly while he mixed a potion and spoke an incantation over the brew. Then he lit four candles at the quarters around Wilson's chair with sigils marked in between them. Finally, he walked widdershins around the chair, murmuring under his breath.

"Drink this." He handed Wilson a goblet filled with the elixir. "Together with the magic, it should do the trick."

Wilson looked from Elian to the cup, apprehensive. He received the cup with both hands, wrinkled his nose at the look and smell of the potion, and then closed his eyes, drinking it all in one gulp.

Elian walked the circle in reverse, snuffing each candle as he passed it, quietly intoning more words Jake didn't catch.

Wilson's eyes rolled back, and his face went slack as his limp body slumped from the chair onto the floor. Jake and Conroy moved forward, but Elian held up a hand. "Don't. It's the curse departing. Give him space."

Jake watched, worried, as Wilson trembled, shuddering with a seizure. His eyes opened wide, and his mouth gaped as he groaned in pain. Elian watched, nonplussed, features damnably difficult to read.

"The curse dug in deeply," Elian said as if guessing their worry. "Removing it is neither easy nor pleasant but far better than the alternative."

Wilson stilled, but his chest rose and fell.

"It's done. He will recover. When he wakes, give him tea and broth until he can keep food down, and let him sleep. Once he's able to eat, the worst has passed," Elian instructed.

"Thank you." Jake had not met Elian before the previous day, though he came well-recommended by both Conroy and Andreas

Thalberg. Now he could see why they thought so highly of the witch.

"You are most welcome. I hope such a situation does not arise again," Elian replied.

Conroy stayed with Wilson while Jake and Elian walked toward the back corner of the walled compound where Wilson was supposed to have handed off the clock.

"It's a long shot, but can you pick up on anything?" Jake saw that the grass still lay flattened where Kovach had tackled Wilson, and footprints marred the ground. Since the payment was supposed to be passed through the gate from outside, Jake wasn't sure much, if any, evidence would remain, but he figured it was worth asking.

Elian made a careful examination of the area, then shook his head. "There's nothing here. Perhaps if we could go outside the wall, I might find a trace of whoever was to deliver the payment—assuming they ever intended to do so."

Jake summoned two guards to accompany them, and strolled around the exterior of the compound until they were opposite their first location. The security men stood back, giving Elian room to work. Elian crouched, studying a set of footprints. He spoke a few words under his breath and slowly ran his hand, palm down, several inches over the grass, then he stood and looked at Jake.

"Whoever was here had some magic. I think they wore a deflection amulet or cast a spell to make their energy more difficult to identify," Elian told him. "Magical energy is unique to its caster. The identifying variations are subtle. To suspect a match, I would need to be present when a witch used their power. I do not recognize this witch's signature, so it wasn't Cortez's pet, and if Veles was involved, I'm sure he sent a minion."

"If you come upon them and they work a spell, will you remember the energy signature?" Jake couldn't help being intrigued by the complexities of magic.

"It depends. I believe this person was trying to hide or blur their magic to an observer," Elian replied. "So possibly not. Still, it tells us something about the caster. They had some degree of knowledge in the Craft to create and use such an amulet or spell, and they knew what they were doing might lead to a search. This wasn't an amateur or a dabbler. And they expect to encounter us again."

"Are they powerful enough to be a threat?" Jake didn't like the implications of Elian's analysis, although he wasn't surprised by the conclusions.

Elian chuckled. "In the hands of someone with malice, any magic is dangerous. Just like one doesn't need to be a sharpshooter to kill with a gun. The clock was clearly meant as an attack against you. That suggests that whoever bribed your worker knew exactly what the clock could do and meant to kill."

"That doesn't help figure out who included it in the cargo. Is it related to the other attacks, or is this a different enemy?" Jake asked. "Unfortunately, we've acquired several."

"Perhaps the theft is unrelated to recovering the *Vincente* cargo," Elian agreed. "But I find the timing to be suspicious, and I am wary of 'coincidences.'"

They walked back to the gate with the guards close behind, but nothing struck Jake as dangerous or triggered a warning from Elian.

"Next stop—the warehouse," Jake said. "Before we go out on the salvage run, I'd like to have the rogue crates locked down as much as possible so they don't cause trouble. It needs to be done before we close the warehouse, increase the magical protections, and post guards."

"What's your plan?" Elian asked.

Jake took him to a small building near the warehouse where they usually stored the compound's maintenance equipment. The cement block construction had been able to withstand hurricanes with its solid metal roof and lack of windows. Jake hoped it could be made equally magic-proof.

"Can you ward the questionable crates? Put them on magical lockdown?" he asked Elian.

Elian nodded. "Yes. At least, long enough for us to get to the bottom of what's going on."

"Good. We know which boxes weren't in the manifest and which ones you and Liliana thought might be dangerous. With your protection, I'd like to open the 'extra' boxes to make sure there's no smuggling going on.

"We don't need to risk opening the bad magic boxes now, or maybe ever. If you can wrap them in a spell to let us move them from the main warehouse into the equipment shed, then they'll be in 'quarantine' and should be less likely to hurt anyone," Jake continued.

"That works. Let me get the wardings set up here while you pull your crew together to move the crates," Elian replied. "This shouldn't take too long."

Jake knew that the witch made a complicated process look deceptively simple and was grateful for his help. Without Elian and Liliana, he shuddered to think how many of the compound's workers could have been hurt by the cursed or haunted crates.

Conroy had workers and the mechanized wagon ready to move the crates. It took time to move the non-magical, rogue crates out of their stacks. Conroy and Jake used crowbars to pry off the lids, wary that someone might have tried to smuggle out weapons, money, or illegal substances using the airlift for camouflage. Jake had no desire to get mixed up in any of that or to be drawn into the war more than they were with the *Vincente's* salvage.

"Soapstone carvings." Jake carefully picked through the first crate's contents. The hand-cut pieces lay nestled in a bed of straw. Jake used the crowbar to nudge enough of the packing aside to guess that at least a hundred crudely-featured statues of animals and people filled the box.

"There's a metal plaque," Conroy pointed out. "*HMS Centurion.*"

"That's not a ship I recognize. Strange."

They replaced the lid, and workers hefted the box onto the wagon. The next unlisted crate held a similar cargo, this time with a yellowed crew complement of the same *HMS Centurion.*

"This can't be a coincidence," Jake said. "And while the contents didn't trigger Elian or Liliana, it's giving me the creeps. Let's put these with the 'ghost' boxes."

The contents of the next crate were even more perplexing. Inside was an oil painting with a name plate that read "Lost City of the Great Swamp." It showed a small village of wooden buildings painted in firelight hues, surrounded by massive mangrove and cypress trees and the thick vegetation of a tropical wetland. To Jake's eye, the town in the painting looked disreputable, maybe sinister, like a last outpost for people who didn't want to be found.

"This just keeps getting weirder," he muttered.

"Guess we need to brush up on naval history," Conroy replied. "This has to mean something important."

The last rogue crate held old maps, leather-bound journals with yellowed pages and faded ink, loose papers, and a small portrait of a man in a dark coat with a printed scarf around his neck. The man had a thick mustache and trimmed beard, and from his clothing, Jake guessed he had lived in the last century. Another miniature portrait showed a different man dressed in rich brocade with a powdered wig, after the fashion of a wealthy man in the late 1600s.

On the top of the packing material lay a handwritten note addressed to "J.D." Jake glanced at Conroy and picked up the envelope. "I'm guessing this is for me." He was torn between curiosity and foreboding as he found a letter inside.

Mr. Desmet,

Please forgive the unorthodox communication and the arrival of four unexpected crates with the cargo shipment. The situation in Havana is dire. Spanish ships have bombarded the harbor, and nowhere is safe. Rumors abound, and no one is sure what is really happening.

We have withstood several attacks, which I believe were ordered by Drogo Veles, but fortunately, the wards repelled the worst of the magic. His operatives are known in Havana. They have tried to harm our workers, and he has attempted to slip cursed objects onto the property. So far, we have stopped his efforts, but everything is falling apart here, and I fear we will not be able to protect ourselves much longer.

Materials have come into my possession that may be valuable depending on the course of the war. You are the only one I trust to receive them, and I believe you will know how to get them into the right hands if necessary.

Some believe the legend of the ghost ship HMS Centurion, whose gentleman-pirate captain was a sworn enemy of the Spanish fleet. Perhaps items from his ship and crew may be of use to you, given your many connections. Pay close attention. Its ghosts may be helpful as well.

Old stories hold that the pirate José Gaspar eluded capture in the Florida swamps, hiding his treasure in a secret base. I have sent you everything that was entrusted to me regarding both stories, including a coded message I could not decipher. May you discover the truth of them in time of need. A seer I respect warned me that you will need these objects in the near future and that they may turn the tide of your battle.

I do not wholly trust my workers, but I am not certain who among them may be against us. The men I will send on the airship are of unquestioned loyalty. I will deal with the others here in Havana.

We may be forced to fall back from the warehouse for our safety if the bombardment continues. I will make sure all protections are in place for what goods remain before we leave and will get word to you when it is safe to do so.

I beg your prayers for us and hope to greet you again in better days.

Sincerely, Raul Hernandez

Jake shared a worried look with Conroy. "I recognize Raul's handwriting. This explains—at least partially—why there were extra boxes that weren't dangerous. He thinks that the pieces fit together like a puzzle and hold clues to something important."

"He must have believed the seer that the legends had some truth to them to go to the effort, given the situation," Conroy said.

Jake nodded. "I think he was being careful with what he wrote, in case the cargo didn't make it to Florida. He clearly felt unsafe, so he didn't say what he meant plainly. We're going to have to do some sleuthing to figure out exactly what was so important."

"He knew his operation had been infiltrated," Conroy observed. "Which would explain how the cursed and haunted crates got onboard. If they were under siege, the packing may have been more frantic and disorganized than usual. Raul could personally ensure which men came with the airship, but he couldn't keep an eye on the entire loading operation. Someone with access would be able to get the malicious crates on board pretty easily."

"That was my thought," Jake agreed. "Although we still don't know for certain who was behind it or why. If Veles's people were causing trouble, did they smuggle the crates onboard? Did they want to cause an incident hoping that the airship would wreck? Did they mean to sabotage our base here or kill our people?"

"I don't know, but I'm glad we're locking up the bad stuff. I've got no magic at all, but having them in here makes me worried," Conroy admitted. "The guards will be grateful as well."

"Veles might be hiding in Eastern Europe, but he's got his fingers in every pie," Jake said. "Of course he'd look for ways to turn the war to his advantage—and our disadvantage."

"I'd say your theory sounds very reasonable," Conroy replied.

The crates sent by Hernandez were set to one side so they could be more carefully examined later. Just as Jake was about to go in search of Elian, the witch strode into the warehouse, seemingly unaware of how the workers stepped back to give him more space.

"The other building is protected," Elian said. "Show me which boxes to ward, and they can be moved as safely as possible."

Jake consulted his list and the notes Elian and Liliana had made during their walk-through. He led Elian to each of the crates, then stood back as the witch set spells to temporarily bind the magic of the items in the boxes.

Jake could tell the whole effort made the warehouse workers nervous, and he shared their apprehension. Still, they stayed at their posts and followed Elian's instructions, making sure the questionable boxes were safely moved and unloaded in the other shed.

Once that was done, Jake locked the building and gave the key to Conroy. Elian spoke another incantation, and to Jake's eyes, the shed glowed brightly for an instant, then settled back to drab gray.

"No one goes in or out of the shed," Jake ordered. "No one has any reason to come near this building. If you think you see anything unusual, let Mr. Conroy know immediately. We'll deal with the boxes when things calm down a bit."

Conroy and the workers remained behind, closing up the main warehouse, as Jake walked Elian to his carriage.

"Thank you again for coming back for this. We should be ready to board the ship tonight after dinner," Jake said.

Elian climbed into the carriage and nodded in response. "I will be ready. I suspect Liliana and Nicki have plans of their own while we're gone."

Jake chuckled. "I don't doubt that. Let's just hope explosions aren't involved."

Conroy and Jake headed for the dining room, where the pages of the airlift's manifest were spread across the large table. A servant brought coffee service, and they paused to savor a hot cup before diving into the next task.

"What did you make of all that, with the witch?" Conroy asked.

Jake shrugged. "Too soon to tell. I believe that Elian told us what he could, and that his power is real. The thing I've learned about working with witches—and others with abilities—is that magic isn't the cure-all we like to think. It helps—just like any specialized skill—but unfortunately, it doesn't just go 'poof' and wrap everything up with a neat bow."

"It's a real shame, that is," Conroy commiserated. "It would be nice to just wave my hand and say 'abracadabra' and have problems solved."

Jake laughed. "I agree completely—but no such luck, I'm afraid."

They turned their attention to the lengthy manifest, splitting the pages between them. Jake picked at the plate of tropical fruits and Cuban pastries that soon joined the coffee. He jotted down the list of crates they had found in the warehouse that didn't match the manifest and looked for any other deviations from the expected cargo.

After an hour, Conroy leaned back to stretch. "Are you thinking what I'm thinking?"

Jake nodded. "I agree with Hernandez that at least one person on the Havana side of the operation sold us out. We know now why there are some of the extra boxes he sent, but that doesn't explain the bad magic crates."

"My thoughts too." Conroy toyed with the spoon in his coffee cup. "Of course, the real question is—like with the cursed clock—is this related to the *Vincente* or something separate."

Jake twiddled his pencil. "I think the 'extra' items with bad magic are definitely a threat—or a warning. We still haven't figured out what's missing from that open box."

"I've got men searching the warehouse and the grounds," Conroy replied. "So far, no one's reported finding anything."

"And now we know why we haven't heard from the Havana crew," Jake said. "There's enough going on with the *Vincente* salvage, it would be nice not to have something else to worry about too." He managed a wan smile. "Goes back to wanting a little abracadabra, I guess."

In less than half an hour, they had finished going through the rest of the pages, confirming their count and polishing off the pastries.

Conroy handed Jake his list. "What's your next step?"

Jake sighed. "I need to talk to someone in Havana—preferably Hernandez if he hasn't gone into hiding. The warehouse there is essentially a bunker—the staff should be safe under most conditions, but we never expected direct bombardment. Moving the objects in the airlift was really compensating for client paranoia—I thought. Now, I'm not so sure. I believe that most of the clients just wanted to safeguard their precious collections and had the money to do so. But someone got wind of it and had other plans."

"How well do you know the manager in Havana?" Conroy asked.

"Father hired him a decade ago. Raul and I have had quite a few phone conversations—especially over the airlift—but never any problems. Seems to run a tight ship."

Jake put down the pencil, realizing he'd been twirling it between his fingers. "I'll send a telegram setting up a phone call—if everyone hasn't gone into hiding." Phones were still new and expensive, making them relatively rare. That meant calling Hernandez at the Havana warehouse.

He left to send the telegram to their agent in Cuba, who would get the message about the call to Hernandez. Conroy gathered the papers and slipped them into a folio, clearing the table.

Jake returned, frowning. "I sent the telegram, but didn't get an acknowledgment. There's supposed to be an operator twenty-four hours a day. This doesn't bode well."

"There is a war going on," Conroy observed.

"We set our people up with a safe house for just that reason. I'm worried about our staff—and whether they're in danger from more than the shelling."

"Brand and Desmet offered to bring any of the Havana warehouse workers on the airlift if they wanted to leave," Conroy pointed out.

"Most of them didn't. They had family to care for or were worried about getting back," Jake replied. "But maybe I can learn something from the ones who did accompany the cargo."

"They're all still here in the compound. We'd been a little short-staffed, and had plenty of work for them. They weren't in a hurry to leave and have to deal with the authorities, and since they were already vetted by Brand and Desmet, I trusted them. We've been working on getting their paperwork done, depending on whether they plan to stay or go back. I can have them meet with you after lunch if you like," Conroy offered.

"Sounds good. I'd like to not be worrying about Havana when we ship out tonight. The *Vincente* is going to be enough of a headache on its own, I'm sure," Jake agreed.

He checked his watch. They'd gotten an early start with Elian, and the manifest review had gone more quickly than he'd expected, so it was still mid-morning. Jake rubbed a hand across his eyes and glanced remorsefully at his now-empty coffee cup.

His gut was telling him they were missing crucial information. Unfortunately, it didn't give him any hints on how to obtain it.

Kovach and Adam were waiting for him in the parlor when they entered the house, chatting with Rick and Nicki. Jake had suspected as much when he heard the motorized wagon arrive and glanced out the window to see a large, tarp-covered object in its bed.

Adam had brought a wheeled corkboard from the library and

pinned it full of maps, ocean charts, and schematics. Ben stood to one side, ever the silent sentinel. Jake startled at what he first thought was a second automaton and then realized it was Adam's new diving suit.

"I was afraid I'd need to drag you over to join us," Rick teased, although Jake knew his business partner would read his worried expression for what it was. "Adam's about to fill us in on the exciting stuff."

"He wouldn't show us the rest of his techno turtles until you were here, so hurry up and have a seat," Nicki urged, eyes glinting with excitement. "Liliana begged off. She has a headache."

Kovach leaned against the wall, arms crossed. While staunchly on their side and in favor of the salvage operation, Jake knew that Kovach distrusted technology in general and was particularly unsettled by Adam's untried inventions, which did have a rather distressing safety record.

"Farber was just about to tell us how going down to the bottom of the ocean in a metal bathtub is a good idea," Kovach said in a droll tone.

Adam endured the good-natured teasing. Kovach had saved his life more than once, and while the two enjoyed verbal sparring, they closed ranks and faced down fearsome enemies side by side when needed.

"All right, if we're heading out tonight, I need more details," Jake said, and Rick nodded in agreement. "Lay it out."

Adam smiled. "Happy to do just that. Miska and I have gone over all the equipment, and Ben made an extra check. Everything made it here okay and works after being reassembled. Next, we go down to the docks and meet up with Harry Boyers. He's the captain of the wrecking ship, and he's going to ferry us over to Calusa Key with our equipment so we can load everything onto the *Diligence*. They've added some special equipment to handle the submersible. Fortunately, this isn't their first time with diving suits, so they knew they needed to tweak things a little to work with mine."

"Maybe a little more detail, please?" Rick asked, and Jake was glad

Spark of Destiny

he didn't have to. Adam had a habit of having half of his conversations in his head and forgetting that he hadn't spoken out loud.

"Oh, sorry. Okay," Adam said with a slight blush. "This is the *Diligence*." He pointed to a picture of a large tugboat outfitted with cranes, hoists, and pulleys. I'll spare you all the stats, but she's strong enough to lift very heavy pieces of wreckage. We aren't trying to recover the *Vincente*. We just need to get into the hold and bring out the right pieces of cargo."

"That's *Oceanus*, the submersible." Adam pointed to an odd contraption that looked like a large keg with a propeller.

"I hope I'm wrong, but don't people try to go over Niagara Falls in something like that?" Rick asked.

Adam gave him a look. "Very funny, but no. The *Oceanus* is a one-person submersible that can stay down four hours at a time and has mechanical arms that can grip and drag heavy objects. Ben can accompany me, and he'll have more dexterity to open doors or locks. Also, with special goggles, I can see what he sees, so I don't have to get as close with the *Oceanus*."

"What about the diving suit?" Nicki nodded toward the strange one-piece coverall fitted with hoses, valves, and a bulbous helmet.

"That's just insurance," Adam admitted. "I'm hoping we don't have to use it. Diving with the suit is more dangerous because hoses can get caught or snagged. Also, in the suit, I need time for decompression so I don't get the Bends. In the submersible, it's always pressurized, so that's not a worry."

"Who are these wreckers?" Jake asked. "I know Andreas Thalberg vouched for them, and Conroy checked their background. But we're betting a lot on them—as well as trusting that they won't sell us out. Are we sure?"

Kovach cleared his throat. "I did my own research, not that I didn't trust our other sources," he added, although clearly that trust had limits. "Salvage operations on the Keys goes way back—some of it legal, some not so much. Calusa Key has always been a favorite base, and the Boyers have been 'wreckers' there for five generations."

"On the legal or not-so-much side?" Nicki asked. Rick snickered.

"Probably both depending on the circumstances," Kovach replied. "Wreckers are a tight-knit bunch—usually family and found family. The Boyers are rare because they have experience working with supernatural items. Jacob Boyers is the granddad. He doesn't go out on as many salvage runs as he used to. Stays at the base and runs the rest of the operation."

"Harry is Jacob's son, the day-to-day boss of the operation and captain of the *Diligence*. Harry and his father are weather witches," Kovach went on. "Albert is the first mate, and Ralph is the chief engineer. They're both Harry's sons. Albert's magic is in locating wrecks. They say Ralph can do astral projection and 'walk' through the wrecks."

"Impressive." Jake quirked an eyebrow. "I'm really curious about this 'walking through wrecks' stuff. You mean he gets psychic visions?"

Kovach shrugged. "The people I talked to said that Ralph can somehow send his 'consciousness' over a distance and see things there that he remembers when he wakes up. Sounds pretty crazy to me, but everyone I talked to swore it was the truth."

Jake knew how much Kovach disliked magic on general principles. He preferred things that were clear, easy to understand, and solid enough to punch. Given his long time with Brand and Desmet, Kovach didn't doubt the reality of the supernatural. He just preferred not to deal with it himself if he could avoid it.

"The *Diligence* has a cook and four deckhands who have specialized salvage skills," Adam picked up the story. "We'll be two to a cabin on board—Jake and Rick, Miska and Elian, Ben and me. The *Diligence* has a full kitchen and fairly comfortable quarters. That's good because we're likely to need to spend more than one night at the wreck."

"Right now, we don't have reason to think anyone else has pinpointed the location," Kovach picked up the story. "Hence the trip at night. We don't want to sit there bobbing like a buoy to tell everyone where to go. We'll salvage at night, pull back to another location for the day, and come back in again to finish at dark. If everything is straightforward, we're looking at two days, maximum."

Spark of Destiny

Jake noticed that Kovach didn't say "with luck." Superstition ran strong with the security chief, and Jake didn't blame him for not tempting fate.

"We know other people are going to be looking for the *Vincente's* cargo. That's why I created these." Adam held up something that looked like a metal turtle.

"You saw one of these on the train, but not all of what they can do. The turtles are outfitted with cameras and can transmit when they spot a boat." Adam's pride in his inventions was clear in his voice. "They float on the surface, and they can dive for short periods to avoid notice. We can use them as sentinels to watch our perimeter while we're working on the wreck, and when we pull back, they can help us keep an eye on the location in case any poachers come along."

Jake couldn't help smiling at Adam's enthusiasm and love for mechanical creatures. His clockwork carrier pigeon had come in handy, and his *werkmen* had endearing eccentricities despite being automatons.

"Those look amazing!" Rick was always quick to pick up on Adam's excitement. "That's a great idea, and it means we don't need extra people in boats watching to make sure we aren't surprised by intruders."

Jake turned to Nicki. "While we're gone, I need to ask you and Liliana to do some research for me." Jake filled Nicki and the others in on what he had learned about the rogue crates, both the ones Hernandez had sent with the letter and the malicious boxes locked in the warded shed.

"I still haven't gotten a telegraph response from Havana, so I have to think our base there is damaged or compromised and that Raul is in hiding." Jake refused to allow the possibility that the workers who remained in Havana might have been injured, captured, or killed.

"Of course. What can we do?" Nicki looked distressed.

"Raul's letter was cryptic. He was probably afraid it might be intercepted. Unfortunately, I can't figure out why he sent the items that were included and what we're supposed to do with them.

"I need you two to read the journals and go over the maps and

87

documents he sent and try to understand how they connect with what's going on. If he thought it was important enough to put the boxes together while the base was under bombardment, then there's something valuable there we need to understand," Jake explained.

"Yes, whatever we can do to help," Nicki assured him. "And if there are codes, I'll get Cady involved. She's great at figuring out the ciphers."

"Thank you. I'll admit that I'm boggled," Jake answered.

Despite the generally pleasant atmosphere of the house, Jake couldn't shake a strange foreboding as if something was watching them. He thought about mentioning it, but figured his nerves were getting the best of him.

Kovach frowned and sniffed the air. "Does anyone else smell smoke?" He and the others fanned out, searching nearby rooms. Shouting and banging drew them to the kitchen.

Jake found Edward and the cook stomping out several burning kitchen towels. Pots and pans were scattered on the stove and floor.

"I'm so sorry—I swear I saw a swarm of huntsmen spiders coming out of the stove. They were right there on the counter, too. I know the stove was off. I tried to get them with the pan, and somehow the towels ended up on fire." Edward coughed. "I don't understand. I have no idea what happened. I promise…" Edward was short of breath and looked as if he might have a heart attack. While the private train cars were in Key West, Edward and the rest of the Pullman staff joined the staff at the compound.

"Did you get them?" Jake helped pick up the blackened towels with a meat fork. He didn't see any trace of large spiders or any insects. He was glad Edward got the fire out; it could have gone badly if it had spread.

"There were so many." Edward looked truly rattled. "But… then they were gone. I didn't see them leave—they just vanished. I'll have the maintenance man put down chemicals to make sure they don't come back."

"They were gone by the time I returned after hearing Edward yell," the cook added.

"What the hell?" Kovach asked when Jake returned from the kitchen.

Jake shook his head. "It's taken care of, but there's something strange going on." He told Kovach about Edward's spider sighting and his own disquieting feelings.

"We all just searched the house. There's no one else here," Kovach protested.

"Last I checked, ghosts don't show up as spiders and can't start fires, so there's got to be something," Jake replied.

A knock on the doorframe announced Conroy's presence. "I've gathered the Cuban workers in the dining hall. And I can translate if you need me to."

"Rick and I will be right there." Jake told Conroy about the spiders and odd fire. "Have someone look things over. Something's fishy."

Conroy went to find Edward and get the process started. Rick and the others joined them, and Jake filled them in, then turned his attention back to the main problem.

"I want to find out more about the situation in Havana before we go out to the *Vincente*. I have a feeling everything is tied together somehow." Jake turned to Nicki as he stood. "I'll fill you in before I go if there's anything useful. Nice work, Adam, Miska. I have a feeling this is going to be a memorable trip."

Rick fell into step beside him as they walked to the crew quarters. The large dining area was empty except for four men who sat nervously at one table and Conroy, who chatted quietly with them in Spanish. From Conroy's tone, Jake suspected he was trying to set the men at ease.

Jake and Rick spoke enough Spanish to get by under normal circumstances, but he didn't want to miss any nuance from the men's account, so he was glad Conroy was willing to translate.

"Thank you for meeting with us." Jake took a seat at the table as Rick sat next to him. "We're glad you're here."

He paused, waiting for Conroy, then went on. "I'm worried about Raul Hernandez and the others who stayed behind in Havana. Apparently, we didn't realize how bad it had gotten there with the war. Do you know where he went and what plans were made by the ones who stayed behind?"

A man in a blue shirt spoke up. Conroy waited until he finished his answer, then turned to Jake.

"This is Carlos. He says that Mr. Hernandez planned to stay with family on a farm far from the coast. Hernandez took a couple of workers with him who didn't have anywhere to go. The others were also going to try to take their families to safety."

Jake had no way of knowing whether their efforts were successful, but the answer boded well and was far better than other alternatives.

"Good," Jake replied. "Before you left Havana, were there any workers—maybe new hires—who seemed suspicious? Someone on the inside had to have smuggled the crates with dangerous magic onboard the airship."

Jake figured the men probably understood English at least as well as he did Spanish, but they waited for Conroy's translation, then murmured among themselves. Finally, a short man with a thick mustache launched into an explanation. Jake tried to keep up and couldn't, so he had to wait for Conroy to explain.

"Mateo says that a couple of the long-time employees had to leave to take care of family because of the war, and Hernandez brought in a few new dockhands. There were also new people at the airfield. He thinks they could have smuggled the other boxes on board," Conroy said.

"Did you have the feeling that the base was being watched? Did anything strange happen? Were there attacks on the warehouse or any of our people?" Jake pressed.

Carlos and Mateo conferred with the others, who seemed okay with letting the two speak for them. Carlos looked up and gave a long answer.

"He says that Mr. Hernandez told them to be careful because there had been a lot of looting with the war. They heard other people say they thought they'd been followed when they went outside, and twice it looked like someone tried to break the lock on the back door," Conroy said.

Mateo jumped in with more. Conroy listened and nodded before sharing with Jake and Rick.

"According to Mateo, Mr. Hernandez intended to close the warehouse for a while after the shipment so they could all leave the harbor area. During the last week or so everyone slept in the building because it was strongly built. Some of the places nearby were hit by the shelling."

"Anything else?" The men shook their heads and Jake stood. "Thank you. Your information was helpful. I hope you'll be comfortable here."

Conroy stayed behind with the workers while Rick and Jake returned to the house. "I wish Raul had told me how bad it had gotten," Jake said.

"He probably didn't want to worry you over something you couldn't control," Rick replied. "And if other people were staying at their posts in the city despite the danger, he might have thought it was a point of honor to ride it out."

Jake sighed. "I hope they're all right. There's not going to be any way to find out until it's all over, but maybe if they can go to ground in the countryside, they'll be okay."

I've been thinking of this war as Spanish and American gunships blasting at each other in the ocean. Not bombarding the island and shelling the city. We can't let the Spanish get their hands on the Vincente's *cargo and become even more dangerous.*

Kovach was waiting for them when they got back to the house. "I just got word from Mitch and Jacob—they've dug up details about Sombra. You need to hear this."

Mitch Storm and Jacob Drangosavich were agents with the Department of Supernatural Investigation, one of several secret agencies that tried to keep tabs on all things paranormal. Jake and Kovach shared a bone-deep mistrust of official organizations, but Mitch and Jacob had proven their integrity many times over and were a pipeline for hard-to-get information.

They walked into the kitchen, and Jake poured himself a cup of coffee. "Okay—spill."

Kovach leaned against the wall as Rick straddled a chair. "Apparently Sombra has been meddling in the affairs of the islands where the witch dynasties are based. That hasn't gone well, and—no surprise—the witches are winning. But it's fueled old rivalries between the witch families who are always vying for more control over the trade routes, or competing for the rum, sugar, or tobacco markets."

"Not surprising," Rick said. "And disappointing. All that magic, and they're squabbling like common merchants."

"I guess even witches need to make money. Cursed relics aren't cheap," Jake added.

"Sombra is clearly betting on the Spanish to win. Lucky for us, Tesla-Westinghouse and Edison-Bell are mostly putting aside their rivalry to support the Americans," Kovach replied. "That means both sides are fairly well-matched, although we've got a slight advantage."

"But Sombra getting to the *Vincente* cargo first—if it's what we think it is—would tip the scales," Rick ventured.

"Yeah, and Mitch says that right now, the witch dynasties aren't taking sides. There's no love for Sombra, but they aren't keen to see the Americans have more control in the Caribbean after they've been trying to push the European powers out. Of course, that doesn't mean individual witches haven't thrown their lot in one way or the other," Kovach continued.

"And there are other witches, like Elian, who dislike the dynasties as much as either of the warring sides," Jake pointed out.

"The longer the hostilities go on, the more likely it becomes that one or more of the dynasties will wade into the fray—officially or not," Kovach said. "I think Mitch is hoping that by helping us, it increases the odds of Sombra losing."

"That makes sense. After all, secret agents are supposed to be sneaky," Rick agreed.

"I also can't tell, but I suspect Mitch and Jacob aren't exactly working through official channels on this," Kovach added.

"Which brings me to their tip about Javier Cortez. Their intelligence suggests that he's after the same thing we are—the *Vincente*. The wreck is in international waters, but close enough to the US that I

Spark of Destiny

don't think our side would give it up without a fight. Sombra technically owns the cargo, but given the war, a US court might not be so willing to uphold that. In other words, it's going to get messy," the security chief warned.

"It always does." Jake polished off the rest of his coffee and relished the burn. "Elian believes that Cortez's witch was behind the attack on Nicki's carriage. If he's right, then Cortez is already in Florida and busy meddling. Thanks for the update. Now we have even more to worry about, but it's helpful to know where the next hit might be coming from."

"Shit—we need to get ready." Rick glanced at the clock. "It's getting late. Better pack a duffel so we're ready to head to the ship."

"I DON'T LIKE SPLITTING UP," Jake grumbled as their carriage rumbled toward the waterfront.

"It's more like we're the diversion to keep attention off Adam and Miska," Rick replied. "Not the first time we've been the bait to draw fire away from our boy genius and his toys."

They had agreed to have Adam and Kovach travel separately. Adam's equipment needed its own heavy wagon. To avoid attention, Adam would be meeting Albert Boyers, the son of the *Diligence's* captain, to load the tools, submersible, and Ben onboard a smaller ship that would take the technology, plus Adam and Kovach out to Calusa Key. Ralph Boyers, the captain's other son, would pick up Jake, Rick, and Elian in another boat and meet them at the island.

Conroy had obtained more practical clothes for them, suitable for the salvage work aboard the wrecking ship. Canvas pants, linen shirts, socks, and ditchers' boots, plus jackets and hats, meant Jake and Rick didn't look out of place on the dock with their duffel bags.

The carriage dropped them off a few streets from the docks to avoid prying eyes. Rick and Jake hefted their bags and headed toward the waterfront.

"A bit different from our usual gangways, isn't it?" Rick said as they walked through the bustling, narrow streets. Jake and Rick were no strangers to ocean travel but usually ventured out on ocean liners or private boats.

Those docks were many blocks away. The pier where they were to meet Ralph Boyers was in the commercial section, full of fishing boats, shrimpers, cargo ships, and delivery skiffs. The sidewalks were filled with the men who crewed those boats, not passengers. Establishments that catered to the sailors and fishermen lined the streets, everything from saloons and brothels to barber shops and places to buy clothing and gear.

"If everything goes well, we don't have to be here long." Jake gripped the straps of his duffel just a bit tighter. He hoped he didn't need the gun holstered beneath his coat or the knife hanging from a sheath on his belt, but knowing they were close at hand made him more comfortable in rough company.

Piano music sounded from the juke joints, vying with the sound of the waves and the creaking of boats. The air smelled of seawater, fish, boiled cabbage, and cooked sausage, a nauseating combination that made Jake glad he hadn't eaten dinner.

The sun hung low in the sky, and it would be dark soon. No one seemed to notice them, for which Jake was grateful. He had his hat pulled low and his collar turned up, just in case. The men who jostled past them didn't make eye contact, and Jake wondered if they were just as happy to be anonymous.

"We're early, but not by much." Rick stole a glance at his watch.

"Let's hope Ralph is on time. I don't want to hang around too long," Jake replied.

Despite the day's mild weather, the brisk wind off the ocean made Jake glad for his coat. His foot slipped when something beneath the sole of his boot squashed, and Jake did not look down, not wanting to know.

"There it is. Dock 35." Rick pointed with a nod toward a slip not far ahead of them. The dark shape of a boat bobbed in its berth, but Jake couldn't make out any details. He scanned the people walking nearby but didn't see Elian.

Jake and Rick stepped out of the alley and started across the wide dock siding. Halfway to their destination, three burly men closed ranks to block their way. Rick and Jake stepped back, trying to avoid a confrontation.

"Jake Desmet and Rick Brand," a fourth man said, joining the others. From what Jake could make out by the light of the gas streetlamps, the large men had the look of hired toughs, while the newcomer's coat, trousers, and shoes were expensive.

Jake opened his mouth to deny the greeting, but the newcomer, a shorter man with Macassar-smeared hair and a goatee, held up his hand. "Don't bother to deny it. I don't have time for games."

"Who the hell are you, and why are you in our way?" Jake snapped. Rick fell back a step so they could easily stand back-to-back if a fight broke out.

"I am Javier Cortez. I believe you've heard of me—and of my employer, Sombra."

"If you wanted an appointment, you could have met us at the compound." Jake tried to size up the danger. Cortez didn't look like the type to get his hands dirty. His three bodyguards were large brawlers. Jake suspected they were armed as well.

Rick and I might win if it came down to a fight, but I'd rather not test our luck. Even if we got away from Cortez, I don't want to get the cops involved.

"Don't interfere in Sombra's affairs," Cortez warned. "The *Vincente* is our ship, and you've got no right to the salvage. Your company has nothing to gain by getting embroiled in this war."

"Why are you here?" Jake sidestepped Cortez's warning. He'd been expecting Cortez to show up sooner or later. What bothered him was that the other man knew enough about their plans to know they would be here on the docks at this time.

We've got another traitor. That's the only way for Cortez to have found out.

"I'm here to warn you to mind your own business," Cortez told him, his expression hardening. "And to make it clear that we're keeping an eye on you. This is not a fight you can win. Go home."

Jake managed a cocky half-smile. "Can't do that. Already made reservations."

Cortez stepped back, which was the signal for the goons to pull their weapons and move toward Jake and Rick.

"Last chance," Cortez said from behind the toughs. "Leave now, and you won't be harmed."

Jake saw the glint of the streetlamp on gunmetal and the steel of blades. He reached for his Peacemaker. "Go to hell."

The three toughs advanced and then stopped in their tracks.

"Enough." Elian emerged from the shadows, a slim figure dressed all in black.

"What did you do to my men?" Cortez demanded.

Elian regarded him with annoyance. "I stopped them from committing a crime."

"Let them go."

"Eventually. Once we have gone about our business." Elian moved closer. Cortez's eyes widened in fear as he struggled but appeared unable to move.

"Leave us alone. Stay out of our concerns. Get out of Key West and don't come back," Elian told him.

"You don't have the right—" Cortez's argument cut off mid-sentence as his mouth continued to move, but no more sound came out.

"Come along," Elian said to Jake and Rick. "We're expected."

Jake cast a look over his shoulder as they followed Elian toward Dock 35. Neither Cortez nor his ruffians had moved or made a sound.

Dim running lights illuminated the boat, and Jake could see the silhouette of a man in the cabin.

"That was a very handy trick back there," Rick said.

Elian gave him a look of wan amusement. "A lifetime of magic makes the complex look simple. Far more than a 'trick' was involved, but I no longer waste breath on people who won't see reason."

"What happens when the spell wears off?" Jake asked as they hurried toward the dock.

"They'll regain their ability to move and talk, but we'll be long gone," Elian replied. "I imagine they'll have terrible headaches as well, which will keep them out of our affairs for at least a day."

Jake looked at their companion, even more impressed with his magic than before and deeply thankful to have Elian on their side.

"Hurry!" A stocky man with dark hair gestured from the top of a gangplank. The *Marlin* looked like a modified patrol boat.

Jake hung back. "Blue skies," he said, repeating the code phrase Kovach had given him.

"Red skies," the man replied, sounding frustrated. "Now get your asses onboard so we can get the hell out of here."

Jake and Rick hurried up the ramp. Elian managed to quicken his pace without looking rushed.

"I'm Ralph," the man said as two others started to cast off lines, and the engine rumbled. "Get into the cabin, sit down, and hold on. We're going to put some distance between us and the wharf."

They found seats inside the small cabin as the boat roared to life. As soon as they were clear of the harbor, they picked up speed, hurtling across the waves.

After a while, Ralph poked his head into the seating area. "Don't worry—someone's got the helm, and I've got scouts watching to make sure we aren't followed."

"How did Javier Cortez know we'd be on the docks at a certain time?" Jake asked.

Ralph's face darkened with anger. "Son of a bitch. I don't know, but I'm going to find out. Is that what held you up?"

"Cortez and three of his men tried to intimidate us," Rick said. "Elian persuaded him to let us go."

Ralph looked at Elian and raised an eyebrow. "Persuaded, huh? I bet. I can tell you that no one from my crew left the boat from the time we got to port. But the docks are full of people, and Cortez could have had spies watching for one of our boats."

"How would he know to look for your boats? There are a lot of wreckers in Key West," Rick asked.

"First, Cortez is a known quantity around here. Sombra's good little soldier. Sombra is always looking for a way to poke their nose in where they aren't wanted," Ralph said, disdain clear in his voice. "Second, he knows what's in the *Vincente's* cargo—I guarantee it. So if magic is involved, we're one of the very few wrecking crews that will handle that kind of job and the only one anyone but a fool would trust. That narrows down the list."

Someone called to Ralph from the deck, and he yelled back in acknowledgment before he returned his attention to Jake and the others. "Gotta go. We can talk more at the Key. Just stay in the cabin—we're moving fast, and the water's choppy. I don't want to have to fish you out if you go overboard."

"You think Kovach and Adam had any trouble with Cortez's people?" Rick asked when Ralph was gone, clearly worried.

Jake shrugged. "Don't know, but I doubt it. That's why they left from a different place. Cortez has no reason to recognize either of them—you and I have been a little higher profile," he said with a wry smile. "And honestly, Miska's a shoot-first kind of guy. If someone did try to get in the way, he'd make sure they regretted it."

Jake looked to Elian. "Did you pick up on any magic back there? Is Cortez a witch or a psychic?"

Jake's question seemed to pull the other man out of his thoughts.

"Cortez?" Elian replied. "He's got some magic but nothing powerful, and by all accounts, he's neither trained nor experienced. That can still be a dangerous combination, but one we can work around. His witch, Ramon Escarra, is strong enough to be dangerous."

"What's your theory on how Cortez knew to look for us?" Jake asked.

"The simplest answers are usually closest to the truth. Both sides want to salvage the wreck as quickly as possible, so it's not a stretch that you'd find a wrecking company and go to Calusa Key," Elian replied.

"Ralph is correct that few salvagers will work a wreck that's said to have a magical cargo. Ghosts don't bother them, but wreckers are a superstitious bunch around anything paranormal," he continued. "Cortez could have spies watching for those wreckers, waiting for you to make contact. No doubt he and Sombra already have their plans underway."

"Do you think he'll cause trouble for the compound?" Jake hated being watched or followed.

"I suspect that Cortez had something to do with the clock incident. If he's connected to Drogo Veles, then Cortez might have also gotten those cursed and dangerous crates onto the airlift in Havana. The sender was probably counting on them triggering in mid-air, or once they reached Key West, and now he's pulling out his hair, wondering why nothing happened." Elian gave a cold laugh. "Which is why I'd already strengthened the protections on both the airship and the warehouse ahead of time."

Jake felt Rick shift in his seat and glanced at his friend who clung to the armrests with a white-knuckled grip. "Are you going to be sick?"

Rick had paled, and he kept his mouth clamped tightly shut as he vigorously shook his head.

"Calusa Key isn't far, and at the rate we're going, we should be there soon."

The engine throttled back, the boat slowed to a more normal speed, and it stopped bouncing on the waves. Rick slumped in his seat, still with an iron grip but no longer looking like he might heave at any second.

Ralph stuck his head in again. "Everyone okay?" Jake and Elian nodded. Ralph looked askance at Rick. "Your buddy doesn't look too good."

"He'll rally," Jake promised. "He does this on airships, boats, and fast carriages."

Rick made a rude gesture in Jake's direction but didn't bother to argue.

"If you say so. Tell him if he pukes, he has to clean it up," Ralph warned. "I sent a telegraph to the office letting them know we had you and were heading home. If you need it, there are crackers and tonic water in the cabinet. I'm sure there'll be food waiting when we get there."

Ralph ducked out, leaving them alone once more. Rick groaned and closed his eyes, but still didn't lose his lunch. Jake and Elian sat quietly, each lost in thought.

How are we going to stay one step ahead of Cortez and Sombra? Cortez and his witch could be a serious problem.

More worries rose in the silence. *I'll let Conroy know that Cortez is poking around to make sure our people are protected. That goes double for Liliana and Nicki because Nicki never stays out of trouble if it's to be found. I trust them and Conroy—they know what they're doing.*

But it would be a mistake to underestimate Cortez. He's not going to give up without a fight, and it's likely to get bloody before it gets better.

Chapter Five

Darkness fell early, making it appear later than it was. The *Marlin* docked, and Ralph led them off the boat after he'd given instructions to the crew. "Welcome to Calusa Key. Home to wreckers since at least the 1600s. Our family's been at it for over a hundred and fifty years. It's in our blood."

He pointed to a hulking dark shape of a ship a little farther down the dockside. "That's our tug, the *Diligence*. Your friends are already on board. I'll help you stow your gear."

Jake looked in the opposite direction, where a path ran from the dock to a rambling, one-story house. The pink stucco walls likely hid cement block construction to withstand hurricanes. Steel Bahama-style storm shutters covered the windows. Bougainvillea climbed trellises up the walls next to large oleander bushes.

"The central section was the original house, which has been added onto over the years, becoming the compound for the whole family," Ralph told them, noticing Jake's interest. "It's made it through a lot of storms."

Shouting near the dock drew their attention. Jake recognized Kovach's voice. He and the others ran toward the pier, where it looked like a brawl had broken out.

"What's going on?" Ralph's voice cut through the clamor.

Kovach and two other guards stopped roughing up three black-clad strangers. All six men were soaking wet. "We found these guys underwater trying to put explosives on the boat," he told the others. "Thank Adam—he had one of his turtles on patrol. It gave the alert, and we hauled their asses up to find out who sent them."

"And the explosives?" Ralph demanded.

"Found, removed, and set aside to be safely detonated," Kovach replied.

"They didn't swim here," Ralph said to a nearby dockhand. "Take one of the boats out and look for a small craft. Go armed." The man headed toward another dock where skiffs were tied up.

Kovach gave his prisoner a shake. "Who sent you?"

The man looked wet and miserable and was sporting a bruise that would likely be a black eye. "I don't know, mate. A guy on the docks offered us good money to come with him, swim over to the big boat, and stick a couple of things on the side. Said he'd pay us as soon as we got back to the wharf. I didn't ask questions, and he didn't explain."

"What did he look like?" Kovach pressed.

"Nothing special. He's someone I've seen around. Don't know his name."

Jake and Rick exchanged a look, and Jake knew they were likely thinking the same thing—that whoever piloted the craft that brought the saboteurs would have detonated the explosives before the men got clear, eliminating witnesses and removing the need to pay for their services.

"Wait until we've left for the wreck, and then hand them over to the police," Ralph told his guards. "We've got a schedule to keep."

Jake didn't expect the craft that transported the saboteurs to be found, and he wouldn't be surprised if they met with "accidents" in jail so they could never identify who hired them.

"I sent the turtle around the boat twice—no more bombs," Adam reported breathlessly, running to join them.

"Nice work," Jake told the inventor. "I'm now a techno turtle fan."

He looked to Kovach. "Thanks for handling that. Let's get on board and get you into dry clothes."

Ralph stopped to give quiet orders to his guards, then jogged to rejoin them. "Now that we aren't going to blow up, let's get going."

They followed Ralph up the gangway onto the *Diligence*.

"Did you have any trouble on the wharf?" Adam asked. Ben was nowhere to be seen, so Jake guessed the automaton was already in Adam's cabin.

"We had a run-in with Cortez but got away from him thanks to Elian," Rick replied.

"Glad you made it." A broad-shouldered man with salt and pepper hair strode toward them and shook their hands. "I'm Harry Boyer, captain of this fine vessel. You've already met Ralph. Albert, my other son and our first mate, is busy getting us ready to shove off. Go ahead and stow your gear, then come up to the mess hall for dinner."

He bustled off before they even had a chance to introduce themselves. Ralph watched his father walk away and chuckled.

"Don't worry—he'll know your names by the time we finish dinner. He's got a single-minded focus until we're in open waters. Part of what makes him a good captain." Ralph turned back to them. "Come on. I'll show you to your quarters and give you the quick tour before I'm due on the bridge."

"They've got the *Oceanus* rigged with its crane real slick," Adam gushed, pointing toward where the submersible hung at one side of the ship. "I've been all around the boat and down to the engine room. And I showed Albert and Harry the maps so they can fine-tune where we're going."

"Albert's good with locator magic," Ralph reminded them. "Once we get to the site, I can astral travel to the wreck to help Adam know exactly where to go."

Their cabins were clean and comfortable, despite their small size. Bunk beds left room for a small desk and chair, and cabinets provided a place to store their duffels. Jake noticed oilcloth rain slickers hanging from pegs on the wall, with two pairs of high boots right below.

"They're not calling for bad weather, but things can change fast out here, so if we get a storm, you'll want gear for it," Ralph said.

"There's a shared bathroom with everything you need down the corridor," Ralph told them. "Even hot water. All the comforts of home."

After they left their bags in their rooms, Ralph walked them through the main areas, giving them a quick run-down of basic procedures. He ended with the galley.

"Once we're underway, Cook will have dinner ready. The food isn't fancy, but it's filling, and our boys never go away hungry."

Ralph took his leave for the bridge. Jake and the others found their way back on deck as the tugboat cast off.

"I thought we'd be roughing it more. Those cabins are pretty nice." Rick leaned against the railing, watching the lights of Calusa Key fade in the distance.

"It's too damn dark out here," Kovach grumbled.

"That's the whole point," Jake teased. "We're being stealthy."

Kovach's muttered reply made his opinion clear on the matter. Rick stared off toward the open water. "I always forget how big the ocean is. And how hard it would be to find a person if they got lost."

"What's with all the gloom and doom?" Adam countered. "We're heading for a shipwreck. I'm going to get to put the *Oceanus* to a real test and see how well Ben does underwater. We're going to recover sunken treasure. It's like something out of an Allan Quartermain novel—or even Jules Verne."

Jake smiled at his friend's fondness for the famed fictional adventurer and Verne's fabulist science. "Like our lives aren't dangerous enough?"

Adam gave a dramatic sigh. "It's *fiction*, Jake. The good guys win, the bad guys lose, and the main character lives to fight another day because if he didn't, there would be no more books. It's much tidier than having adventures in the real world."

Adam, Rick, and Jake had plenty of experience being chased by monsters, shot at by assassins, and nearly blown up by rivals. Jake had enough excitement to last several lifetimes, although he suspected that the current situation was bound to add to the total.

"I rather fancy biographies of the explorers myself," Rick noted. "I consider it good luck to read about people who had all kinds of adventures and lived to a ripe old age to write their memoirs."

Jake's taste ran to mysteries, especially the sort without a lot of ruckus that featured a detective who solved the cases in relative safety through deduction and intelligence. Given the dangers of real life, he found the stories tidy and soothing.

"How about you?" Jake asked Elian.

"When I'm not studying grimoires, I'll admit a fondness for Dumas's stories, as well as Poe and Defoe." Elian smiled as if admitting to a faux pas. "Potboilers, I know. But there you have it."

Jake chuckled. "Nicki's the one who loves books like *Dracula* and *Frankenstein*—and Dr. Jekyll. I don't know how she manages to sleep after that."

Elian's smile broadened. "She shares that penchant with Liliana, who told me that in finishing school they used to stay up late and make up scary stories for the other girls. Such tendencies, so firmly ingrained, are hardly likely to be changed now," he added with mock chagrin.

Jake shared Rick's discomfort with the vast, dark ocean that on the tugboat seemed far too close than it did aboard an ocean liner. The wind whipped around them, much colder than it had seemed on land. He shivered, not entirely due to the temperature.

"Let's go get dinner." Jake was unsurprised when the others were quick to agree.

They followed the smell of food to the mess hall, a compact space dominated by a table and benches bolted to the deck.

"You're the passengers? Come on in." Cook gestured toward the large stew pot in the center of the table. A big bowl of rice sat next to it. "I'm Danny, but the crew call me Cook."

"Help yourselves. There's the ladle. It's fish and seafood stew. Goes good with the rice. There's plenty to go around. Everyone else will wander in when they get a break in their duties."

"This is fantastic," Rick said after a couple of mouthfuls.

"It reminds me of dinners in Cuba," Elian replied, clearly pleased with the meal. "So good."

The flavors were new to Jake, and he noted Adam's curious expression, but both men dug into their meals after a few hesitant early bites.

"I think I have a new favorite." Adam reached for a second helping.

"There's plenty of black coffee to wake you up after you're full," Cook said. "You've got a long night ahead."

When they finished eating, Jake and the others went back up on deck. He couldn't help feeling nervous about the night's work and sensed the same jitters in his companions.

The *Diligence* clipped along through the waves at a good pace. More than an hour after leaving the dock, their speed slowed, and the engines idled.

Ralph came down the steps from the bridge. "Albert says we're close, based on your maps." He nodded to Adam. "And what he's picking up from his magic. We're going to get a little closer, and then I'll do my thing."

"Any sign of company?" Kovach scanned the horizon, always alert for threats, although the darkness made it difficult to see very far.

"Nothing yet," Ralph told them. "Once we're in position, I figured you'd send out your 'turtles.'" He glanced in Adam's direction.

"They're ready to go," Adam assured them. "If I had to guess, I think we're a couple of days ahead of Sombra in figuring out the wreck location. With a bit of luck, we'll be in and out before they get here."

Jake knew that things never went that smoothly. Still, he held his peace, hoping for the same, but he knew it was unlikely. "Our friends at the Department of Supernatural Investigation are looking closely at Sombra and Javier Cortez. I'm expecting a file from them when we get back. Normally I don't like working with the officials, but finding the *Vincente's* cargo is too important to risk Cortez beating us to it, and DSI can't step in without causing more of an international incident than we've already got with the war."

Rick looked at Elian. "Picking up on any magic?"

Spark of Destiny

Elian's gaze went unfocused for a moment as he stilled, staring out into the darkness. "I don't sense magic actively being cast other than by those aboard our ship," he replied when he came back to himself. "But I feel something beneath the water. It must be powerful for me to be aware of it at this distance."

"Can you tell what it is?" Jake asked.

Elian shook his head. "No. But we must be near to the wreck."

"That's my cue," Ralph said. "I'd prefer to do this where I can lie down."

They followed him to the now-empty mess hall. Ralph lay down on one of the bench seats, and Jake guessed this was a familiar part of a salvage run for him.

"Most of the time when I 'travel,' it's nothing to be concerned about," Ralph told them. "Keep an eye on me, don't let me fall off the bench, and don't worry if I make some odd noises. When I come back, I'll need someone to grab me some water and sweets—there should be a tin box with goodies on the counter. Cook leaves them for the crew to eat at odd hours."

"How do we know if something goes wrong?" Jake asked, anxious about the idea that Ralph could send his consciousness wandering away from his body, far enough to reach a shipwreck on the ocean floor.

"If I start shaking and take a fit, put a belt between my teeth, and get Albert." Ralph turned to Elian. "I don't know if you could do anything to help with your magic. I hope we don't have to find out."

Ralph closed his eyes, took several deep breaths, and relaxed. It looked to Jake as if Ralph had fallen into a deep sleep, but he suspected that was the trance necessary to do his astral travel.

"Interesting," Elian mused. "His magic has a very different 'feel' than mine, but I sense that he has begun. There's a shift in the energy that's most unusual."

Minutes passed. Jake and Rick exchanged a glance, both of them increasingly nervous the longer Ralph's trance continued. Adam watched from a few feet away, looking both scared and intrigued.

Ralph made a few faint grunts as if he were dreaming. His fingers twitched, and one foot moved from side to side. Rick and Jake stayed close by in case Ralph slipped from the bench. Kovach retreated to stand with Adam while Elian backed up just enough to give Ralph some breathing room.

"He's been gone for a while." Jake checked his watch. "How long is too long?"

"Give him a bit more time," Elian urged. "I'm not sensing danger or distress. He might have needed to search for the wreck if we're not right on top of it. Or he might be looking for the best path for Adam's submersible to access the cargo."

After what seemed like forever, Ralph's eyes snapped open, and he jackknifed to sit up, gasping for breath. Jake and Rick took a step forward to steady him if necessary. He waved them off, still trying to compose himself.

"I'm okay. I'm sure it's strange watching that for the first time. The crew has gotten pretty familiar with it. Usually Cook or Albert stays with me. Give me a minute, and I'll tell you everything."

Adam came forward with a glass of water and the tin of sweets. Ralph gave him a grateful look and downed the water, then chomped through several cookies. His breathing evened out, and he nodded to the group of anxious watchers.

"That's better. It takes me a few minutes when I get back to… settle into my skin again. That's not really accurate because part of me is still here even when I'm…there…but it's how I think of it."

Jake didn't envy Ralph the experience. Elian also wore a sympathetic expression, and Jake supposed that a major outlay of magic also required recovery time.

"We're near," Ralph confirmed. "I can give Dad directions to nudge us so we're directly overhead. The *Vincente* must have twisted as it sank. The bow and the stern are in two pieces a few hundred feet apart. It looked like something blew a hole right through the side. The good news is that between the blast and the way the ship tore apart, getting into the cargo hold shouldn't be a problem, especially if you have your mechanical man to help."

Adam nodded his approval. "That's better than what I expected. Did it look like cargo had spilled out?"

"I'm not sure. I wasn't looking for that—my attention was on the condition of the ship," Ralph said. "The wreck hasn't been down long, so that means tides and storms haven't had a chance to carry loose pieces far. I hope your little ship has a bright light because it's black down there."

"It does," Adam confirmed. "Plus, Ben's eyes are fitted with some experimental night vision lenses, so he should be able to see pretty well. And I designed a special techno turtle that can handle the water pressure to scout for us. It can feed what it sees back to Ben and from Ben to me. It's also got a bright light—and a few surprises."

After what they saw on the train, Jake figured the turtle could hold its own in a fight. He suspected that the ones deployed as sentinels were also armed.

"Does that mean we're ready to get moving? Because the night isn't getting any younger," Kovach observed.

Albert came to the door. "We've got a problem. There's a storm coming in, fast. It either wasn't there earlier or changed directions. It's not safe to deploy until it's past."

Adam looked stricken. "How long?"

"No telling. If it keeps moving at the current rate, it could cost us a few hours. If it stalls, we could lose the whole night. There's no helping it." Albert looked worried enough that Jake didn't second-guess his opinion.

Kovach looked at Adam. "You really don't want to be down there in rough seas—or if the ship has to pull back."

"Harry's a weather witch. Can he *nudge* the storm to a different course?" Jake asked.

Albert grimaced. "Maybe. Depends on the size and power of the front. It's one thing to whip up a waterspout or push back the edge of a storm to hurry past it. But relocating or neutralizing an entire storm would take enormous energy—possibly fatal for the witch. That's a last-ditch emergency move I hope we never have to use."

Adam's crestfallen expression made his disappointment clear.

"Sorry," Albert said. "I know we're trying to beat Sombra to the prize. But if the boat or the equipment gets damaged, we're out of the race. We'll keep an eye on the weather and keep you updated." Ralph excused himself to follow Albert to the bridge, leaving the others in the galley.

"Let's make sure everything is secured and try to get some sleep." Jake felt as disappointed as Adam looked. "I don't like the delay, but Albert's right—if we get damaged, we'll be even further behind."

The *Diligence* pulled back from its position to wait out the storm. Unfortunately, the rough weather lasted until just before dawn. Since the plan had been to work at night to reduce their chances of being spotted by Sombra, that meant losing a full day.

Jake risked another telegram to keep Nicki and the others from worrying. "Delayed."

Adam puttered in his makeshift lab, with Rick and Kovach dropping in to help and Jake stopping by to chat. Offers to help around the ship were politely declined. After a while, Jake returned to his quarters, read a book, and tried to sleep, hoping that calm seas would mean working all night.

BY LATE AFTERNOON, Albert and Harry gave the "all clear," meaning the storm front had moved off, and they could move forward that night with the dive. Ralph did another astral session to ensure nothing below had moved due to the rough water and confirmed that conditions remained good for the salvage.

"I'll adjust our position, and then I'll be down to help get Adam into the *Oceanus* and send his turtles out to stand guard," Ralph told them once evening fell.

If Ralph seemed to find any of the night's work strange, he took it with remarkable aplomb, as if an experimental submarine, mechanical spy turtles, and a waterproof automaton were all in a day's work.

Then again, he can astral project. His father and brother have water and

Spark of Destiny

locator magic, and this isn't their first supernatural salvage run. Maybe it *is* just another day for him.

"Hey, Adam. I understand how you're going to get Ben down to the wreck. He weighs enough to sink like a stone. How are you going to bring him back up?" Kovach asked as they walked toward where the *Oceanus* hung in its cradle.

Adam grinned. "That's easy. He's got blasters in the soles of his feet. When we're done, he'll fire up and shoot right to the surface. Then he's got an airbag he can deploy to keep him afloat until we haul him on board."

Kovach shook his head, grinning. "I should have known you'd have it figured out, Wonderboy."

"Are you sure that special weird radio of yours will work?" Jake asked.

Adam's experimental device used extremely low frequencies that traveled better and farther through water than radio waves.

"Mostly," Adam admitted. "I sank one in the deepest quarry I could find, and it transmitted just fine. Although I'll admit that's not as far down as the *Vincente*."

Jake knew the power of the equipment was limited, mostly for emergency use, so chatter wouldn't be an option. "Tell us when you get down there, and check in once an hour. We're all going to be on pins and needles until you're back."

Adam nodded. "Will do."

"I can't be of any help deploying the submarine," Elian said. "So I'm going to get out of the way and scan for other ships."

Jake, Rick, and Kovach moved to the side to give Adam, Ralph, and several deckhands room to maneuver.

Adam fussed over Ben, checking the *werkman* over carefully before clapping him on the shoulder. "Don't take any chances," he warned the metal man. "I'm counting on having you come back without getting hurt."

Jake wasn't surprised that Adam spoke to his clockwork creation as if it were human. He knew how fond the inventor grew of his *werkmen* and had spent enough time with them to know that their individual quirks made them seem almost alive.

Adam and Ralph opened the gate in the railing where the gangplank would normally rest. Ben stepped off the deck and plummeted into the dark water with a splash.

"Now it's my turn." Adam wore the diving suit as a precaution and carried the round helmet under his arm. Ralph helped him run a last check of the systems when he powered up the *Oceanus* and gave him a hand to climb inside. Adam looked to his friends and snapped a jaunty salute before sealing the hatch behind him.

"All clear!" Ralph yelled once the submersible was ready to be deployed. Wally and Sid, the deckhands, worked winches to slowly lower the *Oceanus* to the surface, then opened the cradle to let it sink below the waves.

Kovach crossed himself. Not for the first time, Jake wished his Presbyterian upbringing afforded him a similar warding gesture. Rick absently stroked his watch, a telltale clue to his anxiety.

"Now, we wait." Ralph stared down at the sea, looking pensive.

Jake, Rick, and Kovach returned to the mess hall where Adam had rigged up his special radio. Elian chose to remain on deck, and Jake felt better knowing the witch was watching for trouble. Ralph promised to let them know if anything changed on the bridge and went back to his duties.

"Guess that leaves us with cards and coffee." Jake pulled a deck from his pocket. They filled their cups and sat at the table, silent while Jake shuffled and dealt.

Rick fiddled with the box that Adam swore would pick up signals from the *Oceanus*. He moved it around until he detected the constant sound of static on the channel Adam designated.

"How off the books do you think that is?" Kovach nodded toward the radio.

Jake snorted. "Very. Top secret, Fort Knox stuff. Adam always gives us his best experimental gear first."

"That's what I figured," Kovach replied. "I'll give him credit for guts. I'm not keen on swimming, and less so going underwater. No way in hell you'd get me inside that tin can at the bottom of the ocean."

"I'll admit I wouldn't volunteer for it." Jake studied his cards. "But it's all a big adventure to Adam."

Rick returned to his seat, apparently satisfied with the way the radio had been tuned. "Unfortunately, there's no way for us to contact him," he fretted. "But if it works the way Adam says it will, he should be able to share short bursts. Obviously, it's never been tried at that depth before."

"Hell of a shakedown cruise," Kovach remarked.

They played poker for a handful of dried beans Jake found in the pantry. Conversation focused on the game, and no one seemed interested in talking. Jake fought the urge to fidget. The game served as a better distraction than reading, but losing several hands in a row—given his usual skill—only served to demonstrate just how much his focus suffered.

About an hour after the *Oceanus* submerged, the static crackled louder. Jake and the others dropped their cards and gathered around the box, straining to hear.

"…can see it. Turtle is inside. Ben moving boxes. All good."

Jake wasn't the only one who breathed a sigh of relief, although Adam still had several hours before retrieval.

"It's working." Rick stared at the box with a look of wonder. "Holy hell, it's actually working."

Ralph stepped in, along with Elian, and Jake told them about the transmission.

"We don't have a visual on any other ships," Ralph said. "This spot is at the edge of the shipping lanes, so it's not in the main traffic flow. That tells me the *Vincente's* captain wanted to avoid patrols and other ships. It might have left them isolated for an attack, but it helps us keep a low profile."

"I will stay alert, but so far there hasn't been any hint of magic other than the faint, odd energy coming from below," Elian told them.

"I wish Adam's 'techno turtles' could show us what they see, but that's probably asking for too much," Rick said.

One of Adam's turtles had been modified for deep diving. The others floated around the ship, helping to keep a lookout.

"The *Diligence* is running with minimum lighting for safety," Ralph added. "We don't want to attract attention, but we also don't want to get hit in case another ship happens to come our way."

He glanced back toward the hatch. "I've got a feeling that the weather might be changing again. I hope your buddy doesn't run late. We don't want him down there in another storm."

Ralph went back to the bridge while Elian returned to his vigil. Jake suspected that Elian's surveillance was his way of dealing with the stress of waiting.

"You think Ralph's right about the weather?" Rick sounded nervous.

Jake shrugged. "Things can change fast out here. Let's hope Adam doesn't get lost in the moment and remembers he's on a deadline."

THEY PLAYED HALF-HEARTEDLY, paying little attention to the game but unwilling to sit with nothing to do. After a few hands, they even stopped counting their winnings.

On the hour, the radio squealed again.

"Nearly ready…carry what we can…one more dive…ship is haunted…be on time."

The radio went dead again, and the three men looked at one another.

"The ship's haunted? Guess that's not a surprise, but does that mean the ghosts are bothering Adam?" Rick echoed the questions in Jake's mind.

"I wish we'd have brought Liliana," Jake said. "Although I don't know if her abilities could reach that far under the water."

"That's something she never tried." They looked up to see Elian in the hatchway, and they filled him in on Adam's latest update, unsure how much he had heard.

"She deals with the sea ghosts from the shore. This part of the ocean is full of wrecks," Elian went on as he entered the room. "The ghosts of the deepest places don't often stir. I wonder if *Vincente's* secret cargo contained something that agitated spirits or gave them more power."

"That's a lovely thought," Kovach muttered.

Harry Boyer, the ship's captain, stuck his head in. "We have a situation. There's fog rising, and the water is rough, but it started all of a sudden. Normal weather doesn't do that."

Elian met his gaze. "It's not magic. Something has disturbed the ghosts."

Harry's eyebrows raised. "Ghosts? Are you kidding me?"

Elian shook his head. "I'm afraid not. I don't detect magic, but I sense the energy shift. Unfortunately, my wife is the medium, not I."

"Shit. We can ride this out for a while—long enough to bring your friend up from the bottom—but it would be a whole lot safer if we didn't have to do it in a storm." Harry passed a hand over his face. "I'm a weather witch. But like I told y'all before, that doesn't mean that I can turn a hurricane around, although I can usually temper what's going on in the immediate area around the ship for a little while."

"That's also how you know what's going on isn't normal?" Jake confirmed.

Harry nodded. "Yeah, it's pretty freakish. Never figured ghosts could do that."

"I don't think 'normal' spirits can," Elian said. "I may not have my wife's talent, but I have learned a lot from her over the years. Certain objects and circumstances can rile spirits or give them more energy, enabling them to impact the world of the living."

"Do we think there's something in the cargo annoying the ghosts?" Kovach asked.

"That would make sense," Harry agreed. "But it doesn't change that the fog and rough water is going to make hoisting the mechanical man and the submarine more difficult than it already would be."

"I can help." They all turned to look at Elian. "I'm not a water witch, but I can channel energy to strengthen your magic and stamina.

Make you a little more powerful. If we time it right, you and I together might be able to clear the fog and quiet the waves just long enough to get Adam and Ben back onboard."

"Okay." Harry gave a daredevil grin. "That's just crazy enough to work. I'm in."

Jake and the others gave up on their game as the clock counted down the last hour. Jake played solitaire while Kovach rolled a fifty-cent piece between his fingers, and Rick stared at the radio as if he could will it to speak.

"Coming up…water's rough…got a load. Ghosts aren't happy. Stand by." Adam's voice broke up as he spoke but was still understandable through the static.

Jake and the others left the mess hall in search of Harry and Elian, who were standing by the railing, staring out at the ocean.

"It's time. Adam's on his way up." Jake felt breathless with anxiety. "Anything you can do is a big help."

Ralph and the deckhands showed up right on time, standing by the rendezvous area with a searchlight directed at the water.

A metallic gleam caught Jake's eye as one of the turtles bobbed to the surface. Ralph scooped it up with a net and set it out of the way on deck, doing the same as others made their way back to the ship.

The water had grown increasingly choppy in the past two hours, ever since Adam's vehicle reached the wreck site. Jake glanced at Elian and Harry, who stood at the rail with their eyes closed, faces taut with concentration. Elian laid a hand on Harry's shoulder.

Something large and shiny popped through the water. Ben's metal head broke the surface, with a cloud of white airbags supporting him. The deckhands dropped a loop of cable that went under the automaton's arms and began to winch him up with another turtle catching a ride.

"There's Adam!" Jake yelled when the *Oceanus* emerged.

All around the tugboat, the fog had thinned, although Jake could see it blanketing the water a little farther out. The sea wasn't placid immediately around the ship, but it looked to be wilder several dozen yards away as if a protective bubble surrounded the *Diligence*.

Spark of Destiny

"We've got him!" Ralph called as the sling and hoist closed around the *Oceanus*.

Ben landed on the deck with a thump. A container was clutched in each hand, holding small pieces from the *Vincente's* cargo. As the submersible rose from the water, Jake could see that its metal claws held a crate next to its underbelly.

A sudden flare lit up the sky in the distance. Jake squinted at the bright light and made out the image of a dark boat before the light faded. Shots rang out, sounding like a Gatling gun.

"What the bloody hell?" Rick looked at Jake, confused and worried.

"Get us out of here," Ralph yelled into a speaking tube to the bridge. "Everyone's aboard, might be trouble where that light went up."

Rick and Jake hurried toward the submersible, where Ralph and Kovach were already pulling the crate away from the edge of the deck and standing by for Adam to open the hatch. Ben and the turtle stood off to one side, awaiting further instructions.

"Did you see that?" Adam stumbled out of the submarine, looking exultant and wild-eyed, hair completely askew. "It worked! It really worked!"

Jake glared at him. "You didn't expect it to?"

Adam had the good grace to look chagrinned. "There was always a chance," he admitted, then brightened immediately. "But the *Oceanus*, the turtle, Ben—it worked!"

Rick took Adam's arm and steered him toward the hatch to the interior of the boat. "What the hell was that light, and who's shooting at us?"

Adam's grin broadened. "Those were the turtles. When they sensed an intruder, they were supposed to light up and fire blanks."

"Blanks?" Kovach asked.

"Mostly," Adam admitted. "Some of the turtles have real bullets in case of emergency. Those require a manual override."

"How are they going to find us?" Rick asked until a metallic *clunk* sounded near the ladder that went down the exterior of the tug boat.

"Son of a bitch," Kovach muttered under his breath as they

watched all of Adam's mechanical turtles climb aboard as the ship's engines came back online.

Adam made a quick count. "All here. We can go now."

Ralph just shook his head, incredulous. "That's all really…something."

"I figured out what cargo we need from the wreck, but even with Ben's help, I couldn't get it all at once, and I didn't think we wanted to try again until tomorrow," Adam told Ralph. "I'm afraid we'll have to come back—but I think we can finish up with one more dive."

The *Diligence* began to move, and it seemed to Jake that since they'd brought Adam's sub onboard the fog lifted and the water calmed.

Harry and Elian joined them in the mess hall as Kovach helped Adam out of his cumbersome dive suit.

"I don't think we'll have any more weather trouble tonight," Harry said. "Especially not once we pull back from the area. We'll go out far enough to confuse anyone who's looking for us and come back here tomorrow night."

"And I'll send the turtles back to watch the area so we'll know if anyone gets close," Adam replied.

"You two make an impressive team." Jake turned to Adam. "When the ghosts got grumpy, they used their magic to calm things down."

"Thank you." Adam dropped onto the bench seat like his strings had been cut. "I think the ghosts were protective of the wreck, especially once we started moving and taking things. It's also possible that something in the cargo I haven't brought up yet—like that mysterious relic—affects them too."

Elian frowned. "Did you happen to pick up anything that might have been a personal belonging for the crew?"

Adam smiled. "I had a feeling you'd ask. Just in case, I had Ben pick up a shoe and a pocket watch."

"Good. While Liliana is the medium, my magic can petition Papa Legba and the Baron to ease the passage of the drowned men's spirits," Elian replied. "I was not prepared tonight. By the time we return tomorrow, I will make sure the ritual is ready. That should avoid what happened tonight and let the ghosts move on."

Harry and Ralph exchanged a look, and Jake wondered if they realized their guests were more unusual than they had expected.

"I knew this was going to be an interesting job when we took it." Harry broke into a grin. "You didn't disappoint."

Chapter Six

The faint sound of a child's distant laughter woke Nicki. She opened her eyes, blinked at the light coming in through the sheer curtains at her windows, and took a moment to place where she was.

"Must have been dreaming." Nicki yawned and stretched, listening for the laughter again, but heard nothing. "Definitely my imagination."

She gathered her things, donned a robe, and padded to the bathroom. Jake and the others left the previous evening, so she and Liliana were the only guests. Since Elian was out with Jake and Rick, and given everything that was going on, Liliana had agreed to stay at the compound until the others returned from the salvage attempt.

Nicki looked at her reflection and noticed something at the corner of her eye. She leaned in and pulled at what she thought was a piece of white fuzz. It was soft but not what she thought. It tugged at her eyelid as she tried to remove it, and she bit back a cry as she realized it was a little worm. She put it in the palm of her hand and watched in horror as it bore into her, moving under her skin.

Nicki glanced back to the mirror, thinking perhaps there might be tweezers or a blade in the medicine cabinet and saw several more wiggling white forms at the corners of her eyes.

"*Mon Dieu!*" She startled and her foot caught in her robe causing her to fall. Nicki looked at her hand to see if the worm was still there but there was no sign. She tentatively touched her eyelids and found nothing unusual. *Get a hold of yourself.* Nicki took a deep breath and stood, afraid but determined as she checked her face in the mirror.

"I must be losing my mind," she muttered before getting ready. No one could blame her for the chill down her spine every time she saw her reflection.

On the way downstairs, Nicki glanced at a bookshelf, thinking there might be a novel to read to ease her mind if they had a slow moment.

Sudden screaming filled her head, so loud Nicki clapped both hands to her ears. Her foot slipped, and she pitched forward. She let out a cry of surprise as she flung herself at the balustrade, barely catching hold in time to keep from nosediving down the rest of the steps.

Conroy hurried toward her. "Are you okay?"

Nicki nodded, breathless from the close call. "Something weird is going on. I had a vision in the bathroom, and just now I heard screaming that made me lose my balance. I didn't just slip."

Conroy frowned and helped her to a chair, then went back to the stairs for a closer look. "I don't doubt your experience, but there's nothing wrong with the steps. Your experience sounds like Edward's sighting of non-existent spiders yesterday. We'll get to the bottom of this."

Nicki nodded, still catching her breath. "Are you sure the house isn't haunted?"

"Not that I know about, but perhaps your friend could tell you better than I," Conroy replied. "Can I get you anything?"

Nicki waved him off. "I'm just flustered. Let me gather my wits and I'll meet Liliana in the kitchen."

Conroy left with a backward glance as if he wasn't completely convinced that she was undamaged. Nicki had to admit that she wasn't entirely sure of that herself.

A child's laugh again startled her and she quickly glanced around, confirming that she was alone. Nicki chided herself for an active imagination and took a deep breath. To take her mind off her near-accident, Nicki focused on the details of the room. She noted the seashells and scrimshaw carvings scattered on the shelves among the books that were in keeping with the house's beach theme, although she wondered about the old doll.

A chill went down Nicki's spine as she stared at the poppet. It was crudely made, like something crafted, not bought. The felted face and hands had yellowed with age, and the clothing looked homemade.

When she had first spotted the doll, she thought it might have had sentimental value to Conroy or someone else in the house. But now that she lingered near it, she felt unsettled and vaguely afraid.

Nicki thought of the odd laughter she'd heard—more than once. *There aren't any children in the compound. Could it be the doll?*

And as crazy as it sounds—did the doll try to kill me?

She shied away from the thought of touching the doll but resolved to ask Conroy about it as soon as she saw the man.

Liliana was already in the kitchen, savoring a cup of coffee as she lingered over the newspaper. She frowned when she saw Nicki's expression.

"Are you okay?"

Nicki told her about the vision and the strange sounds, as well as her near-miss on the steps. She didn't mention Edward's spider incident just yet.

"*Dios mio*," Liliana said. "I'm glad you're not hurt. Sit. I'll bring you something to drink."

"Did you make the coffee?" Nicki hoped for more of Liliana's Cuban recipe.

"No, sorry. It's still good, just very American," Liliana replied.

Liliana took a plate from the counter and heaped it with sliced fruit and pastries. She carried that and a cup of coffee to the table and set them in front of Nicki, who murmured her thanks.

"Has Mr. Conroy come back inside?" Nicki asked.

"No—he seemed to be in a hurry, probably looking into what caused your fall. Before that happened, he said he would bring in the crates Señor Hernandez sent from Cuba for us to have a look. Said that Jake mentioned it before they left."

Nicki grinned. "I'm excited about seeing what's in the boxes. Mr. Hernandez must have had a good reason to send them. We get to be detectives."

She remembered the doll, and her good mood faded. Nicki grew quiet as she picked at the food on her plate. Liliana watched her in silence for a moment before folding the paper and setting it aside.

"Was there something else? I'm sure it was quite upsetting." Liliana said.

Nicki fortified herself with a few sips of coffee before answering. "Have *you* heard anything strange since you've been in the house? Sounds that don't belong here? Anything like I described?"

Liliana frowned. "No, but I haven't been here long—just last night. After everything that went on yesterday, I was so tired that I had a nip of brandy and went right to sleep."

Nicki looked down, doubting it had all been in her imagination.

"You've thought of something. Tell me," Liliana urged.

"Are there ghosts in the house? You'd know, right?"

Liliana closed her eyes and stilled for a few minutes with an expression of deep concentration. She looked up and shook her head. "I don't think the house is haunted. I'd notice if there were ghosts strong enough to do something that drew your attention."

Nicki toyed with the edge of her napkin for a few seconds before she answered. "I'm not crazy. Between the vision and the screaming and the times I've heard a child laughing when there was no one around—certainly no children. It sounded far away, but I know that's what I heard. It wasn't a happy sound. There's something scary about it. And I wonder if it's linked to that creepy doll…and maybe the visions?"

Liliana frowned. "Doll? Where did you see that?"

Spark of Destiny

Nicki got up and motioned for Liliana to follow her. "It's on the bookshelf." She retraced her steps from earlier. "Right over—"

The doll was gone.

Nicki turned to Liliana. "I swear it was right there." She pointed to the spot on the shelf. "I saw it just this morning on my way down to breakfast, and saw it yesterday too. It's rather ugly, which made me wonder why anyone would display it, but I thought maybe there was sentimental value."

Liliana moved closer and closed her eyes, concentrating on the spot where Nicki had seen the doll. "I'm picking up very strange energy. Like a spirit mixed with magic somehow. I've never felt anything like it."

"So I'm not imagining it, right?" Nicki felt a tangle of emotions. Relief that she may not have been hallucinating coupled with uneasiness now that the creepy doll was real.

Liliana laid a hand on Nicki's shoulder. "I believe you. But now I'm wondering where the doll came from and how it was able to get inside all the protections that Elian placed on the house."

"Maybe it walked in the front door since it seems to be able to move around by itself." Nicki was only partially joking.

Liliana made a protective gesture. "That would be a very bad thing. Let's hope not."

The door opened, and Conroy walked in. "I have my people checking all over the house and the compound for an intruder, although I don't know how anyone could have gotten in. Someone will be bringing the Cuba boxes into the library so you can have a look at them with more comfort and better light than in the warehouse. Are you feeling better?"

"What do you know about the doll?" Nicki felt encouraged by Liliana's belief.

Conroy looked confused. "What doll?"

Nicki repeated what she had told Liliana and showed Conroy where she had spotted the figure earlier that morning. To her chagrin, he had not seen the toy nor heard the laughter.

"I don't like the sound of that," Conroy said when Nicki finished.

"You know, we never did figure out what was in that opened crate. Maybe we've found the missing object."

"A doll that moves around by itself has to be animated by magic and sent from someone we don't know—that's dangerous. It got past the protections. Now it's hiding. We need to find it and lock it up until Elian can have a look," Liliana said.

"I agree," Conroy replied.

"Do you think it made Edward see the spiders—the ones that almost caught the kitchen on fire?" Nicki asked.

"It's possible," Conroy mused. "It could be a spy as well as being ordered to cause damage or injury. We haven't seen the doll actually do anything, but we need to assume it's dangerous."

"I'm already quite certain of that," Nicki murmured. "Are we going to look for it?"

"Yes—but let me get some equipment first." Conroy hustled out of the room and back outside.

Nicki wrapped her arms around herself and shivered. *"Mon Dieu.* I have seen much worse working with Jake and Rick. I don't know why I let a little poppet upset me."

"You're probably picking up on bad energy without realizing it." Liliana gave a reassuring smile. "Our brains have ways of warning us that we don't always understand. And dolls are supposed to be for fun and comfort. Having one turned into something evil makes it even scarier."

Conroy returned with a harpoon, an iron fireplace poker, and a pole with an odd gray sack on the end. "We're going hunting. The sack is woven with silver and iron threads through it, for strength and to dampen magic or ghostly energy. If you see the doll, spear it and I'll scoop it up in the net."

"You're assuming it's still in the house," Liliana pointed out.

"I have people on the lookout around the compound," Conroy replied. "I suspect it's still in here, where it has the most opportunity to do damage. When I get a chance, I'll ask Wilson if he knows anything about it, although I'd have hoped he would have said something when we confronted him about the cursed clock."

Spark of Destiny

Conroy took the pole with the net. Liliana chose the fireplace poker while Nicki reached for the harpoon.

The trio moved silently and communicated by gestures. Nicki didn't know if the doll could hear or understand them, but she didn't want to take any chances.

The kitchen was clear, as was the pantry. They checked under furniture and in cabinets, and made sure the doll hadn't ensconced itself on one of the shelves. As they cleared a room, they closed its doors, trapping the doll in a smaller and smaller space.

The library now held the crates Hernandez sent with his cryptic clues, but no sign of the doll. In the sitting room and dining area, the sheer number of possible hiding places slowed their search.

Nicki saw a flash of something tan as she poked beneath a chair. "I saw it!"

Liliana whirled, aiming with her poker for the blur of motion that scurried from beneath the chair toward the couch, then shrieked and stepped back. "A snake!"

Nicki didn't see a snake, but a huge roach skittered from beneath the sofa. She forced herself to ignore the vision and jabbed under the sofa with the harpoon, but the doll eluded her and let out another scary peal of laughter.

Nicki cursed loudly in French. The doll zipped past Liliana and eluded the swing of her poker, and Liliana muttered under her breath in Spanish. Conroy blocked the doorway, cutting off the doll's escape.

"It's the doll. The damned thing is playing with our minds," Nicki warned. "Whatever you see, it's not real."

"Drive it toward me," Conroy told Nicki and Liliana. "It's running out of places to hide."

Nicki and Liliana moved in tandem, poking under furniture and into corners. The poppet let out a shriek and raced like a cornered rat, driven from its hiding places time and again, herded toward Conroy.

The doll was too quick to stab, but Conroy brought the net down fast, pinning it to the floor. He slid a control on the handle, and the net pulled closed, trapping the doll inside.

Nicki took a step back. "I don't need to get close. I've seen it already. Is it a zombie? I've heard of such things in the islands."

Liliana's eyes narrowed. "I don't think so. Elian can confirm, but I doubt the doll was ever alive. If I had to guess, I think magic animates the creature, and gives it sentience."

Inside the bag, the doll threw itself from side to side, shrieking.

"I'm going to put this in one of our lead boxes, just in case," Conroy said. "That should hold it securely until the others return. I apologize for the inconvenience."

Once he left, Nicki collapsed dramatically onto the couch. "I have been chased by vampires, werewolves, and vengeful spirits, but I was nearly killed by a haunted doll." She knew she was exaggerating but felt like she had earned the indulgence.

Liliana sat with less theatrical flair, although Nicki thought the hunt had jangled her as well. "If I'm right about the nature of the poppet, dark magic could trigger deep instincts—the way you get alert for danger when you're walking at night. It's nature's way of warning us."

Nicki fanned herself with her hand. "It's a most unpleasant feeling. I'll sleep better knowing that awful thing is locked up. Who do you think sent it? Drogo Veles? Cortez's witch?"

"I don't know," Liliana replied. "And while causing harm might have been one goal, I suspect that spying was the main purpose. We should get a telegram to Elian and the others in Calusa Key to let them know our plans may have been overheard. We are well rid of it."

Nicki nodded in agreement, for once at a loss for words. The incident had scared her more than she liked to admit.

"Coffee," Liliana declared, rallying. She rose and went to the kitchen, rummaging through the cabinets and muttering in Spanish. Nicki followed, lingering at the doorway.

"I'm going to make us Cubano coffee. It makes everything better."

Nicki moved closer so she could watch and learn. Liliana found what she needed even in an unfamiliar kitchen and set to work.

"The more I think about it, I'm sure the doll was from that opened crate." Nicki felt better in the bright light of the kitchen, with the smell of ground coffee filling the air. "So that's one mystery solved. Among many."

"Once we've fortified ourselves with coffee and another pastry, we'll go through the books and maps in the crates." Liliana's unshakable confidence buoyed Nicki's mood. "Señor Hernandez went to considerable effort to get those items out of Havana and into our hands. We'll just have to figure out how to use them."

After they'd gathered their wits, Nicki and Liliana retreated to the library. The crates had been set around the edges of the room, lids pried off, and each sitting on the floor instead of stacked for easy access.

"Journals, soapstone carvings, papers, and oil paintings," Nicki murmured. "Such a puzzle. Where do we begin?"

Liliana moved from crate to crate, her hand hovering over each without touching. "Leave the carved soapstones for last. I didn't pick up on it in the warehouse with all the other ghosts and magic, but they're definitely haunted. There's a faint presence, very old, and I don't sense any threat. Perhaps we'll learn more about the carvings and the ship in the journals."

Nicki and Liliana unpacked the crate filled with maps, papers, and diaries, placing each item carefully on the large study table in the center of the room. Nicki also removed the paintings from the crates and leaned them against the bookshelves.

She studied the painting of the ship, wondering whether it had been commissioned by its captain. The dramatic scene showed the *HMS Centurion* on a stormy sea with dark clouds and lightning.

The two men's portraits were less appealing. The man in the older style of clothing had an arrogant lift to his chin and a cruel slant to his mouth. The newer portrait was more crudely drawn, matching its subject, who looked like a ruffian.

"I'm happy never to have met either of them," Nicki said.

After examining the maps and charts, Liliana settled at the table with one of the journals. "I don't think we need to worry about that. They're long gone, and whatever spirits cling to the soapstone figures,

I doubt it's those men. Have a seat. Let's be detectives." Liliana gave a mischievous smile.

Nicki made herself comfortable, kicking off her shoes and gathering her feet under her skirts. Even with the library's ample lighting, making out the cramped, faded ink made her squint. The smell of dust, old paper, and packing sawdust sent her into a sneezing fit.

Once Nicki settled in, it didn't take long to figure out the nature of the journal she had chosen. "This book must have belonged to a historian studying the *HMS Centurion* and its captain." She glanced up at Liliana. "They were obsessed with winning their war with Spain. The *Centurion* took quite a toll on the Spanish navy before it was sunk during a battle."

Liliana tapped her pencil against the table, quiet after Nicki's comment. "Someone must have salvaged at least part of the ship for us to have those boxes of carved figures. They wouldn't have been cargo—more like what sailors made to amuse themselves between chores and battles. But why make such a great effort to send them to Jake and Rick right now? There must be a connection we aren't seeing."

"What's your book?" Nicki asked.

Liliana carefully marked her place with a piece of paper, then she put down the slim volume and stretched. "It's about the pirates that roamed the Keys, especially José Gaspar. The stories have been embellished into tall tales, but allowing for all that, he must have been clever and wily to be successful for as long as he eluded capture. Having a secret hideout in the swamps had a lot to do with it. His people had flat-bottomed boats that could navigate among the cypress roots. The larger ships couldn't follow him in."

"Which swamp?"

"From what's written here, the Everglades, but he probably had more than one hiding place—there are a lot of swamps here," Liliana replied.

They went back to reading. Nicki skimmed through the history of the *Centurion*, impressed at the clever tactics and sheer determination of the ship's captain to fight the Spanish navy for territory. The retelling of the ship's sinking based on witnesses' stories made her wonder about the fate of the men who had carved the soapstone carvings, although she feared that many of them had been lost at sea. She even found a partial list of the crew among the papers.

Liliana had taken to pouring over the maps. "There has to be a connection between all this stuff and what's going on now that Hernandez didn't dare spell out. Let's boil it down to the main points. Number one—the *Centurion* played merry hell with the Spanish navy until it sank. They were the king's worst nightmare. No doubt the Americans would love to have an ally like that now. I can sense that some of their ghosts are still present with the carvings."

Nicki nodded. "Number two—José Gaspar knew the swamps and used them to escape from the authorities. He had hiding places and at least one secret base."

Liliana pulled the painting of the "Lost City of the Great Swamp" toward her. "This seems different from Gaspar's hideouts. Let's see if we can find a mention anywhere."

They dug through the materials from the crates, looking for clues. Liliana rose and walked around the library, studying the shelves to see if she could find books that might relate to the topic.

"This might be helpful." Liliana pulled a book, an excited gleam in her eyes as if she had found a treasure. *"Legends of the Florida Keys."*

Nicki hadn't had time yet to explore the compound's library, but the number of volumes packed into the room impressed her. "Given Brand and Desmet's business, we might find plenty of books here on magic and supernatural things. Now we just need to know what to look for."

While Liliana skimmed through her newfound tome, Nicki studied the maps. "One of these has a mark for where the *Centurion* sank." She paused. "I could be wrong, but it looks to me like it should be fairly close to where Adam said the wreck of the *Vincente* was located."

Liliana looked up. "Interesting. That makes it even clearer that Hernandez is trying to send a message. We just need to read between the lines."

Nicki frowned as she turned back to the maps. "These are maps of the swamps, both the ones in the Keys and parts of the Everglades. They're old, and they look more hand-drawn than printed. Do you think they could be related to Gaspar's hiding places?"

"Maybe. Or the Lost City. Listen to this." Liliana's eyes sparkled.

"Deep in the Everglades is a lost city, so many people claim. Rumor has it that pirates, bandits, wanted criminals, and people who needed to disappear have found their way through the Great Swamp in search of sanctuary. Most were never heard from again, presumed to have fallen prey to the swamp's many dangers," Liliana read aloud.

"A very few have reappeared, years later, claiming to have found the Lost City and been welcomed. Notably, none of them were able to lead a search party successfully to find the city again, or they claimed to have lost their memory of the route. The story persists, and occasionally reckless explorers seek it for adventure and glory, but like so many, they disappear."

She set the book down and looked at Nicki. "Lost city? Hidden bases? Hideouts? That has to mean something."

"I know you've tried to reach the *Vincente* ghosts and not been able to make contact," Nicki said. "But we have plenty of items from the *Centurion*, like the carvings. Even a crew list. Would it be worth trying to reach them?"

"They died a long time ago," Liliana mused. "Ghosts often fade or move on after centuries. But with the relics from the ship, it's worth a try."

Nicki helped Liliana prepare. They cleared part of the table, moving the valuable old maps and journals out of the way. They carefully carried some of the soapstone carvings and the brass plate with the ship's name over to their seats.

Liliana put the carvings and the nameplate between her and Nicki, then reached out to take Nicki's hands in hers. "Don't let go, and don't react, no matter what you see."

Nicki squeezed her hands. "I'll be fine. Just be sure to let me know what *you* see."

Liliana closed her eyes and hummed, rocking back and forth with

Spark of Destiny

the melody. Nicki guessed she was sliding into a trance and watched as all the tension seemed to leave her companion's face and shoulders.

"Crew of the *HMS Centurion*, I would like to speak with you," Liliana murmured. "We mean you no harm. Come and talk to me. Many years have passed."

For several moments, nothing happened. The room seemed eerily quiet as if all the normal sounds had been stolen. Nicki felt goosebumps rise, and the temperature in the room dropped to a wintry chill.

The air shimmered, and the faint outline of a man dressed in a frock coat with frilled sleeves struggled to appear. He wore a powdered wig and several rings with large gems adorned his fingers. The scowl caught Nicki unprepared.

"Why does a Spaniard dare summon us? My crewmen were Spain's sworn enemy, and their ships sent us to the bottom." The faint voice held a strong English accent.

Nicki's eyes widened, angry at herself for not anticipating the reaction from the *Centurion's* ghosts.

"Almost four hundred years have passed since then. The world has changed. The land you knew as La Florida is now part of a large new country, currently at war with Spain. I support the new country against my homeland," Liliana replied calmly enough that Nicki guessed the medium had suspected she might receive a harsh reaction.

"What do you seek?" The man's skeptical expression and clipped tone made it clear he would not give his trust lightly.

"We have many pieces of carved soapstone taken from the wreck of your ship. How many of your crew remain, and why have you not moved on?" Liliana asked.

The man's image flickered, and Nicki knew it cost Liliana to lend the ghost energy to maintain his visibility.

"All of us remain. We want vengeance," the ghost replied. "We will wait forever to avenge ourselves on the accursed Spaniards."

"You may get your chance," Liliana told him. "A new war rages between Spain and the United States—the country that claims La

Florida. There may be a way for your crew to be of help. If you could get your revenge, would your people move on?"

The ghost had lost some of his bluster, and now he looked tired. "Yes, I believe so. We did not want to die in vain."

"Stand by," Liliana told him. "If there is a chance for your crew to turn the tide of the battle, I will call on you. Afterward, I will help you cross the Veil."

"I believe you are an honorable woman," the ghost replied. "I will listen for your call."

The ghost vanished. Liliana slumped in her chair. Nicki squeezed her hands again, then let go and moved around to the other side of the table to gently pat Liliana's cheeks.

"Come on, wake up," she urged. "Let me know you're okay, and I'll bring you something to eat and drink."

Liliana's eyes fluttered open. She managed a tired smile. "You saw?"

Nicki nodded. "Quite impressive. I know you spent extra energy to let me see and hear him. Thank you—but you shouldn't drain yourself on my account."

"Sometimes it helps to have a second opinion." Liliana sounded spent. "Can't get that if you only hear second-hand."

Once Nicki had assured herself that Liliana wouldn't fall out of the chair, she gave her a pat on the shoulder and straightened. "Stay right there. I'll be back."

She hurried to the kitchen, poured a fresh cup of coffee and took a bowl of candied fruits from the counter.

"Here. This should help." Nicki placed the cup and bowl in front of Liliana. "Eat. We can talk once you're revived."

Liliana gave a grateful smile and sipped the strong coffee, then nibbled at the fruit. Nicki thought she could see the color return to the medium's cheeks.

Finally, Liliana drained her cup and pushed the bowl away. Nicki took a couple of the candies and sat back. "Well?"

"Considering how much he hated the Spanish, that went better than expected." Liliana didn't look offended by the ghost's opinions, which had nothing to do with her personally.

"He seemed…tired," Nicki ventured. "Is it normal for a ghost that old to still remember so much?"

Liliana shook her head. "Quite the opposite. I think that their vengeance has given them an anchor and a reason not to fade away."

"Could they help? We're a long way from the salvage operation."

Liliana shrugged. "I don't know. Having the soapstone carvings and the items from the ship should certainly give them more energy than if we just called to them without those things. Maybe they can be reinforcements in a pinch, and we can give them peace."

Nicki glanced at the crates. "Do you think that's what Mr. Hernandez intended by sending the *Centurion* relics to us?"

"It seems likely, although how he knew about the ghosts, I have no idea."

"Maybe that's one mystery solved. But we still have all the other stuff to figure out." Nicki popped another piece of candied fruit into her mouth.

"Before we go back to the books, let's take a walk. It's nice outside, and I need to stretch my legs."

Nicki and Liliana grabbed shawls and headed outside. Despite the late-morning sunshine, the air was cool for Florida. The Brand and Desmet compound was a commercial location, but care had been taken to add trees and flowers around the house and near the dormitory, as well as in a few spots where the plantings wouldn't be in the way.

"I wonder how things are going for Jake and the others," Nicki mused after they had walked for a while. "I hope last night's delay wasn't anything too serious."

"Right now they're probably sleeping—pulled out to sea so they aren't marking the spot of the wreck," Liliana replied. "If anything important had happened, I suspect we'd have had another telegram unless they're keeping silent to avoid anything being picked up by Sombra."

"I'm hoping they can find what Adam needs and leave quickly,"

Nicki said. "This whole situation wears on my nerves." She looked to Liliana. "Are there other ghosts here? Besides the soapstone spirits?"

She knew enough of Florida's history to know that between the native tribes and the waves of colonizers, the area had been settled and fought over for centuries. Plenty of reasons for ghosts with a grudge to stick around.

Liliana gave a faint smile. "Ghosts are near us all the time. Fortunately, most don't wish harm to the living. Some have forgotten themselves and are barely a wisp of energy. Others have reason to remain behind. A few fear what might come next. I bid them well, and they let me be."

A commotion near the front gates drew their attention. Nicki hurried toward the noise, motioning for Liliana to follow. They slipped around the side of the house, then hunched and ran to the cover of Conroy's parked mechanized wagon. That put them within sight of the entrance while screening them from easy notice.

Conroy and three beefy security men formed a line several feet from the high iron gate.

"This is the last time I'm saying it—go away," Conroy barked at the armed group outside the fence.

"Mr. Cortez said you're here to steal from the company. Go back where you came from!" The leader of the mob of gun-toting men brandished his weapon to underscore his demand.

"This compound is private property," Conroy replied, remarkably calm. "You are trespassing."

"Go get your boss."

"Mr. Desmet and Mr. Brand are very busy. If you'd like to make an appointment—"

"We aren't going away, and we aren't going to make a damn appointment. Leave Key West, and leave the company alone," the leader demanded, and the ruffians raised their guns.

"I wish you hadn't done that." Conroy raised his right hand and let it fall.

Machine gun fire blasted from the observation tower, kicking up dirt just inside the iron gate—a clear warning and a distraction that enabled Conroy and his guards to take cover in case the ruffians decided to fire back. The mob fell back a few paces but did not disperse as if daring the man on the tower to mow them down.

"Are there any loose ghosts who might like to put a scare into those asses?" Nicki hissed.

Liliana blinked. "Loose ghosts?"

"Some of those spirits you were talking about before, who just hung around. Now would be a good time for them to earn their keep," Nicki returned.

"I can't compel them, but I can ask for help." Liliana closed her eyes and took a couple of deep breaths.

Yelps and frightened squawks from outside the gate told Nicki the ghosts had accepted the challenge.

"Holy shit! What was that?"

"Something touched me. I swear, I felt something."

"Sweet Mary and Jesus—that's a ghost!"

The toughs panicked, running despite their leader's shouts. He looked ready to stand his ground before a gray figure appeared from nowhere to loom over him, sending him sprinting after the others. Another blast of machine gun fire aimed at their heels reminded them not to return.

To their credit, Conroy and his guards handled the whole thing with aplomb.

"You did it!" Nicki exulted, beaming at Liliana when the medium opened her eyes. "You got rid of the lot of them without bloodshed!"

"We were lucky," Liliana said as they stood. Conroy caught sight of them, and Nicki saw an understanding of what had just transpired in his expression.

He hurried over. "Those ghosts—you did that?"

Liliana nodded, and Nicki stepped closer, realizing her friend had paled again.

"Thank you," Conroy said. "It could have gotten bloody real fast. I'd like to think we would have won, but I'm glad we didn't test that theory."

"Let's get you back to the house," Nicki suggested. Liliana gave her a grateful look and didn't object to taking Nicki's arm to steady herself.

"It's the second time she's called spirits today, and that takes a lot of energy," Nicki explained as Conroy accompanied them.

"Second time?"

"Long story, but we made a lot of progress on those boxes from Cuba," Nicki told him, steadying Liliana on the steps to avoid a fall. "We can fill you in later."

"Lunch will be ready soon." Conroy checked his watch.

Liliana shook her head. "I need to rest. Maybe something light could be sent up to my room in an hour or two, please?"

"I'll bring it up myself," Nicki assured her. "You should eat, but I think you need to drink some water and sleep first."

Conroy lingered behind them as they climbed the steps to the second floor in case Liliana faltered. When they reached the top, Nicki gave him a nod to let him know she could take it from there.

"What can I get to help you feel better?" Nicki didn't leave Liliana's side until the medium was seated on the edge of her bed.

Liliana stretched out, bothering to remove only her shoes. Nicki found a light throw and spread it over her.

"My head is pounding," Liliana confessed.

"I'll bring up willow bark tea and a cool compress," Nicki promised. "Then you can rest as long as you like. Whenever you wake, I'll get you something to eat."

"Sorry for the inconvenience," Liliana replied.

"You just stopped a gunfight, and before that you called up an ancient privateer's ghost," Nicki countered. "You deserve a nap—and lots of cookies."

Liliana didn't protest as Nicki fussed with her blanket and pillow, then adjusted the shades to dim the light.

"I'll check on you, but yell if you need anything," Nicki told her. "I won't be far away."

She closed the door with a quiet click and went downstairs. Conroy was in the kitchen, speaking with the cook. He looked up when Nicki entered the room.

"Is Señora Delgado all right?" he asked, concerned. "I was just talking with our cook about possibly needing to make some adjustments for dinner."

"She's resting. I think sleep will do wonders. I promised to bring her a cold compress and some willow bark tea," Nicki told them. "I'm not sure if she'll want a big dinner, but she needs something easy to digest and nutritious. Connecting with the ghosts twice in such a short period drained her."

"I'll make the tea and get some ice right away," the cook replied, turning to the pantry and ice box. "I can send it up with someone when it's ready."

"I appreciate that, but I'd like to take it up myself," Nicki said. "I want an excuse to check on her."

She took a seat at the table to wait for the water to boil, looking up as Conroy paused beside her.

"I'd like to talk after you take that up to Señora, if you don't mind," Conroy said. "I have the feeling that everything that's happening around us is connected somehow, but it's like a jigsaw puzzle without all the pieces."

"I'll be glad to tell you everything. We had a very interesting afternoon." Now that the adrenaline rush had faded, Nicki felt her energy flagging.

"You look like you've had a day, ma'am," the cook said, putting a hot cup of coffee in front of Nicki. "Take care of yourself, and you can care for your friend better."

"Thank you." Nicki was grateful for the kindness. "There's been a lot going on."

By the time she finished the coffee, the cook returned with a tray that held the willow tea, some sugared ginger, and a hunk of ice wrapped in a towel. Nicki carried the tray upstairs, glad to find Liliana hadn't moved.

"Get the tea into your system and put the ice on your head. Then you can sleep as long as you want." Nicki helped Liliana sit up to drink and then made sure she was comfortable nestling back into the bedding.

"I'll check on you and bring food when you're ready. In the meantime—sleep," Nicki admonished. Liliana just smiled and closed her eyes as Nicki let herself out.

She wasn't surprised to find Conroy waiting in the sitting room. Nicki sat on the couch opposite his chair.

"Fill me in," he said.

Nicki told him about their morning spent with the maps and journals, their insights and discoveries, and the decision to reach out to the ghosts of the *Centurion* as well as the unanswered questions about the Lost City in the swamp and the pirates' hidden bases.

"You covered a lot of territory." Conroy sounded impressed. "Nobody expected you to solve all the mysteries in one day. Jake and Rick might have new insights when they return from the wreck."

"Have you heard anything more?" Now that she wasn't busy, Nicki's worry for the salvage mission team grew.

Conroy shook his head. "Nothing since the telegram that said they had been delayed. But I didn't expect any unless there was an emergency. The less we communicate, the fewer chances Sombra and Cortez have to intercept the information."

"Those men at the gate—they were Sombra?"

Conroy frowned. "I doubt it. I think they were toughs hired by Cortez to do his dirty work. Cortez seems to have a great deal of leeway in how he does his job, and we're not completely sure what his job actually involves. My money says he's just a smooth enforcer, one step up from the ruffians he employs, but able to intimidate with his words instead of his fists."

"Once Liliana feels better, we have more to do with the contents in the crates," Nicki told him. "Mr. Hernandez's letter was like a puzzle within a puzzle. Normally I like solving riddles, but I can't help feeling like the clock is ticking for us to keep something bad from happening."

"I have the same feeling, and I pray that I'm wrong," Conroy replied.

A knock at the door startled them. No one outside the compound had access to the house, and Conroy hadn't given permission for anyone to enter. Nicki saw him pull a gun from a hiding place in the kitchen and slip it into the waistband of his pants as he approached the door.

She peeked out the window and saw one of the workers hand an envelope to Conroy. They exchanged a few words, but Nicki couldn't hear what was said. She returned to her seat before Conroy came back into the room.

"Interesting—Rafael, the butler from Señora Delgado's house, brought this letter that arrived in today's mail." Conroy must have noticed the look of concern on Nicki's face. "Don't worry—I'm sure he used one of the bespelled carriages for safety. The man said to pass the letter along to Señora Delgado and that it was extremely important."

He noticed a lump in the envelope. "There's more than just a letter inside. Curious. I'll put this on the table in the dining room. If you see her before I do, please mention it."

Nicki promised to do so, and Conroy resumed his duties managing the compound. Nicki selected a book from the house's ample library and curled up in a comfortable chair to read, still jangled by everything that had gone on.

She startled awake sometime later, chagrined she had fallen asleep in the chair and let the book slip from her grasp. A glance at the clock confirmed that she had slept for nearly an hour and that they were closer to dinner than lunch.

The quiet house told Nicki that Liliana was still sleeping and that Conroy was tending to the compound. She retrieved the book from the floor and bookmarked her place, feeling too jittery to read. Taking a walk was appealing, but she didn't want to leave Liliana alone in the house in case she needed assistance.

Nicki went to the kitchen and found a pot of coffee still warm on a back burner and a plate of cookies under a glass dome. She poured a cup for herself and took a cookie, trying to figure out what to do next.

When she finished, Nicki returned to the library and sat at the study table, spreading the maps out. On impulse, she browsed the shelves until she found a modern map of Florida as well as a close-up of the southern tip of the peninsula and the Keys.

She placed the new map next to the old ones, looking for differences. The newer map was drawn with more attention to detail, showing the contours of the islands and the shoreline more clearly. The latitudes and longitudes also showed a subtle shift, no doubt due to more precise instrumentation.

Nicki looked closely at the maps that showed swampy areas in the Keys or the Everglades. The newer maps showed roads and some changes to the size and shape of the wetlands. She squinted at the small writing that marked "Fort Harrell" deep within the Everglades, surprised to find a fort in such an inaccessible location.

On a hunch, Nicki scribbled down the coordinates for Fort Harrell and made a note to find out more about the remote outpost.

Is the fort near Lost City? Did stories about the two get mixed up together? There's not much else deep in the swamp. What was Mr. Hernandez trying to tell us?

She walked over to the painting of Lost City and took it to the window, where she could see better. The landscape was not fine art, closer to what Nicki had heard called "folk art," done by someone with talent but no formal training.

Despite the fiery sunset and the shadows of the mangroves and cypress trees, the painting didn't look fanciful. The wooden buildings—a few houses and businesses—weren't idealized or pretty. They looked hard-worn and weathered, enduring but not prosperous.

I can't imagine someone just making this up. The town's homeliness was its most persuasive argument for the painting being based on a real place.

The late afternoon light was fading, and lamplight was scarcely brighter, making it difficult for Nicki to find a signature on the painting. She resolved to examine the artwork and its frame in more detail when the light was better.

Nicki replaced the painting and went back to her notes. *Where is Fort Harrell, and does it have anything to do with Lost City?* she wrote. *Examine the painting in bright light. Search for more in the library books. Did we miss anything in Hernandez's letter?*

Nicki set her pen and paper aside and stretched, trying to get the kink out of her neck from when she had fallen asleep in the chair.

"I'd better go check on Liliana," she murmured and headed upstairs. She could already smell dinner cooking, which made her stomach rumble, reminding her that she had mostly skipped lunch to care for her friend.

At Liliana's door, Nicki hesitated, unsure whether to knock and risk waking her. She eased the door open, giving a belated rap when she saw that Liliana was sitting up in bed, reading a book.

"Feeling better?" Nicki asked.

Liliana nodded. "The tea and cookies helped. Thank you for taking care of me. We had a busy day."

"Dinner will be ready soon—you're probably famished." Nicki perched on the side of the bed. "I think it will be just you and me, so don't bother being fancy. A good meal will perk you up."

"Have we had any more word from the salvage party?" Liliana's worry for Elian was clear.

"Nothing new," Nicki said with forced cheer, pushing aside her own worry. "They'll be back before we know it."

"What have you been up to?"

"Started reading a book, took a nap, and poked around in the library some more. I found some interesting tidbits that we can look at tomorrow when the light is better," Nicki summarized. "And before I forget—your butler delivered something that came for you today. It's on the dining room table."

Liliana frowned. "For me? Did you see what it was?"

"Just an envelope, but Conroy said it felt like it had more than paper in it."

"*Dios mio*, do you think it might have something to do with Luis? Maybe he's finally gotten in touch." Liliana's eyes shone with a desperate hope that broke Nicki's heart.

Nicki felt ashamed that with everything else going on, she had forgotten about Liliana's missing brother. "I don't know. It could be anything. Please—"

Liliana managed a sad smile and laid a hand on her arm. "I promise not to get my hopes too high. But it's not like Luis to leave without communicating. Something's gone very wrong. I just want my brother back."

"Why don't you come down when you're ready?" Nicki swallowed a lump in her throat. "We can sit on the porch rocking chairs until dinner's ready."

Minutes later, Liliana joined Nicki on the porch. She had changed her dress and piled her hair in a fresh updo. Nicki was pleased to see that she looked more rested and less drawn.

"You found it?" Nicki nodded toward the letter clutched in Liliana's hand.

"Yes, but I'm too chicken to open it alone," Liliana confessed.

"That's what I'm here for."

Liliana took a deep breath and then opened the envelope. She pulled out a note and frowned as a man's ring fell into her palm.

"It's Luis's handwriting, although I don't recall this ring."

"Don't keep me waiting—what does it say?" Nicki leaned over in her seat to see. Liliana translated the Spanish to English as she read aloud.

"Dearest Liliana,

I've gone away to protect both of us. Contact Alvaro Ramirez, the owner of this ring, and he will tell you everything. Be careful. I'll come home when it's safe to do so. One way or the other, I will talk to you again.

Love, Luis."

Liliana's voice caught at the words. "He's in danger. That's what he means by 'one way or the other.' Either the danger will pass, or he'll come to me as a spirit."

Nicki's eyes widened. "How are you supposed to find Alvaro Ramirez from just a ring? There's no address."

Liliana shook her head. "I don't need an address. Alvaro Ramirez is a ghost. I can feel his presence."

Spark of Destiny

"Do you think you should try to contact him today? You've already done so much—" Nicki couldn't help worrying.

"How can I delay when he has news of Luis? I'll be all right. I've recovered a bit, and I'll make an early night of it."

"How about after dinner at least, so you have a good meal for fortitude?" Nicki coaxed. "If you push yourself and collapse, it does no one any good—including Luis."

Liliana nodded with reluctance. "All right. But I'm definitely doing this tonight."

Just then, the cook called for them to come in for dinner. They found the table set for the two of them.

"Mr. Conroy said to send his regrets that he wasn't able to join you," the cook told them. "He's taking his dinner in his office tonight. I'm supposed to tell you to enjoy the food and save room for dessert."

The meal began with a chilled mango soup. Baked grouper with an orange glaze lay on a bed of fluffy white rice accompanied by peas and pearl onions.

Nicki dug in with gusto, surprised at how hungry she was. Liliana ate slowly, but Nicki noted with satisfaction that her friend ate most of her serving.

"And homemade banana pudding for dessert." The cook placed a generous serving in front of each of them. "Enjoy!"

When they finished, both women took cups of coffee to the sitting room. Liliana's gaze drifted to the letter and ring on the side table. Nicki didn't say anything, letting her friend use the moments while they savored their drink to collect her nerve.

"I'm ready," Liliana said with determination.

"If it's less stress for you, it's okay if you don't make the ghost visible. You can tell me about it afterward," Nicki said, still concerned.

"Let's see how willing he is to appear. Some ghosts are eager to tell their story."

She set aside her cup and took the letter and ring in her hands. Nicki watched the now-familiar ritual as Liliana closed her eyes and breathed deeply.

"Alvaro Ramirez. I'm Luis's sister. He sent me your ring and told me you had information. Please make yourself known. Luis is missing, and I'm very worried."

Liliana sat quietly, waiting. Far more restless, Nicki tamped down on her agitation, trying to keep her leg from jiggling and her fingers from drumming.

After what seemed like forever to Nicki but was probably only a few minutes, the gray figure of a man flickered into sight. He looked to be in his early thirties, with short dark hair and a mustache.

"Your brother looks like you," the ghost said, using Liliana's gift to be heard. His ghost seemed nearly solid, and Nicki wondered if he had enough energy on his own to be visible.

"How did you know Luis?" Liliana asked. Nicki tightened her fists in her skirt to keep still.

"We were kidnapped together," Ramirez's ghost replied.

Liliana and Nicki gasped.

"What happened?" Liliana breathed.

"They took us to a locked laboratory and forced us to work on an experimental engine from pieces and parts with only fragments of drawings," Ramirez replied. "Luis told me about you. He knew you'd be frantic."

"Do you know who the kidnappers worked for?" Liliana pressed.

"No. They were careful not to let that slip," the ghost answered. "They knew we were engineers. Taking us wasn't random. I don't know where we were, but it was a long ride by carriage. They shut us in the lab, told us to do what they said."

"What happened?" Liliana asked. Since Ramirez was dead, clearly the prisoners hadn't been safe.

"An accident with a propeller prototype. I bled out fast. Luis couldn't save me, but he asked me to find you. He must have gotten someone to smuggle the ring and letter out for him."

"Thank you." Liliana's voice stayed steady despite the tears in her eyes. "Do you need my help to cross over?"

"No. I just needed to keep my promise to Luis. I hope you find him. Tell him I kept my word." With that, the spirit faded until nothing remained.

Spark of Destiny

Liliana covered her eyes with her hands and folded forward, sobbing.

Nicki moved closer and put an arm around her shoulder. "I'm so sorry."

"He's locked up and scared, and now his friend is gone," Liliana said in a choked voice. "And I don't know how to find him."

"One step at a time," Nicki coaxed. "At least you know that he didn't go into hiding on his own or run away. He probably fibbed about that in the letter in case it was intercepted. And if someone is kidnapping engineers to work on engine pieces from strange drawings, that's got to be Sombra. Maybe they have some of the same sort of things that are in the *Vincente's* cargo, and they need the rest to finish the project."

Liliana dried her tears and sat up, squaring her shoulders and setting her jaw. "We'll find him."

"Of course we will," Nicki assured her. "Jake and the others will be back soon. Maybe there will be something in the *Vincente's* cargo that helps us figure out where the secret lab is."

"I just want him to come home safe."

Nicki rose and poured them both a few fingers of scotch from the decanter on the sideboard. She handed Liliana a glass and sat next to her once more.

"Drink. Let it help you sleep. You're going to need your strength to help Luis—and figure out the stuff in the library. There's nothing else to do tonight."

Liliana accepted the drink with gratitude and didn't speak until she had taken several sips. "If we can narrow down where Luis is, I can ask nearby ghosts to spy for us. Someone must have seen something that could help."

"If it's Sombra, then they have witches of their own," Nicki reminded her. "That's going to make it more difficult. But once Elian is back, he can help plan."

Liliana took Nicki's hand in hers. "Thank you. You're a good friend. I'm glad I don't have to deal with this alone."

Nicki gave her hand a squeeze. "I'm here. Elian loves you. Jake,

Rick, and Miska will have ideas on how to find Luis. Maybe their secret agent friends can help too. We'll figure it out."

Liliana begged off shortly afterward, claiming a headache. She took her scotch with her. Nicki didn't blame her friend. Hearing from Luis was a shock and even more so to find out he was kidnapped. Despite the optimism she mustered for Liliana's sake, Nicki had no idea how they would find Luis even if Sombra did turn out to be behind his abduction.

Outside, the wind had picked up. Nicki walked to the window. Rain lashed against the pane, and clouds hid the moon. She shivered and hoped that the storm didn't affect the salvage efforts.

Her thoughts turned back to Luis. *Did Javier Cortez order his kidnapping? I'm sure of it. Maybe Liliana can bedevil him with vengeful ghosts to make him tell us.*

She sighed. *Probably not. But Agents Storm and Drangosavich surely have access to other sources. Maybe they've had their eye on Sombra and Cortez, and they already know where their lab is. I'll get Jake to ask for a favor.*

Now Jake and the others just have to make it back safely with what was on the Vincente. *Once we're all together, we'll figure it out. We have to. Because whatever's going on, this is much bigger than Luis or a sunken ship. And we might be the only people who can stop it.*

Chapter Seven

"I hope there's a lot more coffee." Rick joined the others in the mess hall for breakfast. He had let Jake have the shower first and went in search of food and caffeine before attempting to shave.

"We run on it out here." Albert moved over to make room at the table for Rick to join them. "There's more than enough for everyone."

Rick sat and Cook brought him a cup of java and a plate full of scrambled eggs with ham, bacon, and toast. Between the sea air and the physical work on the boat, Rick's appetite surprised him.

"You've got great food onboard," Rick said between mouthfuls.

"I don't think I've ever seen you dive into breakfast like that," Kovach joked, savoring his coffee over his empty plate.

"Lots going on. Gotta keep my strength up." Rick made short work of the bacon.

They had been up all night, not leaving the dive site until just before dawn, so everyone slept in once the ship moved off to a distance. Between exhaustion and the rocking of the ship, Rick had slept hard and discovered sore muscles from lending a hand with the pulleys and ropes.

"Where's Adam?" he asked when the coffee hit his system, and he looked around the table. Albert, Ralph, and Kovach were seated with him, along with Elian, who looked as impeccable as ever despite their circumstances. Rick assumed Harry and the deckhands were keeping the *Diligence* running and that Adam's techno turtles helped keep an eye out for danger.

"He grabbed a couple of hours' sleep, carried off what was left of the night shift coffee and a handful of cookies, and said something about being in the cargo hold," Cook told them. "I tried to get him to wait until I could fix a plate for him, but he said he had what he needed."

"Sounds like Adam." Rick tucked into the rest of his food like a starving man. "He runs on sugar and caffeine."

"The good news is that we didn't spot any other ships in our vicinity or heading toward the *Vincente*," Kovach said. "Wally, Sid, and I split the watch. Along with Adam's tin turtles."

"I did not sense any interference with the wardings I set before retiring," Elian told them. "That only proves no one attempted to bother us, not that we went unnoticed."

"That's cheery," Kovach replied.

"What did I miss?" Jake walked in, hair wet and askew from his shower but otherwise looking annoyingly chipper. "Looks like I'm just in time for brunch."

"Apparently nothing news-wise, but I might fight you for the rest of the coffee," Rick said.

"Have a seat," Albert replied as he rose. "I need to get back to the bridge."

Jake took the empty spot on the bench, and Cook brought out his plate and coffee. "Everyone okay after last night?"

"Sore," Rick admitted. "But not as much as I thought I'd be. And I didn't fall out of the bunk bed, so that's a win."

"I asked Harry to send a wire to Conroy to let him know we're safe," Jake said between forkfuls of egg. "It might keep Nicki and Liliana from swimming out to find us," he joked.

"That is a wise precaution," Elian said with a faint smile.

"What's the plan?" Rick poured himself another cup from the pot on the table.

"I figured once we ate, we'd head to the cargo hold and see what Adam and Ben brought up from the wreck last night and what to make of it," Jake replied. "They've had a look at the *Vincente* now—and so has Ralph, after a fashion—so they should have opinions about what's left to salvage. We've still got a long night ahead of us."

"I'm going to give Adam a hand before he hurts himself or blows us sky high." Kovach excused himself.

"Unless I'm needed to take a look at the cargo, I'd planned to stay on deck today, scanning for intruders," Elian told them, taking his leave.

Jake finished the last of his food while Rick poured them both refills of coffee. "Penny for your thoughts," Rick said.

Jake pushed his empty plate out of the way and leaned forward, resting his elbows on the table and letting one finger toy with the rim of his coffee cup.

"I'm on edge for no reason," he admitted. "Harry said the morning watch didn't pick up on anything, and neither did Adam's turtles, but I can't shake the feeling that the peace and quiet won't last."

"Elian said he hasn't sensed magic or anything supernatural nearby, but we don't know the full scope of Sombra's capabilities," Rick replied. "If they've got a witch who can scry or psychics who are far-seers, they could still be keeping an eye on us."

"Yeah, I thought of that. The sooner we're back on dry land, the better."

Jake and Rick headed down to the hold. The ship had pulled back once more from the wreck site, marking time until darkness fell. The regular crew went about their chores, doing repairs, cleaning, and touching up paint. Wally and Sid nodded as Jake and Rick passed them and returned just as quickly to their tasks.

"Just another day for the crew, I guess, until we're back at the salvage site," Rick observed.

"I suspect everyone's going to grab some extra sleep before dark."

Jake stifled a yawn. "I used to be able to be out until the wee hours in college and bounce back just fine the next day."

"That was a few years ago," Rick pointed out. "And I dare say partying and drinking goes less hard on a body than real physical work."

"You're probably right about that," Jake admitted. "What do you think Nicki and Liliana are up to?"

"As much trouble as they can sneak past Conroy," came the quick reply. "I'm curious to see what they can find out about the boxes Hernandez slipped into the airlift and whether it ties into the whole *Vincente* situation."

"If Cortez gets wind that we're disturbing the wreck, he could take us to salvage court," Jake said. Wrecking could be a contentious business with competing claims over valuable cargo. Special courts administered the laws designed to determine the rights to disputed cargo. Tempers often flared over the large sums involved, leading to fistfights, duels, and on occasion—murder.

"I don't think he'd dare," Rick replied. "He'd have to reveal the cargo manifest, and that could lead to messy questions. And which jurisdiction would hear the case? The wreck is on the edge of US waters. We're at war with Spain, so the US is going to do its best to exert authority, especially if there's valuable technology involved."

"I'm as worried about running afoul of the military as I am with Sombra," Jake admitted. "I just want to finish this and go back to Key West."

They found Adam, Kovach, and Ben in the hold, carefully unpacking a couple of waterlogged crates.

"I wondered when you'd join us." Adam's sandy brown hair stuck out at angles from his habit of constantly running his fingers through it as he thought. Rick spotted the nearly-empty urn of coffee from the galley, responsible for fueling his twitchiness.

"Did you even sleep?" It was a constant topic of conversation between he and Adam. Rick knew how prone the inventor was to forget to eat and rest when he was chasing an idea.

"Some. Enough," Adam replied, and the light in his eyes told Rick

Spark of Destiny

that his friend was far too involved in the cargo to bother with trivial things like seeing to his own health. "I'll catch a nap before I go back down in the *Oceanus*. But I couldn't wait to get a look at what Ben and I brought up."

Ben stood to one side, awaiting instructions. The turtles had been redeployed as an early warning system, although Rick hoped that in daylight they would be less likely to shoot at passing ships.

"What's in the box?" Jake asked. "Is it what you expected? Worth the trouble?"

It wasn't lost on Rick that the cargo hold had been spelled and warded, walls marked with runes and sigils. Elian had checked on the integrity of the supernatural protections on their first night, adding a few of his own to the mix. All of their party, as well as the crew, wore amulets designed to deflect dangerous magic. Rick knew those precautions didn't guarantee their safety, but he felt a little better knowing that they weren't going in cold.

"Thanks to Ralph's astral travel and what I could see with the help of Ben and the techno turtle, the short answer is, 'yes.'" Adam flitted back and forth between the open crates and his notes on the table.

"We didn't bring up what I think is the main stuff last night because I wanted to check these crates first to make sure we aren't on a goose chase." Adam's attention remained fixed on the pieces he kept removing from the boxes even as he spoke.

"Our information appears to have been correct. There's a piece of experimental technology in the *Vincente's* hold and one occult piece I'm still not completely sure about," Adam said.

"The prototype is an accelerator, using some interesting workarounds I haven't seen before to incorporate tourmaquartz into engines for greater power and speed. But there doesn't appear to be any tourmaquartz in the boxes—that would definitely have a telltale energy signal." Adam glanced up as if to confirm his audience hadn't left, then went back to his work.

"By accelerator, you mean—" Rick prompted.

"A way to make things go really fast." Adam's tone was matter-of-fact instead of mocking. "What we would consider to be abnormally fast."

"What kinds of things?" Rick knew from long experience that the easiest way to get information out of Adam was to keep asking questions and tease out the details, little by little. That was doubly true when the inventor was focusing on his work to the point of obsession.

"Big things like trains or ships." Adam tossed the details out carelessly as if they didn't have the potential to cause a major change in transportation and warfare. "Faster than we can move objects using steam or diesel and without the need to refuel."

Kovach paled. "I can see why something like that would be worth fighting over."

"I didn't bring up the engine accelerator yet because I wanted to make sure it wasn't somehow going to interfere with the boat's systems." Adam returned his attention to the crates. "But from what I've found, I can piece together enough information to feel certain it's safe to bring the other stuff aboard."

Kovach turned to Rick and Jake. "Technology like that could turn the tide of the war—any war. Even one super-speed engine in a warship, a zeppelin, or a train could be a huge military advantage. We absolutely can't let the Spanish get ahold of this."

"If Sombra created the items, can't they just make more?" Rick asked.

Adam frowned. "Not necessarily. From the markings on the crates and some of the paperwork I found in a waterproof folder, Sombra itself didn't invent all these pieces. I don't know whether they hired out the work, bought it from individual inventors, or outright stole it, but these are hand-built prototypes, not manufactured. Sombra might or might not have the knowledge to build them again. That's especially doubtful if the original inventors aren't working with them voluntarily."

"Should anyone have these?" Jake asked.

Rick could have predicted his partner's moral quandary. They'd run up against more than one situation where a new piece of experimental equipment or an occult relic was so powerful to pose a threat to the world. When that happened, Adam had been good about making sure such breakthroughs were buried in the depths of bureaucracy, or their vampire witch friend Andreas Thalberg had locked the item away with magic.

"That's a hard call. If there was a train or a ship carrying food or medical supplies in an emergency, you'd want to go as fast as possible. If it's moving troops for a war, speed could be good or bad." Adam stood back and rested his hands on his hips, surveying the pieces laid out on the table, before reaching for his coffee.

"And the supernatural cargo?" Jake asked. "Do you have an idea of what it is yet?"

"Ralph and I already debated some possibilities early this morning. I think the relics are ocean-related, but I haven't gotten further than that yet."

"That all sounds exciting—and rather terrifying," Jake admitted. "Then again, all of your inventions would be frightening in the wrong hands."

And those are the ones we know about, Rick thought. Adam's work for Tesla-Westinghouse involved secret government projects for groups like the Department of Supernatural Investigation. Adam did his best to funnel his greatest—or most dangerous—experimental technology to Brand and Desmet, but Rick didn't doubt that his friend had supplied some game-changing innovations to the government.

He slept better when he didn't dwell on that thought.

"What are you working on, and can we help?" Jake asked.

"I'm documenting what's here—sketches, descriptions, copying any instructions that survived being dunked in the ocean," Adam told them. "I'll store a copy in the *Oceanus* because I'm a paranoid SOB and I don't like to have all my eggs in one basket."

"Makes sense," Kovach agreed.

"And Ben is recording everything he sees, so that's a second copy." Adam smiled at his mechanical assistant. "You should have seen Ben last night. He did a fantastic job—everything I'd hoped for and more."

Rick thought he saw a glint of light in the automaton's eyes as if he understood praise, and chalked it up to his overactive imagination.

"When I'm done, I'll pack everything up to go back to the compound," Adam added. "That's the safest place for it. No one officially knows we have it, and it's probably a good idea to keep it that way."

During the next few hours, Kovach, Rick, and Jake took turns helping Adam while the others made plans for the night's work before catching a late afternoon nap. Dinner came early, and the *Diligence* chugged back to the wreck site as soon as darkness fell.

Rick tried to ignore the gut feeling that something bad was going to happen. The *Vincente's* location was void of other ships, and the lone techno turtle Adam had left behind didn't reveal any unwanted company during the day.

"Don't take longer than you absolutely have to," Jake told Adam as the inventor suited up before getting into the submersible. "We got lucky last night."

"Don't worry. Ben and I already know where we're going and what we want to bring back. We'll be up in a jiffy."

Elian stood watch on the deck outside the bridge, scanning the horizon. Kovach hovered around the deckhands as Wally and Sid worked the controls to lower the *Oceanus* into the water. Ben walked off the deck and plummeted, a sight Rick didn't think he would ever witness without feeling visceral panic as if a person had gone overboard.

Adam scattered the techno turtles again, sending them into the dark waves to keep sentry. Rick knew they had taken all possible precautions, but it didn't melt the ice in the pit of his stomach.

Tonight, clouds hid the moon. The sky and ocean blended in a black curtain, and the *Diligence's* running lights were dimmed to avoid attracting attention, making the night oppressive.

Jake and Kovach talked quietly at a distance. Wally and Sid waited for the signal to retrieve Adam and his *werkman*. Rick let his fingers drum on the railing and tried not to think about sea monsters.

The cool breeze ruffled Rick's hair. He wondered if Nicki and Liliana had broken the code of the strange boxes back in the warehouse and what those secrets held for them. Not for the first time, he wished he was back on dry land, and for that matter, back in New Pittsburgh.

In an instant the night came alive. A ball of indigo fire struck Elian in the chest, and he fell to the deck. Someone grabbed Rick from behind, strong enough to keep him pinned in a chokehold.

Jake and Kovach had their guns in hand. Wally and Sid drew wicked-looking knives from their belts. The man behind Rick tightened his hold and pressed the muzzle of a gun against his temple.

"Don't move," Rick's captor said. "We're just here for the cargo." More men descended on ropes from the sky.

The moon broke from behind the clouds, and Rick caught a glimpse of an airship with a dark balloon, making it nearly invisible in the night sky.

That's why we didn't see them coming. We were focused on the surface of the water or below. We forgot to look up.

"Let him go," Jake said, gun raised. "Nobody needs to get hurt."

Kovach's murderous expression suggested that he had other opinions, but he stayed where he was without lowering his revolver.

Rick heard the shuffle of people moving behind him and guessed they were heading for the cargo hold. The runes and sigils were designed to repel bad magic and contain the energy of whatever was stored in the rooms. They might deter a witch, but they would do nothing against regular thieves.

Rick glanced toward the bridge. Elian still lay on the deck where he had fallen. Two men with guns stood at the bridge entrance. Rick spotted four men in front of him on deck, his captor, plus several more who had gone to retrieve the cargo. He didn't doubt that Cook was armed, as well as Harry, Albert, and Ralph, but they were outnumbered, and without Elian, outgunned.

"Send a signal to the guy in the little ship," the man behind Rick shouted. "Tell him to bring his crates up now, and no one gets hurt."

"We don't have a way to contact him." Jake's voice dropped into a quiet cadence, trying to forestall a tragedy.

Rick's captor tightened his hold, nearly cutting off Rick's air. "You'd better find one, or we'll make this a ghost ship."

Maybe Ralph can astral travel and warn Adam not to surface. We can't risk letting that cargo get into the wrong hands.

"We got two boxes, Boss," a gruff voice said from behind Rick.

"Get them up to the airship," Boss replied.

The wind picked up as the temperature dropped. Rick wondered if Harry was using his weather magic to make it harder for their attackers since the sudden change buffeted the pirate airship much more than the *Diligence*.

"Bring that little ship up now!" Boss demanded, glaring at Wally and Sid.

"It's not in position," Sid protested. "We can't—"

Boss fired a shot, nearly deafening Rick, who thought for an instant the bullet was meant for him.

Sid crumpled. Wally started toward him, but a wave of the gun stopped him in his tracks.

One of the pirates came up behind Boss. "We can't keep our position much longer in this wind. It's going to be hell getting lifted aboard as it is."

"You got the boxes?" Boss asked.

"Yeah, they're up. And they dropped nets to get us back."

"Stand by," Boss said.

"I'm running out of patience," Boss shouted above the wind. "Bring up that sub!"

Rick knew that as much as Adam cared about his friends and the crew, he would realize that handing over the dangerous technology and magical relic would lead to even more tragedy. Rick agreed with Adam's morals, but he hoped the inventor's commitment didn't cost them all their lives.

"We would if we could," Jake yelled back. "He could be down there for hours. We can't reach him."

Everything seemed to happen at once. Rick heard a shot behind him, and the man who had been talking with Boss fell. Boss pivoted, keeping his stranglehold on Rick, and fired back at the hatchway that led to the mess hall, confirming Rick's suspicion that Cook had their backs.

Jake and Kovach opened fire on the other pirates. Wally jumped one of the attackers, wrestling the gun away and sinking his knife into the man's chest. The techno turtles surrounding them in the water blazed with light and opened a barrage of gunfire pointed skyward. Someone on the bridge lit every light on the *Diligence* and set off its deafening alarms.

Rick fought the hold Boss had on him, kicking and jabbing with his elbows, but couldn't get free. Boss threw them to one side, landing in a net made of wide canvas strips that immediately closed over them and lifted them into the air.

"I've got you, so they're not going to shoot," Boss growled, nearly making Rick pass out from the pressure on his neck, jamming the gun against his side just in case Rick thought of trying anything. "And once we get to the ship, I'm going to blow them out of the water. Then your buddy in the sub won't have any choice except to come up for air, and we'll be waiting."

The net spun crazily in the wind, swinging like a pendulum. Rick wondered if Boss would shoot him for puking.

The gunfire on the ship had stopped, and Rick wondered whether that was good or bad. Boss had abandoned his henchmen, but he was still getting away with part of the *Vincente's* cargo—and had Rick as a hostage.

The wind stopped as abruptly as it had started. Rick hoped someone had gotten word to Harry that he was in the net being hoisted aloft. Seconds later, an iridescent scrim covered the *Diligence* like a protective bubble. Rick figured that whatever that ball of light had done to Elian to disable him, the witch had survived and was back in action.

Bay doors opened wider above them as they reached the pirate airship, then shut when the net had cleared the opening.

"Don't try anything stupid." Boss pressed the barrel against Rick's temple. "You're valuable as a hostage, so don't be more trouble than you're worth."

Rough hands yanked Rick from the net, slapping cold steel cuffs onto his wrists. He saw nothing to identify who had taken him prisoner. *Probably Sombra or someone working with them. Cortez wouldn't get his hands dirty doing this in person, but piracy is his style.*

I am so screwed.

"What about the others?" a large man with a dark beard asked as he gave Boss a hand to get out of the net.

Boss shook his head. "They didn't make it back. Tell the bridge to open fire. Blast that damn ship out of the water."

"Open the bay," Boss told a man by the controls. "I want to watch." He looked toward the two men who had Rick pinned between them. "Bring him closer. Let him see."

Rick's heart thudded, and he held his breath, fearing that he was about to see his friends die.

The airship's guns blazed, unleashing a hail of bullets. Boss cursed as they bounced harmlessly from the glowing bubble. "What the hell?"

He wheeled to glare at a painfully thin man in a deep blue long coat. "I thought you struck down their witch?"

Boss's witch had the look of a moody scarecrow, all jutting bone and sharp angles. He regarded Boss with an expression of annoyed superiority. "I did 'strike him down.' Clearly he didn't *stay* down. He must be more powerful than we expected. What I sent would have killed a lesser warlock."

"Can you break through his protections?" Boss demanded.

"If I could have, it would be done by now. What he's constructed absorbs the energy sent against it, making it stronger. Like a knot that tightens when the prisoner struggles."

Boss grew red in the face like he might burst a blood vessel. "Get out of my sight," he roared at the witch. "Close the hatch, and break off the attack. Head for base."

He rounded on Rick. "You're my winning card. They'll bring me what I want to save your life."

Rick feared Boss was right, although his friends should leave him to his fate and take the *Vincente's* perilous cargo to safety.

But they won't. And if they don't succeed, we'll all die, and the experimental technology will get sold to the highest bidder.

"Throw him in the brig. Put a guard on him," Boss ordered. "Don't let him out of your sight."

The two ruffians shoved Rick out of the bay, frog marching him down a corridor and into an area that held a cell and a small office. They pushed him inside so hard he stumbled. The door slammed behind him, locking with a *clank*.

"Don't cause trouble and maybe we'll remember to feed you," one of the guards told him. "Sit down and shut up."

A slew of taunts raced through Rick's mind, but he kept his jaw clamped shut, not wanting to make a bad situation even worse. He settled for swaggering bravura he didn't feel and a defiant glare, maintaining the façade until the outer door closed and he was alone.

Rick sagged to the floor, drew up his knees, and rested his head in his hands, angry and despondent. *I have no idea where they're taking me or how I can send for help. Jake will bargain to save my life, even if he shouldn't. I should have heard someone behind me, or fought harder, or thrown myself out of the hatch so they didn't have a bargaining chip.*

But I didn't. And now I might have just cost the course of the war and the world's balance of power.

Chapter Eight

"Shit—they've got Rick!" Jake lunged, but Kovach grabbed him and yanked him back as the net hoisted Rick and his attacker into the night sky.

"Let go of me." Jake struggled against Kovach's hold, but the bodyguard held firm.

"You can't save him—right now," Kovach argued. "If you'd grabbed the net, they'd have shaken you off. You'd be dead, and Rick would have seen you die. That helps nothing."

Behind them, Jake heard Wally grieving his dead friend. Everything in Jake wanted to scream, shoot, and fight. His heart raced, and he could barely breathe.

Harry and Elian came thundering down the steps from the bridge. Both witches knelt beside Sid, but Jake knew from the blood pooled beneath the deckhand that he was past saving.

"Fuck," Kovach muttered.

Harry closed the man's eyes and stood. Cook brought a stretcher from the boat's small infirmary and moved Sid's body, covering the dead man with a blanket. They took the body inside.

Harry watched them go with sorrow in his eyes. "They've crewed with us since graduating high school," he said. "They're cousins, a few times removed."

"I'm sorry for your loss," Jake replied, still gutted at Rick's kidnapping.

"And yours," Harry said. "It's personal now, for us. We'll do whatever we can to help you rescue Rick and stop those sons of bitches."

"How did Adam know to activate the turtles?" Kovach asked.

Harry looked toward the bridge, where Albert and Ralph could be seen through the window.

"Ralph did a little 'traveling' and warned Adam. He's probably let Adam know that the pirates are gone, and it's safe to come up now," Harry replied.

Jake turned to Elian, who stared out over the ocean. His usually unreadable façade slipped, and Jake could see his grief.

"I'm sorry," Elian said quietly, his accent thicker than usual. "I failed you all."

Jake shook his head. "You got whammied. We were outgunned."

"I focused on the threats on the surface and below the water, but I did not scan the sky." Elian went on as if he hadn't heard. "The binding spell wasn't powerful enough to kill, but it kept me immobile and unable to use my magic."

"He got the drop on you," Jake said. "I'm glad you're not dead."

"The nature of the spell reveals something about the one who cast it," Elian said in a flat tone that denied the emotion in his eyes. "If the witch had been more powerful, he or she would have killed me outright. That would have been the safest thing to do. He didn't—so I must conclude that he couldn't."

Elian turned to Jake, and this time, Jake saw fury in the other man's eyes. "When I meet him, he will burn."

Kovach came up behind Jake and nudged his arm. "Sorry to intrude, but Adam and Ben are still down there. We need to bring them up and get the hell out of here."

Jake nodded and turned away, leaving Elian at the railing. They heard a loud *clunk* at the ladder on the side of the boat. Jake and

Spark of Destiny

Kovach drew their guns but breathed in relief when Ben climbed aboard.

"I'll drop a net to help Ben get out while the turtles climb aboard," Kovach said.

"I can run the winch, but it helps to have a second person for the ropes." Wally stood by the equipment, pale but resolute. His eyes were red from crying, and he looked lost and angry, but he was at his post.

"Thank you," Jake said. "I'll do whatever you need me to do. And —I'm sorry about Sid."

"When the time comes, I'll shoot the bastard who did it myself. But there's work to do now, so we best get to it."

Jake and Wally got the rig working and slowly lifted the *Oceanus* from the water. The submersible had barely cleared the deck when Adam popped the hatch. He clambered out, stumbling in his dive suit, face flushed with fury.

"What happened? Who was it? How did they get the drop on us? Is everyone okay?" His gaze darted around the deck, noting who was in sight—and who was absent.

"Jake—where are Rick and Sid?"

Jake swallowed, and his silence made Adam gasp and go pale. "Sid's dead. Rick's been kidnapped. They got the boxes in the hold."

"Screw the boxes. How—?"

"Airship. Never saw them coming." Kovach joined them, and his clipped words gave Jake a clue on just how hard his friend was tamping down his rage.

"Ben and I brought up the rest of the important cargo," Adam replied. "Ralph warned me we'd been attacked, so I set off the turtles."

"They helped," Jake assured him. "The pirates didn't know what to make of it, so they panicked. We shot them all—except for the one who got away with Rick."

Adam glanced toward where Elian still stood at the railing. "Is he okay?"

Jake shrugged. "Probably as much as any of us. We need to get out of here, regroup, and figure out where they've taken Rick. Because we're going to get him back—and the tech."

"Damn right we are. And then we're going to make them pay," Kovach growled.

Wally and Harry spoke quietly, and then Wally went back inside, presumably to his quarters, as Harry returned to the bridge.

Adam, Kovach, and Jake headed below decks. Jake and Kovach made a couple of trips to bring the new crates Adam and Ben had just recovered. They helped Adam out of his clunky suit and checked Ben and the turtles for damage. Kovach and Rick usually assisted Adam, but Jake didn't want to be alone, so he kept out of the way.

"Look at this. They made a wreck of the place." Adam stood in the middle of the cargo hold, hands on hips, a grim expression on his face as he surveyed what the pirates had left behind. He had brought some of his own equipment to test the items from the *Vincente*, and what the pirates hadn't stolen, they had thrown on the floor or smashed.

"How bad?" Jake asked.

Adam sighed. "It could be worse." He bent to pick up some of the instruments. Jake and Kovach helped. "Fortunately, they didn't know what they were doing—or looking at. I'll have to see if these still work. I think they're just dented a little, not broken."

He waved a hand vaguely to indicate the empty space. "But they took everything from yesterday."

"You said you put a copy of your notes and diagrams in the *Oceanus*," Jake prompted. "Do you think you can recover anything from that?"

Adam shrugged. "It's better than nothing. My notes—and what Ben recorded—preserve my findings, but I don't know that I could rebuild what they stole just from that. I'd barely started studying the pieces."

"Maybe what's in today's haul will help," Kovach suggested. Despite his rough demeanor, he had a soft spot for Adam and looked out for him.

"It's bad that they stole the stuff. But getting their hands on what we brought up just now would have been much worse," Adam said. "So at least there's that. Cold comfort."

Jake looked to Kovach. "Do you think they'll strike again tonight?"

Kovach frowned. "We killed a lot of their men. I don't know how many they brought with them, but between that and Elian's 'bubble,' I think they'd retreat and regroup." His eyes widened. "Shit. We need to go back on deck and clean up. Between the bodies and the blood, it's going to stink once the sun hits it."

Harry and Kovach conferred and decided to chuck the pirates' bodies overboard. Sid's corpse was in the freezer, awaiting a return to land. Jake, Kovach, and Adam pitched in, sluicing and scrubbing the decks along with Cook and Ralph. When they finished, only a few stray bullet holes in the bulkheads revealed the fight that had taken place.

The late-night snack was a somber affair. No one talked. Jake knew the food was as good as usual, but everything tasted like ash. Finally, the captain stood and lifted a bottle of whiskey. Cook passed around shot glasses.

"To Sid." Harry poured out shots for everyone. "We will always remember the best deckhand to sail on this ship."

They murmured in agreement and knocked back the liquor. Wally excused himself, and Jake wished he could do the same.

"We need a plan," Kovach said what Jake felt sure everyone was thinking. Jake's gut was too tangled up with grief and fury, so he was glad he could count on Kovach to pick up the slack.

"We've got to figure out where that airship is going," Adam said. "They must have a base somewhere. That's where they'll take the equipment—and Rick."

"They intend to come for the rest of the cargo," Harry pointed out. "That's why they took your friend. The good part of that is that they won't just disappear. They'll have to stick close to use him as a bargaining chip. The bad part is…he's in danger, and if they believe you won't make a trade, they have no reason to keep him alive."

"We can't wait for them to negotiate." Jake barely recognized the growl of his own voice. "We have to find their base, rescue Rick, take back the cargo—and make sure the sons of bitches never do this again."

"There's a reason the Florida Keys have been popular with smugglers and pirates for centuries," Harry said. "Plenty of hiding places. Thirty of the Keys are inhabited, but there are nearly two thousand little islands in the archipelago. Those might not be suitable for a permanent settlement, but they'd do just fine for a temporary base with some shelter and provisions."

Kovach frowned. "That might be where they'll fall back tonight, but if they're stealing cargo, then they intend to do something with it. If the bastards behind the attack are Sombra—and I'd bet money on it—they need space to find out what the experimental tech can do. They won't sell off the prototype; they'll need to make more. That requires a lab, maybe even an assembly facility. They'll need to be hidden for that."

"What about swamps?" Adam asked. "There are some in the Keys, right? That could be a good place to hide if there are any places with solid land for a building."

Harry nodded. "It would. The swamps in the Keys are fairly small and remote. But it's a starting point. I'll ask Albert to see if he can use his locator magic to at least find a general direction to search for Rick. Once we narrow the possibilities, Ralph can get a read on the location to look for a base."

"We have an airship of our own," Jake said. "Cullen's been on standby in case we needed him. I'd say we do." The *Allegheny Princess* wasn't technically a military zeppelin, but thanks to Adam it was far better armed than most private airships.

"I need to let Mitch and Jacob know what's going on," Kovach said, mentioning the two agents from the Department of Supernatural Investigation.

"I don't want to have the government come in and take over," Jake warned. "I don't trust the feds to make saving Rick a priority."

Kovach shook his head. "Neither do I. That's not what I meant. I think Mitch and Jacob can offer some off-the-books support that frankly we're going to need."

Jake distrusted secret government organizations on general principles, but he grudgingly made an exception for the two unorthodox agents who had worked with them before.

"Maybe Liliana and Nicki have uncovered something that will change the game," Adam said. "We could use a lucky break."

Except our luck never runs that smoothly.

Harry went back to the bridge. Cook cleaned up the galley since Ralph and Albert had eaten early. Adam and Kovach went to the cargo hold to see what could be reconstructed from his notes and Ben's recording.

Elian hadn't shared the food or memorial with them. Jake went out on deck, needing to get some air. He wasn't surprised to see Elian standing at the railing, staring at the ocean.

"There's plenty of food if you want it." Jake took a spot next to the witch.

"Thank you, but I'm not hungry."

"I wasn't either, but Kovach will force-feed me if I skip eating. He watches over us like a hawk—or a mother hen. Losing Rick is upsetting him a lot more than he's showing."

The ghost of a smile touched Elian's lips. "Liliana does the same for me. We're lucky."

Jake's sigh conveyed his feelings at the moment about "luck."

"Losing a battle doesn't mean the war is lost," Elian said after several moments of silence. "I have lived long enough to know that."

Not for the first time, Jake wondered how old Elian really was. Nicki and Liliana were of an age, but Elian was clearly older. He definitely wasn't a vampire, but Jake had heard that magic could extend a lifespan and slow aging.

"Rick and I have been best friends all our lives," Jake said after another pause. "We always watch out for each other. He's like a brother to me—far more than my actual brother. I'm worried about him. He's alone and in danger. He'll put on a good front, but he's got to be scared."

"He's also clever and persistent," Elian said. "If there is a way for him to escape, he'll find it. And if he can gather intelligence while he's a prisoner, he'll do that too. Don't lose hope too quickly. We still have many cards to play."

Jake nodded, swallowing hard against the lump in his throat. "Thank you. I know that. It's just, right now, my heart isn't listening to my brain."

"Go have some whiskey and try to sleep," Elian advised. "Kovach, Adam, and I will handle the watch. In the morning, we'll be back at your compound and regroup. Paths we can't see now may open for us then."

Jake walked to the galley and poured himself another slug of whiskey. He knew it might help him fall asleep, but his dreams would be dark, regardless.

Nicki's going to skin me alive for not watching out for Rick—and I deserve it. I'm sorry, Rick. I let you down. I promise I'll make it up to you—if it's the last thing I do.

Chapter Nine

Earlier that same day.

"I'm glad you thought to bring your lore books," Nicki said as she and Liliana made themselves comfortable in the library's armchairs. A tray with tea and shortbread sat on a nearby side table.

"It's a good thing I packed so many books. I wasn't sure how long I'd be staying or whether we would be able to go back for more," Liliana replied. "It's not safe now for Rafael and the servants to leave the house or us to leave the compound. At least I can communicate with the house spirits to keep me informed."

Nicki chuckled. "Most people just use a telephone."

"I don't want to bother Rafael, but knowing that the household is running smoothly eases my mind," Liliana admitted. "The spirits also don't shade the truth. Rafael is inclined to gloss over the difficulties to keep me from fretting. I appreciate the intent, but I'd rather know the real situation."

Since Cortez's people had caused a scene at the compound's front gate, things had been quiet. Nicki didn't trust the pause. *Cortez is planning his next move. And whatever it is, we aren't going to like it.*

"How do you think the boys are doing out on the boat?" Nicki asked in an attempt to derail her pessimistic thoughts. "I'm worried that they've lost a whole day."

Liliana looked up and laid her hand on the page of her open book. "If I could reach the sea ghosts from this far away, I would have gladly kept an eye on them. I'm worried too."

"At least we're worried together." Nicki managed a weak smile.

"And we have tea and cookies—and books. That makes everything easier to bear," Liliana agreed.

Liliana read spell books and magical histories, seeking insights into their current challenges. Nicki scoured records of the Keys, focusing on the pirates, smugglers, and wreckers, looking for any mention of the Lost City or hidden bases in the stories of the swamps.

"I wish Cullen were here with the airship," Nicki said. "He could do reconnaissance over the swamps and see if there are any likely places for secret cities or forts. I'm certain that Mr. Hernandez meant to point our attention in that direction. Maybe he couldn't put the pieces together either and passed the information on for us to do better."

"I've been looking into swamp magic," Liliana replied.

"There is such a thing?"

"Apparently so. I shouldn't be surprised. Swamps and marshes are liminal places—spots where the line between this world and the next is thin. They are neither land nor water. Those kinds of locations magnify energy and have potent magic. Since Cortez and Sombra are using their own witches, having a base in the swamp would make a lot of sense."

Nicki rearranged herself in the chair so that her legs were folded under her, and smoothed her skirts. "What kind of base? That might make a difference in the location. Is it just a hideout in case they're on the lam from the law?"

"Nicki!" Liliana chided with a gleam of humor in her eyes. "Such language!"

"I've said plenty of worse things when I was running the Gatling gun on the airship." Nicki gave an impish grin.

"Go on. I just had to tease you."

"As I was saying." Nicki cleared her throat theatrically. "The type of base might make all the difference. If they just need a hideout, one or two buildings might suffice. They'd only need to keep them supplied and have a place to hide a boat. But they want the *Vincente's* cargo, so do they need a warehouse—or a laboratory?"

Liliana raised an eyebrow. "Good question. I don't think Sombra intends to sell the cargo to the highest bidder, not when they could make copies and sell to a lot more buyers. Would they need a factory? Probably not. It sounds like the prototypes were handmade."

"But they might need a space like Adam has back in New Pittsburgh where he can assemble his contraptions and test them," Nicki replied. "It wouldn't be as large as a factory or a warehouse but bigger than a cabin."

"Which might mean Cullen could spot it from the air." Liliana sounded excited as she warmed to the speculation.

"They could still camouflage buildings, and if the cypress and the mangroves are thick enough, it could make them difficult to see from the air," Nicki mused. "But the more space Cortez's people need, the harder it will be to hide."

"Does that help narrow the locations? Some of the swamps might be too small or not have enough stable ground. I'd think that a good base would need water access, so it shouldn't be landlocked."

Nicki hummed as she went back over the maps. "Yes. That cuts it down from a huge number of possibilities to a slightly more manageable, very long list. *Merde*! This is taking too long."

When Liliana didn't reply, Nicki looked up and found her friend sitting up, stiff and straight-backed, staring ahead with a glazed look in her eyes. A sudden chill filled the air, and Nicki knew Liliana had a ghostly visitor.

"Lili?" Nicki felt her heart in her throat, fearing bad news.

Liliana came back to herself a moment later, pale and eyes wide. "There's been trouble at the house. I need to talk to Rafael."

Nicki trooped behind Liliana, heading for Conroy's office. Liliana knocked on the door, and Conroy called for them to enter.

"Something's happened at the house," Liliana told him when he looked up, clearly surprised to see them. "One of the ghosts told me there's been an attack. I need to call Rafael."

Conroy gestured toward the phone on the wall. "Of course. Be my guest."

Nicki stood back, giving Liliana privacy as she rang up her home number. She exchanged a glance with Conroy, wordlessly letting him know that she had no additional details.

Liliana defaulted to rapid-fire Spanish, far too fast for Nicki to keep up. If Conroy could follow the conversation, he didn't let on. Liliana asked a series of questions, then listened with a distressed expression, growing more agitated.

Nicki couldn't catch every word, but she understood "fire," "weapons," and "damage" amid the torrent.

Liliana blinked back tears and clenched her fist. "*Gracias*," she whispered and hung up the receiver.

It took a moment for her to turn back toward Nicki and Conroy. "Someone attacked our house," she said once she gathered her composure. "They used magic and fire. Fortunately, thanks to the wardings and the quick thinking of our household staff, nobody was hurt, and little damage was done."

Nicki could hear tears in Liliana's voice. "Someone tried to burn down our home and kill my people." She sounded furious and heart-broken. "Most of our staff have been with us for decades. They're family to me. I can't abide this."

"They're okay?" Nicki realized she had been holding her breath, needing confirmation.

"Yes. Thank God. But it could have been so much worse." Liliana dropped into a chair and covered her face with her hands. "How did we come to this?"

Nicki shifted closer and laid a hand on Liliana's shoulder. "I'm sorry it happened, but glad no one was hurt. Were there any hints about who did it? Do you think it was Cortez's people?"

Liliana rubbed her eyes and sat up, taking a deep breath before she spoke. "It must be Cortez. Who else?"

"When Elian returns, can he pick up traces of the witch's energy signature?" Conroy asked.

"It depends. A powerful witch leaves more identifying traces—but is also more likely to be able to cover them," Liliana replied. "Whoever's working for Cortez is probably skilled enough to hide."

"Is anyone hurt? Do they need supplies?" Conroy asked. "I can send armed guards."

Liliana gave a bitter laugh. "Oh, the neighbors would love that! As it is, they'll be talking about us for years." She shook her head. "Thank you, but no. We prepared for this sort of thing, although we hoped the preparations would never be needed. They're safe—for now. Although it's taken a toll on their peace of mind."

"I'm sorry," Conroy said. "If there's anything I can do to help, please let me know."

Nicki shepherded Liliana back to the library and poured her a cup of tea. "Here. Tea makes everything better."

Liliana's hand shook as she held the cup. "What happened was too close. I'll see it in my dreams."

"I've been thinking." Nicki took a seat across from her friend. "Can you ask the ghosts to search for Cortez? He and his bully boys have probably added to their number. I doubt they bear him any goodwill or owe any loyalty."

"I don't want to take advantage of them."

"If they agree freely, you're giving them an opportunity to help the cause." Nicki brushed aside Liliana's objection. "If we could find Cortez, it might even change the course of the war. We would certainly be safer with him stopped. And ghost spies can't get caught."

Liliana nodded. "You're right. Elian says I'm always too careful." She finished her tea. "Let me rest and clear my mind. Tonight, we'll recruit ghosts."

When Liliana went to her room, Nicki returned to her chair in the library and buried herself in the maps.

Conroy's knock at the door several minutes later startled her. "We have visitors, Miss. You'll want to meet them."

Nicki set her maps aside and rose. "Are they interesting? I'm not feeling very social right now."

Conroy chuckled. "I believe you'll find them to be very interesting."

"Have you heard anything from the ship?"

"Early this morning. One word, 'safe.' I didn't mention it because there were no details."

"Too long," Nicki muttered. "I'll be glad when they're back."

"In my experience, neither Mr. Brand nor Mr. Desmet prefer the 'safe' choice."

Nicki snorted. "I've known them all my life. I'm quite aware."

She shook out her skirts and followed Conroy to the parlor.

Two men rose when she and Conroy entered. One was shorter with dark hair and a five o'clock shadow, the good looks of a penny dreadful hero. The taller man had blond hair and a long face.

"Agents Storm and Drangosavich." Nicki recognized them from past exploits in New Pittsburgh. "What brings you to Key West?"

The men sat on the couch after Nicki settled into her favorite wing chair, and Conroy took the other armchair. Edward brought a tea tray and cookies and set them on the low table in front of the sofa.

"To be honest, Miss LeClercq, we're here because of Brand and Desmet," Storm replied. "It appears that we have a common interest—and a shared enemy."

"Do tell." Nicki felt a rush of relief at the appearance of the agents from the Department of Supernatural Investigation, sure they could help. At the same time, she knew Jake *mostly* trusted Storm and Drangosavich, passing along information on a "need-to-know" basis.

"We've had a few telegrams from Mr. Kovach, relaying that your group is here to salvage a wreck that might be vital to the war effort," Storm said. "The cargo could change the course of the hostilities—and shift control of the Caribbean."

Nicki paused to give the impression that she had considered what they said. "What do you know about swamps?"

Spark of Destiny

Both agents looked perplexed. "Swamps?" Drangosavich asked. "I'm not sure I understand."

"Wet, mushy places with awful snakes and alligators and mosquitos," Nicki clarified. "Swamps."

Storm cleared his throat as if stifling a laugh. Drangosavich just looked lost. "I am acquainted with the concept, but I don't see the connection."

Nicki sighed. "Does your department know of any secret bases hidden in the swamps near here? Or anything about the Lost City or a forgotten fort? Because I'll bet your bottom dollar that's where Sombra's got their lair."

Nicki knew her mind was prone to skipping ahead, jumping from topic to topic with a link only she could see. Jake and Rick were used to it, although they teased her about her seeming non sequiturs. Conroy had the benefit of knowing the background behind her question. The two agents appeared thoroughly baffled, though their ears pricked up at the mention of "Sombra."

"I have the feeling we may have missed a briefing." Drangosavich gave a patient smile. "What makes you think Sombra is hiding in a swamp?"

"Our Havana office sent some crates that weren't expected." Nicky hedged her answer but was hungry for information. "They had maps and information about a city and a fort that were abandoned deep in one of the swamps. I don't think it was a mistake. It was a clue—but without a cipher. It makes sense if Sombra needs a place to assemble its experimental technology. And since they kidnapped Luis and locked him in their secret lab, we need to find Sombra and stop them."

Storm and Drangosavich exchanged a look. "Luis Delgado Ruiz?" Storm asked. "How do you know him?"

Nicki gave a wave of her hand as if the question were superfluous. "He's the little brother of one of my best friends from finishing school."

Nicki had learned long ago that overwhelming her listeners with important but seemingly jumbled information threw them off their game and made it more likely they would disclose something they didn't intend to share. She found it to be a delightful exercise that gave her the advantage, just like when men underestimated her intelligence because of her bosom.

"Where did you find out about Luis and the lab?" Storm looked confused, as if he was still trying to catch up.

"The ghost from the ring told Liliana," Nicki replied. "Luis got a letter smuggled out of the lab, and the ghost of Alphonse Ramirez gave Lili the rest of the details. It makes sense that Sombra would be after Luis since he's a propulsion engineer, and the *Vincente* was probably carrying experimental engine parts."

Nicki was fairly certain that the agents had come to fill them in on the situation, perhaps pick up a few tidbits. From their expressions, she guessed that she had been the one with the information.

"That's…a lot to take in," Drangosavich admitted.

"You're lucky you got here safely," Nicki added. "Javier Cortez's people have attacked several times, and they just tried to blow up Liliana's house."

Storm pinched the bridge of his nose. Drangosavich had the hint of a smile as if appreciating a game well played.

"Maybe it would be best if we could get everyone in the room and start from the beginning," Drangosavich suggested. "Are Jake and Rick here?"

"They'll be back soon," Conroy said. "And they may have additional news worth waiting for."

"Yeah, that sounds like a good idea," Storm agreed. "Believe it or not, we might even have some details you haven't found yet." Drangosavich elbowed him in the ribs.

"I'm sure you do," Nicki replied with a smile. "Once the boys are back, let's compare notes. We'll probably know more from the ghosts by then too."

Storm looked like he was going to ask a question but seemed to change his mind. Nicki had the feeling that Drangosavich enjoyed seeing his partner thrown for a loop.

The two agents stood. "We'll be back at a reasonable time in the morning, then. Thank you for the tea," Storm said. Conroy saw them out and returned as Nicki poured a cup of the untouched tea and helped herself to a cookie.

"That went well, don't you think?" Nicki gave a conspiratorial smile.

"I must say, I enjoyed that interaction very much," Conroy replied. "I do hope that they'll be able to fill in some of the missing pieces—about Luis and Sombra."

Nicki glanced at the clock and pushed down her nervousness. "I hope Jake, Rick, and the others are okay. I wish Liliana and I had been able to go with them. We've made some important headway, but I don't like missing out."

Conroy smiled. "I'm certain that everyone will be glad to fill in the details—for you and Señora, as well as for the agents." He frowned. "Is Señora feeling better?"

Nicki felt relieved that Conroy shared her concern. "You saw how upset she was about what happened at the house. She went to rest and calm her nerves. We'll return to our research once she feels up to it."

Conroy's expression suggested that he suspected that their "research" might go beyond dusty tomes, but he didn't comment. "Very well. Dinner will be at the regular time. If Señora needs anything medicinal, please let me know."

Nicki thanked him and then headed back to the library. Edward had brought hot tea, and she poured another cup, sitting quietly and sipping the brew to center herself.

I don't have Renate's ability to see visions, or Lili's talent of talking to ghosts, but my intuition has always been good. I can't shake the feeling that Jake and the others are in trouble—or that something is going to happen. But there's nothing specific to warn them about. They're already being careful. All I can do is sit and wait. I hate waiting!

After another hour, Liliana slipped into the library. She still looked worried, but several hours' rest had left her less worn. "What did I miss?"

Nicki filled her in on the agents' visit and their intended return. "They obviously knew who Luis was. They didn't know about the kidnapping, but it makes me wonder why DSI had their eye on him."

Nicki poured a cup of tea and fixed it the way she knew her friend liked, then handed it to her. Liliana gave a grateful nod.

"Luis was aware that his focus on propulsion could be used to do harm," she said after drinking most of the cup. "He skirted offers to join one organization or another because he wanted to use what he could do to improve the world. I don't think he ever considered himself important enough to be kidnapped."

"If the agents can help us search the swamps, and we bring in Cullen and the *Allegheny Princess*, we can find where Sombra's keeping Luis faster, and bring him home." Nicki wasn't at all sure things would go quite that easily, but she knew Liliana needed to focus on positive options.

Liliana smiled, but it didn't reach her eyes. Nicki saw the same doubt about happy endings. "Thank you. That's what I'm hanging onto as well."

She set down her cup. "The extra sleep will help me put out the call to the ghosts. The range of my ability to reach spirits is limited. Most ghosts are tethered to a place—some have more ability to wander than others, but I've never met a ghost that could just go anywhere. The exception are spirits like the ones tied to the soapstone carvings. If ghosts are anchored by an object, then at least in theory they can go anywhere the object is."

"What are you planning?" Nicki set her teacup aside and leaned forward, eager for details.

"Do you remember the 'telephone' game from when we were in school?" Liliana asked, with mischief in her eyes.

"Of course. One person whispered something to the person next to them, who passed it on until it got back to the first speaker," Nicki replied.

"Since I'm limited and the individual ghosts are limited, that's basically what I had in mind. I'll tell the ghosts I can reach, and they'll tell the spirits a little farther out, and so on."

Nicki pursed her lips, thinking. "As I recall, by the time the message got back to the person where it started, everything had changed. That's what was so funny, but won't that be an issue for what you're attempting?"

Liliana sighed. "And that's the problem. Ramirez's ghost was able to travel because of the ring. He was also newly dead so his sense of self and memory was intact. We take a risk with ghosts who have begun to fade. And we're hoping that none of the ones who get the message are malicious."

"There are a lot of leaps in there," Nicki cautioned.

"So there are. But I am going mad sitting still, and I'd rather try and fail than do nothing."

"Then let's do it." Nicki mustered a brave smile. "Nothing ventured, nothing gained."

She helped Liliana prepare for a séance, clearing the small table, setting up candles, and burning incense. They sat opposite each other and held hands. Nicki closed her eyes and tried to still her racing thoughts, taking deep breaths.

"Spirits—if you can hear me, I ask for your help. My brother Luis was kidnapped, and we believe he's being held at a secret place in a swamp. He's in great danger, but we don't know where to look. Please, if you know of such a place, tell me. And if you don't, ask any spirits who might. I will be grateful," Liliana said.

For several minutes, neither woman moved. The library had grown cold, a sign Nicki knew meant that ghosts were present. She peeked her eyes open, but saw nothing amiss—no hovering mist or strange floating orbs.

Liliana remained still, and Nicki wondered whether her friend was hearing from the Beyond or waiting for a response.

The room warmed, and Liliana's stiff posture relaxed. She opened her eyes, and Nicki thought she looked tired but gratified.

"They heard. No guarantees, but a handful of spirits said they would ask others. It's iffy—I don't think Luis is being held close to here, and there's no telling how far the ghosts' range is, but…it's something."

"Let's go back over the things in the boxes Mr. Hernandez sent one more time," Nicki suggested. "We know more than we did on the first round. Maybe we'll see something in a fresh light."

They avoided the soapstone carvings, letting those spirits remain dormant for now. Nicki and Liliana carefully dug through the books and loose papers, taking a closer look at pages that they had originally dismissed.

"Look at this." Nicki held up a page with handwritten notes, sequences of letters that made no sense. "It's gibberish—but why is it here?"

Liliana peered at the strange paper. "If the warships were shelling Havana, maybe Señor Hernandez was in a hurry and just swept everything into the box at the last moment."

Nicki tapped her foot impatiently as she thought. "That doesn't sound right. Here's a guy who had the presence of mind to pull the boxes together with information he thinks is important enough to get onto the last airship out of Cuba. He's going to make the most of every inch of space to send a message."

"Those aren't even words," Liliana protested.

"Not to us," Nicki conceded. "But my friend Cady is a whiz with codes. It's worth seeing what she makes of it."

"You think it's a secret message?" Liliana leaned closer to take a better look.

"What else could it be? Maybe Hernandez found it, or overheard it. I don't think anything was put in those crates by accident, so he had to think it was important."

Nicki gripped the paper and headed back to Conroy's office. "We need to use the phone again," she told him, breathless with the possibility of a breakthrough.

"Did you find something?" He looked as eager for good news as Nicki felt.

"We're not sure. But I need to reach someone in New Pittsburgh."

"Do they have a telephone?"

Nicki didn't fault his question. Phones were still a luxury, although they were growing more common. The new technology was too expensive for most people.

Spark of Destiny

"Not at home—but I'm sure she does where she works."

Nicki rang for the operator, and asked to be put through to the Pennsylvania College for Women in Pittsburgh. She fidgeted as she waited, tapping her toe again.

"Hello? I need to speak to Cady McDaniel. It's a matter of life or death." Nicki figured that her description wasn't too much of a fib, given the circumstances and what was at stake.

Once again she waited, shooting a hopeful glance at Liliana and Conroy. Nicki held the receiver to her ear tightly, as if her grip would strengthen the connection.

"Hello, Cady McDaniel speaking."

"Cady? It's Nicki. We've got a situation. A man's been kidnapped, and we've found a message that looks like a code. It might help us find him. Can you please see if you can crack it?"

"What kind of trouble are you in this time, Nicki?" Cady replied. "Are you with Rick and Jake?"

"Yes. We're in Key West—and don't tell anyone, but this might help swing the war our way," Nicki confided. "Do you have a pen and paper? There are a lot of nonsense words, but I'm positive you can figure it out."

Cady McDaniel was the head librarian at the women's college. She had a fondness for working the puzzles in the *Pall Mall* Magazine for Gentlemen, and recently deciphered a cryptogram thought to be uncrackable.

Her quick wit, sharp sense of humor, and willingness to bend social conventions meant she and Nicki had hit it off right away. Nicki also applauded Cady's penchant for bicycle pants instead of long skirts, as well as her dead-eye aim with a Colt Peacemaker.

"I'm ready," Cady told her. "Go slow. The slightest error could throw everything off."

Nicki painstakingly read off the nonsense words letter by letter, and Cady repeated each one. When the long list was done, they went through it one more time to verify.

"Have you seen anything like it?" Nicki asked.

"Maybe," Cady mused. "One of my friend's brothers was home

from the Navy on a visit. He had a little too much to drink and started arguing with me about secret codes. He told me they used one aboard ship that no one could crack, and I got him to tell me more than he should have. This looks similar."

"I knew you could do it!"

"Not so fast. I could be wrong, but I'll do my best. Give me your number, so I can call you back," Cady said.

Nicki shared the exchange and the four-digit number for the compound. "Thanks, Cady. This really could save a life."

"Glad to help. I'll let you know as soon as I figure it out," Cady promised.

Nicki hung up the receiver and turned back to Conroy. "If anyone can do it, Cady will."

When Nicki returned to the library, she found Liliana with her head cradled in her folded arms on the table.

"Lili—what's wrong?"

Liliana raised her head, and she looked like she had been crying. "The ghosts came back with news faster than I expected. They told me about a warehouse with strange scientific equipment—and a man who looks like Luis."

Nicki went to fetch a glass of iced tea and brought it back to Liliana, along with a cool washcloth. "That's good news, right? It means Luis is alive. Now we just have to storm the warehouse and save him."

"Jake and the others won't be back until tomorrow. Cortez could move him by then," Liliana said, accepting the tea gratefully and wiping the cloth across her face. "And that's assuming that the ghost's information is current—and correct."

Nicki stamped her foot in frustration. For as much as she enjoyed pushing the rules, even she knew that trying to infiltrate the warehouse without backup was suicidal. "Maybe we can't go—but there's nothing preventing those agents from investigating. Tell me all the details."

She burst into the office for the second time in half an hour. "Did

Spark of Destiny

those agents leave their phone number? Lili's ghosts have a lead on finding Luis."

Conroy handed her Storm's business card, and Nicki rang up the number.

"We think Cortez has a warehouse lab on Key West, and he's holding Luis, the kidnapped engineer, prisoner," she told Storm. "Can you get inside and rescue him?"

There was a long pause, and the sound of muffled conversation, as if Storm put his hand over the mouthpiece.

"Do you have more details?" Drangosavich asked, and Nicki guessed Storm had put his more patient partner on the line.

She relayed the information Liliana had gleaned from the ghosts. "No, we don't have an informant, exactly. We have a squad of ghost spies and my friend who's a medium sent them out to do reconnaissance."

Another pause and then muted voices once more. Storm came back on the phone this time.

"That actually squares with what we picked up from sources in town," he said. "*Living* sources. So we'll take a look tonight. Do not—I repeat, do not—leave your compound. Cortez already has his sights on you. We'll handle this and let you know what happens."

Nicki thanked them and hung up. She crossed her fingers and hoped that this time luck would be on their side.

Chapter Ten

"Just my luck; the welds are solid," Rick muttered as he went over every inch of the bars in his cell aboard the airship.

The airship's small brig held one other—empty—cell. A desk and chair were unoccupied in the outer office area. Rick's cell held nothing except a bucket, which he assumed was for necessity. He sighed and sat with his back to the wall in a corner.

How did everything go ass up so quickly?

Rick had looked around as much as possible as his captors strong-armed him to his cell. What he saw of the pirates' airship was similar but less luxurious than their own *Allegheny Princess*. He wondered how well-armed the pirate airship was and whether it included experimental technology from Sombra like the *Princess* had "upgrades" courtesy of Adam Farber and Tesla-Westinghouse.

Shit. This is a real mess.

The pirates had left their dead behind, making off with the two boxes of the *Vincente's* cargo in Adam's early haul and Rick as a hostage.

That's their big mistake. Jake and the others would forfeit the boxes, but they'll make sure there's hell to pay for kidnapping me. Let's just hope that means we all get out alive.

Other than being half of Brand and Desmet and coming from a well-off family, Rick wasn't a prize hostage. He doubted the pirates planned to ask for a ransom, although they might propose trading Rick for whatever new items Adam had gotten from the *Vincente*. Rick's value was emotional—and Boss was betting that Jake and the others wouldn't give him up without a fight.

Maybe they should. I'm not worth losing the war over.

While Rick didn't doubt that an impartial observer might agree with him, he also knew that Jake and the others would never forgive themselves. That meant they were going to mount a rescue, so Rick needed to be prepared to help as much as he could when the time came.

Rick debated whether to use the lock pick hidden inside his belt to break out of the cell, but there was nowhere to go aboard the airship. Getting kidnapped wasn't the best way to spy on their enemy's secret base, but since the die was already cast, Rick figured he'd better make the most of it.

His captors had checked him for weapons but left Rick his watch. He glanced at the time. The ship didn't slow for an hour. Knowing that an airship's average speed was about eighty miles per hour, that told Rick they were far from Key West—which meant they were somewhere on the lower Florida peninsula.

Well, that's something I didn't expect.

Two armed guards showed up not long after the ship stopped. "Get up. Cause trouble and we'll put a bullet in you," the taller man said.

"Don't damage the merchandise," Rick warned as he got to his feet. "My friends won't make any deals if I'm full of holes."

"Want to test that?" The guard raised his gun to point at Rick's chest.

Rick lifted his cuffed hands in surrender. "Whoa. That's not necessary. I'm coming."

He expected the pair to grab him, but instead they kept their guns trained on him. They knew as well as he did that trying to run away aboard the airship was pointless.

Rick thought they'd take him back to the cargo hold. Instead, he

Spark of Destiny

found himself prodded toward the passenger entrance, which he eyed with hesitation, wondering if they had just decided to push him from the ship.

"Walk the ramp—don't try any funny stuff," the tall guard barked. "And if you aren't a fan of heights, don't look down."

The door opened to a gangway leading to a tall metal mooring mast. He guessed the tower to be at least two hundred feet tall, and the ramp shuddered as the wind buffeted the airship.

Rick kept his gaze forward, resolutely refusing to look down or note the gap between the gangway railing and the platform, plenty wide to fall through.

To his relief, the center of the tower had an elevator, with stairs spiraling around it for emergencies. He didn't relish the idea of making his way down the narrow steps with his hands bound in front of him.

"Where are we?" They were surrounded by cypress trees, a thick canopy of branches heavy with Spanish moss.

"Welcome to the swamp," the tall man said. "That's all you need to know."

Rick hesitated on purpose at the top of the tower, trying to get his bearings and spot a landmark. A few dim spotlights lit the single street. The chug of a generator echoed croaking bullfrogs. Nothing but vegetation sprawled as far as he could see.

We flew too long to be in Cuba or to still be in the Keys. Is this the Everglades?

He remembered the odd contents of the boxes Hernandez had slipped aboard the airlift from Havana. *There were paintings of a town in a swamp. Did the place really exist? And have Cortez and Sombra found it and made it their base?*

Overhead, Rick heard the clamor of workers bringing the stolen crates out of the zeppelin for their turn in the elevator. The pulleys and cables creaked. Wind and the tug of the moored ship made the whole structure rattle.

The air grew still and heavy as the elevator descended. Rick could smell wet plants. Insects buzzed. Sweat trickled down his back.

Once they reached the ground, Rick eyed the pirates' base. A small clearing had been reclaimed, and he bet dry land was scarce and not to be taken for granted in storm season. The compound had a few military-style bunkers and dilapidated houses surrounded by a high chain link fence topped with barbed wire. Four Gatling gun bunkers, one facing each direction, pointed out into the swamp.

I don't think a lot of people are going to come from that direction, so I wonder what they're afraid of?

Nothing Rick could see equaled the Brand and Desmet's warehouse, and there was clearly no space for an airship hanger. That told Rick that the zeppelin berthed somewhere else. In a pinch, that knowledge might come in handy. He spotted a few small shallow-bottomed boats at the water's edge and figured that the swamp must have channels that led to the ocean.

"In here." The tall man prodded Rick to enter one of the bunkers, which was larger than he first thought. They bypassed the big open main room, which looked like a laboratory, and headed for a side room where Rick found himself facing another row of cells that appeared original to the facility.

"Home, sweet home." The guard pushed Rick inside. "Give me your wrists."

Rick stuck his cuffed hands through the bars. His captor unlocked the cuffs, and Rick rubbed the sore skin.

"Sleep while you can. There'll be work to do." The guard double-checked that the cell door was locked before he and the others retreated. Rick sighed and took in the same stripped-down accommodations as before, marginally improved with a metal cot that was bolted to the wall. A thin blanket and pillow suggested that he was meant to be here for a while. He sat on the edge of the bed and tried not to think how buggy the thin pad must be given the humidity.

How are they ever going to find me?

"Hey! Who are you?"

The voice startled Rick, and for a moment, he wondered if he had hallucinated it. Then he looked up and saw a handsome, dark-haired man peering through the bars on the other side of the vacant cell between them.

"Are you real?" Rick got up and started toward that side of his cell.

The man laughed. "I think so. Are you?"

Now that he had a closer look, Rick figured the other prisoner to be about his age, possibly Spanish or Cuban from his accent and complexion. "I'm Rick."

"Why are you here?"

"They kidnapped me. And you are—"

"Luis. They kidnapped me too. Must be a popular activity in these parts."

Rick admired the other man's gallows humor. He hoped they could be allies, but experience had taught him to be wary.

"Do you know who they are? Why did they take us?"

Luis sat and leaned against the bars. "I'm an engineer. They've made it clear they want me to build some crazy inventions from pieces and parts they can't identify, without complete plans or instructions. You know, the usual."

Shit. They've got to be Sombra. That's why the pirates wanted the cargo from the Vincente. *They're going to combine it with some of Sombra's other technology and use it to outfit ships for the war.*

"I was in the wrong place at the wrong time," Rick told him, which was true as far as it went. "We were near Key West. They killed people on my boat and stole our cargo, then took me hostage. My friends will be looking for me."

"Good luck. We are so deep in the Everglades that even the alligators have trouble finding us."

A burst of machine gun fire made Rick jump. "What the hell was that?"

Luis looked surprisingly blasé. "I was joking about the gators. They're out there—and so are other creatures that people don't want to believe exist. Not sure if they're monsters or just things that have lived deep in the swamp for so long they've been forgotten, but I don't want to run into them. Sometimes they come in view of the fence, and the guards shoot to drive them back."

I'm stuck in the middle of a swamp with monsters. This keeps getting better and better.

"You'd better sleep while you can," Luis advised. "They'll come for us soon enough."

"And then what?"

"They have me in their workshop, trying to assemble some experimental equipment," Luis replied. "Can you use a screwdriver? I'll ask for you to be my assistant."

Rick sometimes watched over Adam's shoulder in his lab and helped with projects whenever the inventor allowed. He had no intention of admitting that.

"I can at least fetch and carry tools. I'll try not to break anything."

"We work slow and steady. Emphasis on *slow*."

Rick picked up on his meaning. *Delay and distract. Oldest passive resistance technique in history. If you can't refuse, gum up the works.*

He spent a fitful few hours before the guards came for them, exhausted but too agitated to sleep deeply. Rick's dreams were dark, reliving the fight aboard the *Diligence* but with a tragic twist that left no one alive on board. When he woke, sweat-soaked and shivering, Rick guessed from the look Luis gave him that he had been talking in his sleep.

A guard supplied a tray that held a bowl of oatmeal and a cup of coffee. Then he pushed a bowl of water, a rag, and a chip of soap through the bars. "Use this to clean yourself. Be ready when I come for you."

Rick was hungry enough to eat the oatmeal despite its bland taste. He figured that if they wanted his labor and needed him as a hostage that it was unlikely to be drugged or poisoned. The lukewarm coffee was bitter, but better than nothing. *If they're feeding me, it's a good sign.*

His cell afforded him no privacy, but he used the rag to wash himself around his clothing, sluicing off the night's sweat. Rick ran a hand back through his hair and lamented the lack of a razor to shave.

The guards returned before long, armed and wary, one for each prisoner. Much as Rick wanted to escape, he had no idea of his surroundings and no desire to meet either alligators or monsters in a trackless swamp.

Luis didn't look nervous, so Rick took it to mean this was the normal routine. They were led to the large open area Rick had glimpsed on his way to the cell, a makeshift workroom filled with some equipment he recognized from Adam's lab and other pieces that were entirely unfamiliar.

When Rick's guard made as if to take him elsewhere, Luis spoke up. "Where do you think you're taking him? I told Boss I needed an assistant. If he wants the equipment assembled, I can't do it all myself. He's in such a big hurry—I need a helper."

The guards exchanged a look and a shrug. "Fine with me unless Boss says otherwise." They withdrew to the edge of the room but remained where they could watch every move Luis and Rick made.

"What are you trying to build?" Rick's utter unfamiliarity with the purpose of the items ensured that he could easily slow down assembly.

"That's a good question," Luis admitted. "Engine parts, but it's weird stuff, not the usual. The pieces almost make me believe the rumors that they were either magicked or left behind by aliens. The diagrams and schematics they gave me aren't complete, and unfortunately, they haven't sent along the genius who dreamed them up, so it's all trial and error."

Rick had seen some spectacular failures in Adam's lab that had nearly blown the building sky-high. Trial and error sounded extremely dangerous.

"Who are these people?" Rick asked again as he followed Luis around, shuffling tools and trying to look busy.

"Boss isn't really a pirate." Luis kept his voice low but otherwise ignored their keepers. "He's working for Sombra, and his people run guns for the Spanish when they're not stealing the parts for experimental prototypes."

"Have you ever seen Boss's boss?"

"Yeah. Short guy, slicked hair, and an odd goatee," Luis replied. "Javier Cortez. The SOB tried to hire me back in Key West, and when I didn't accept, he tried to intimidate me and threatened my family. I hid to protect them, but Cortez's people found me and brought me here."

"What about the witch? I saw him on the airship." Rick helped Luis lay out tools and set up the work table.

"Skinny scarecrow?" Luis confirmed. "Yeah. No idea what his name is, but he always wears a blue coat, so I call him 'Blue.' I heard someone say he's from one of the witch dynasties in the islands."

"How powerful is he?" Rick moved tools back and forth, hoping he looked occupied. Luis hadn't been in a hurry to do anything productive.

"I don't know. Haven't seen him do much. Even a middling witch is dangerous, but I don't think he's especially strong."

Rick remembered the ball of light that had incapacitated Elian aboard the *Diligence*. "We had a witch with us on the ship when the pirates attacked. Blue threw a fireball and it took our witch out of the fight, but I don't think it killed him."

Luis gave Rick a questioning look. "You had a witch on your ship, and you were near Key West. Was that Elian Lopez?"

Rick's eyes widened. "You know him?"

Luis smiled for the first time since Rick met him. "He's my brother-in-law."

"You're Liliana's missing brother?" It was Rick's turn to stare.

"Were you looking for me? Because this isn't exactly the 'rescue' I had in mind." Luis smirked as he hooked up several gadgets to a panel fed by a large power conduit.

"Rescue?"

Luis glanced over his shoulder at the guards. "The cell between ours used to be Alphonso's. He was another engineer they captured. When he died, I gambled that his ghost might stick to the ring he wore, and I managed to bribe someone to take it and a letter to my sister. I thought maybe—"

"It might have arrived after our ship left." Rick didn't want to discourage Luis since he hadn't heard about any contact. "I was just unlucky all on my own."

"We'd better get to work," Luis said when they had laid everything out on the tables. "I'm going to try to assemble something from the components in the boxes that just came in. Do you know anything about them?"

Rick remembered Adam's theories, but sharing anything with Luis was counterproductive, even though the engineer was dragging his feet with compliance. He didn't want to give Sombra any information they didn't already have.

"It looked like a bunch of junk to me," he replied, which was largely true. Adam hadn't been sure they weren't just a lot of odds and ends, even if he did guess they were to be used for propulsion systems. "I fly in airships, but I don't know how to build one."

That wasn't technically accurate. After all his time hanging around with Adam, he probably knew more than most, but Rick figured no one would expect it from him.

"It might be junk, but I need to see what I can make it into," Luis replied. "So we're going to assemble different versions, and test them out on my equipment. We'll hook them up and see what happens."

"What's the big thing over there?" Rick pointed toward something that looked like a wagon bed with a seat and steering wheel, and in the back, a huge fan.

"Swamp boat," Luis said as he started fitting components together. "Shallow draft, won't get tangled in the cypress roots. Wide enough to be stable and not tip over, not too big to get through the channels. Fast enough—when it's finished—to outrun the gators."

"Your invention?" Rick was impressed.

"Something I worked on at Edison-Bell," Luis admitted. "It was a pet project of Mr. Bell's. I was working on some schematics when I was kidnapped and offered to build one here. Figured this would be the perfect place for a test run. You can't see from here, but it's on a wagon so it can be easily pulled down to the water."

The look he gave Rick suggested that Luis intended to take that run himself, using the swamp boat to make his escape.

"Does it work?" Rick asked under his breath.

"Not officially." Luis winked. "I told Boss that before we test it, his people need to check the depth of the channel between here and the open water to make sure the boat doesn't run aground. That would be bad."

Not to mention slow an escape. Best to make sure the path is clear before making a break for it.

Over the next few hours, Luis tinkered while Rick hooked various components up to several machines and ran "tests." Those resulted in beeps and blinking lights but didn't actually measure anything as far as Rick could tell. The guards didn't care since he and Luis looked busy and produced suitable noise.

"Does Cortez do his arms dealing from here?" Rick asked after a glance assured the guards were out of hearing distance.

Luis nodded. "Yeah. Most of that stuff is in the other bunker. As far as I can tell, the weapons are German—torpedoes, rifles, pistols, machine guns. Probably some naval mines as well—nasty things. Boss showed me once and asked if any of it would help me rebuild the *Vincente's* cargo. I asked for some to study, but they didn't leave it lying around. A pity."

Rick had heard rumors that the Germans were supplying the Spanish with armaments. "What about the witch? Is Blue interested in what you're doing?"

Luis worked on the assemblage as he spoke. "He's obsessed with figuring out how to communicate with the monsters that live in the ocean—or their ghosts."

"You mean sea serpents?"

"Some of the creatures are natural, just uncommon. Others are definitely supernatural. Sailors have told stories about them since boats set to sea. They're destructive enough on their own. Being able to control them—living or dead—and use them as weapons could be brutal," Luis replied.

"Has Blue been able to do that?" Rick couldn't avoid being curious.

Luis shook his head. "Not yet. I don't think he knows how. But he's definitely looking into it."

After they worked for a while, Luis glanced at the clock. "Cortez and Blue should be coming through for their walkabout if they're at the base. Just follow my lead. I'll have something to show them for progress. I've been stalling, but they're getting impatient. I can't hold them off much longer without something to show for it."

Just before noon, the door to the corridor opened, and the guards stopped slouching to look alert. Rick recognized Cortez from the run-in he and Jake had with the man back in Key West. The witch wore a sapphire-colored long coat over a black shirt, pants, and high boots.

I know he's got enough magic to attack Elian, but he looks like he got his outfit from a vaudeville show.

"How do you like the Everglades, Mr. Brand?" Cortez mocked. "I see they've put you to work while you're our 'guest.' If you decide to change sides, I'd be glad to entertain your proposal."

Luis kicked him lightly in the shin, likely a warning to mind his tongue. "I'll keep that in mind," Rick grated and clenched his jaw to keep himself from causing trouble.

"It's good you've decided to earn your keep. If your friends decide not to trade any new cargo for you, there's no reason to keep you alive," Cortez said.

He turned his attention to Luis. "And if I don't see real results in the next four days, I'll have to believe you've been lying about your abilities and therefore are of no use. Should I feed you both to the alligators, or let the monster in the swamp gnaw on your bones?"

Neither Luis nor Rick answered, and Cortez chuckled.

"You've had time to take a look at the cargo we brought back?" Cortez asked. Blue hung back a pace, as if he was wary of whatever Luis and Rick were doing.

"It's mostly spare parts. No tourmaquartz, and nothing that looks witchy," Luis reported. "I can make use of some of the components in the pieces I've been building. I recognize some from the specs we already had for one of the engines. We've been testing the new pieces all morning and running them through the equipment to see what they can do. We're close to having them working."

A cruel smile twisted Cortez's features. "I don't believe you." He glanced to the witch. "Make him tell the truth."

Rick stepped back, fearful of what might happen next. Luis's eyes widened, but he appeared to be frozen in place as the witch made a gesture and muttered a few words.

"Now…tell me the truth," Cortez said in a tone like poisoned honey. "How is your work going?"

Luis's whole body stiffened like he was fighting the compulsion, but the spell tore the answer from him. "I've been stalling. And I'm still not sure what all the pieces do."

"That wasn't so hard, now was it?" Cortez smile held cold malice. He looked to the witch again, whose next gesture dropped Luis to his knees, clutching his gut and writing in pain. Rick tried to go to him, but found that he couldn't move.

After a moment, Luis slumped, gasping for breath.

"You have a new deadline," Cortez said. "Bring me something usable in four days, or the spell will kill you. Painfully." He turned his attention to Rick. "If your friends haven't met my demands by then, you'll die too."

"I expect to have the rest of the *Vincente's* salvage soon," Cortez said. "That should give you everything you need to complete the propulsion units—and the magic required to make it usable."

Blue remained silent, and Rick wondered whether the witch understood the technology or even cared about its uses. Jake and Kovach had seemed certain that Cortez had minor, untrained magic. Blue clearly had more ability, but he had incapacitated Elian, not killed him. His magic also hadn't been able to penetrate Elian's bubble shield.

In a witch fight, Rick's money was on Elian. *But dirty tricks can beat ability unless the more skilled person is wary and smart. And Blue's definitely got enough magic to kill us.*

"The Spanish will pay handsomely for these," Cortez said with an avaricious gleam in his eyes. "And the witch dynasties will be interested as well. This will change the balance of power in the islands, and remove the Americans from the Caribbean once and for all."

Cortez and his pet witch left. Rick ran to help Luis as soon as he could move and knelt beside him.

"Are you in pain? Can you stand?" Rick admired Luis's bravery and his cool defiance under pressure.

Luis groaned and let Rick help him sit up. "The worst seems to be over, but my guts feel like they were set on fire and tied into knots with barbed wire. I wondered when Cortez would think to put a truth spell on me. I guess I've run out of luck."

Rick shook his head. "Don't give up. I know my friends will come for us. And if you have to give him something minor that works to save your skin, do it. We'll find another way to stop them."

Despite their short acquaintance, Rick found that he liked Luis and was as worried for his safety as his own.

"Help me up."

Rick gripped Luis's arm and pulled him to stand. Luis reached beneath his worktable and withdrew a fat metal disk that reminded Rick of Adam's techno turtles.

"What's that?" Despite their dire situation, Rick couldn't help his curiosity.

"My last resort," Luis told him. "A little something I've pieced together that should be able to blow up the bunker next to us, the one filled with ammunition. I had figured that I'd take them with me if they were going to kill me."

Rick heard a low hum and saw the disk rise an inch above the table. "Does it fly? Can it go far?"

"It doesn't have to," Luis said, just above a whisper. "Just over to the other bunker. When the arms stockpiled explode, if your friends are looking for us, they'll know right where to find us."

Chapter Eleven

"Where's Rick?"

Jake and the others had barely gotten inside when Nicki's question brought everything to a standstill.

"Jake? Where is Rick?" Nicki's voice was quiet and frightened.

"They took him." Jake couldn't meet her eyes. *If I'd been faster. If I'd expected the attack. It's my fault.*

Conroy and Edward moved them into the parlor. Liliana hurried to Elian and took his hand, exchanging a glance that spoke volumes of worry, love, and relief. Ben stepped carefully to the corner and went on standby mode. Jake, Kovach, and Adam sat on the kitchen chairs Edward brought into the room, and the others found seats on the couch and in armchairs.

"We were attacked by pirates from an airship." Jake's voice was toneless as he struggled for control. "Their witch dazed Elian, and they had enough ruffians that there was a firefight on deck. That let them steal the first night's salvage; they killed Sid and took Rick hostage."

"Where did the airship go? How do we find him?" Nicki pressed.

"We don't know yet," Kovach replied, picking up for Jake. "But we're working on it."

"We did get the rest of the salvage from the *Vincente*," Adam added, "but it wasn't worth the cost."

The early morning light filtered through the curtains. Conroy and Edward brought fresh coffee and a plate of breakfast pastries. No one moved to partake. Jake figured his group was still grappling with what had happened, and the others were too shocked and upset to think about food.

"Sid, the deckhand, had been one of the wrecking crew for a long time," Kovach continued. "The leader grabbed Rick and escaped to their airship, leaving his henchmen behind to die. Elian's magic kept them from blowing up the ship."

"Rick's clever, and stubborn," Nicki said, raising her chin defiantly. "He'll figure something out."

Jake, Adam, and Kovach took turns telling about their days with the wreckers. When they finished, Nicki and Liliana filled them in on their research into the Havana crates, the *HMS Centurion* and its soapstone carvings, ghost spies, and the secret code.

"This came by courier." Conroy withdrew an envelope with a pressed wax seal embossed with the letter "C" and handed it to Jake.

Jake tore the envelope open and cursed under his breath as he scanned the contents. "It's from Cortez. He says we have three days to turn over the rest of the *Vincente* salvage in exchange for Rick. Miss the deadline or refuse to deal and Rick dies."

The others in the room erupted in dismay. Jake held up a hand and the clamor ended. "We need to find him—fast," he told Kovach.

Conroy cleared his throat. "Might I suggest that our wandering gentlemen eat and then avail themselves of showers and fresh clothing—perhaps a nap might be in order. That way, when we reconvene you'll be rested and have your wits about you."

Jake wasn't hungry, but he knew that his body needed fuel no matter how disinterested his worried brain might be, so he forced himself to eat and washed the food down with coffee. Kovach's appetite seemed untroubled. Adam swallowed down several cups of coffee but only one small muffin to go with it.

Spark of Destiny

The door to Rick's room reminded Jake afresh that his friend had not returned with them.

Hang in there, Rick. We'll find you—we're coming to get you.

The food sat like a rock in his stomach. Jake tried to shut down his damning inner monologue as he ran a tepid shower to wash away the sweat, sea spray, and grime of the past few days. Shaving gave him a familiar routine as he rid himself of two day's stubble. While his sore muscles begged for hot water, the humid air overruled that, and Jake turned the water to cold once he'd gotten clean, letting it revive him.

Jake pulled on pants and then fell across his bed, hoping to make up for the sleep he'd lost being up all night. The trip back to Calusa Key and then to Key West and the compound had been fraught, and they'd all been on edge expecting another attack.

He realized he'd been holding his breath for most of the trip, not able to unclench his jaw until their wagon passed through the gates of their enclosure. Harry and the others had promised their help to find and free Rick, and Jake intended to take them up on their offer once they had a plan.

For as much as Jake had feared not being able to sleep, his body had other ideas, and when he awoke, two hours had passed. He finished dressing, ran a comb through his still-damp hair, and hurried downstairs.

Kovach came down a few minutes later. Adam, to no one's surprise, was in the warehouse going over the cargo boxes once more with Ben at his side.

"Lunch is ready," Conroy told them. "You'll plot revenge better when you don't have an empty stomach."

Jake's stomach growled in spite of himself, self-preservation winning out over grief, worry, and guilt. The conversation was quiet over a meal of cold mango soup, crab cakes, and saffron rice, and chilled, sliced fruit over slabs of angel food cake. While he was certain the food was excellent, he couldn't taste it.

While they were eating, Edward came and spoke quietly with Conroy. Conroy gave instructions, and Edward left the room.

"I regret to inform you that the ruffians from the previous

encounter have returned with reinforcements," Conroy said. "Two dozen or more armed men are blocking the road to the compound, inconveniently just beyond the range of our Gatling guns."

Kovach looked up from his meal. "Beyond the range of the guns on our *towers*. We'd gain quite a few more yards if we use the caisson-mounted guns and pushed them up to the fence."

Conroy paled. "That is true," he agreed, clearly not keen on mowing down the hoodlums as a first choice.

"Let them stand there. It's hot, and there's no shade. No water handy, either. We aren't expecting any visitors or deliveries. And there aren't any neighbors to complain." Jake gave a meaningful look at Nicki, who did not look at all remorseful over the incident in New Pittsburgh.

"Put watchmen and sharpshooters in the towers to make sure the ruffians don't get closer or try to sabotage the fence. If they want to stand there and bake in the sun, let them."

After lunch, Nicki and Liliana brought Jake, Elian, and Kovach up to speed while Adam went to his lab to study the salvage cargo he brought in from the warehouse. Kovach and Jake poured over the maps and clues to the Lost City and hidden fort, while Nicki and Liliana debated calling on the spirits of the soapstone carvings for help. Elian retreated to the lab to help Adam with the occult cargo.

Several hours into their research, Jake heard the phone ring but ignored it. Conroy knocked at the library door a few minutes later.

"Please excuse the interruption, but the agents from DSI are on their way. I alerted them to the ruffians, but they assured me they could handle any problems and asked us to stand by to let them inside," Conroy told them.

Nicki beamed. "This should be fun to watch. Anyone else want to go to the widow's walk and see what happens?"

Kovach excused himself to speak with the guards. Jake wondered if he might also be getting the moveable Gatling gun into position, just in case.

Liliana declined to follow so they could continue their work.

Nicki fairly dragged Jake by the wrist as they climbed the stairs.

Spark of Destiny

"Mitch and Jacob must have some plan in mind." Nicki made good time up the steps despite her skirts. "I want to see those ruffians get their comeuppance—short of getting blown to bits, of course," she amended. Her expression darkened. "Although if anyone hurts Rick, I will lose my Christian forbearance."

Jake had seen Nicki in a gunnery mount, so he knew the fragile limits of that forbearance firsthand.

The cupola atop the house was large enough for at least three people and opened onto a narrow walkway with a railing outside. From that height, they could see over the palm trees and mangroves all the way to the ocean.

"There!" Nicki pointed excitedly as Jake came to stand next to her. He followed her gesture to where a small mob blocked the road not too far from the compound's gates.

"I hope Mitch and Jacob have something up their sleeves," Jake replied. "I don't think those guys are going to just let them stroll past."

A dull roar sounded in the distance, growing steadily louder. Jake recognized the sound before he made visual contact—velocipedes, coming up fast.

"What in the world..." Nicki murmured as the bikes and their riders came into view.

"It's got to be Storm and Drangosavich," Jake answered, although the riders' faces were obscured by odd leather headgear.

The mob turned toward the riders, raising their weapons and shouting. Dark objects shot from the front of the velocipedes, and a cloud of billowing smoke engulfed the ruffians as the bikes shot through the distracted crowd.

Guards at the compound entrance swung the gate open to admit the riders, locking it behind them as they retreated from the smoke.

"Well played!" Nicki cheered. She gathered up her skirts to descend the steps. "Come on—I want to hear what they have to say!"

Jake was a tad breathless from the rapid descent when they burst into the parlor just as Conroy escorted Storm and Drangosavich into the room.

205

"Sorry we missed you the other day," Storm said. "But I'm betting you had somewhere more exciting to be."

Both men looked like they had been in a recent brawl. Storm had a split lip and a row of stitches through one eyebrow, while Drangosavich had a newly blackened eye and bruised cheek.

"Rough night at the bar?" Kovach asked with a smirk.

Storm rolled his eyes. "Not exactly."

Drangosavich elbowed him. "We're glad to catch you at home," he said, and Jake recalled he was the more diplomatic of the two agents. "We have some information for you—and we're betting you have some news for us as well."

Conroy brought coffee and pastries, then he and Edward withdrew after ensuring the parlor had enough seating for everyone with a promise to inform Elian that the agents had arrived. Elian joined them a few minutes later, saying that Adam was busy in his lab.

"Pirates attacked us and kidnapped Rick." Jake's anger was clear in his clipped tones. "They tried to blow up our ship. We need to find out where they took him and get him back alive—and we have four days before they kill him."

The two agents exchanged a look. "Do you have any idea who might have sent the pirates?" Drangosavich questioned.

"Our money is on Sombra and Javier Cortez—and his witch." Jake went on to tell them what happened aboard the *Diligence* and Adam's foray to the shipwreck. "From what Adam observed down there, he thought that someone sabotaged the *Vincente*—maybe with the intention to salvage the wreck and steal the cargo."

"Someone who might want to play both ends against the middle," Kovach said. "Maybe Cortez is hedging his bets, backing Sombra, and taking orders from other interested parties—like the witch dynasties."

"So you were attacked while you were salvaging the wreck of the *Vincente*?" Storm asked. At Jake's sharp look, he held up a hand in truce. "If you want our help to find your friend, we need to know what's going on. Once we heard you and Rick and your friends were headed for Key West, it didn't take much to figure out you wanted the *Vincente's* cargo."

"Everyone wants the cargo," Drangosavich put in. "And we all know that if the US gets it, the first thing they'd do is hand it over to Adam Farber to figure out, so we're all on the same page."

"Are you here officially?" Kovach eyed the two men as if trying to figure out what hadn't been put into words.

"Not exactly," Storm hedged. "We have 'friends' who have a vested interest in keeping the cargo away from Sombra, Cortez, and the witch dynasties, and figuring out how it could help our side. It would be 'messy' if they sent us directly. Jacob and I were given 'vacation' to come down and explore the Keys and meet up with people we knew."

"Figures," Kovach muttered.

"We're here to help," Drangosavich was quick to point out. "The government, Tesla-Westinghouse, and Edison-Bell really don't want the experimental technology falling into the wrong hands. Mitch and I can tap whatever resources we need through back channels. Plus, we've got information."

"We'll take all the help we can get," Nicki spoke up, "if it will help us to find Rick and Luis."

"What have you heard?" Jake asked.

Storm sat back in his chair. "You're not the only ones who figured out what was likely aboard the *Vincente* when it sank. Several powerful players want to get their hands on the prototypes, and on anything witchy that went with it. Including Drogo Veles, who's teamed up with a powerful German vampire and wants to sell weaponry to players on the Continent, which is increasingly politically unstable right now."

"Just the whiff of a high-speed tourmaquartz-fueled super propulsion engine has all the railroad barons in a tizzy," Drangosavich added. "Henry Flagler is racing Vanderbilt and Gould's people for control of the tech because it could change everything for shipping and trains. They're ruthless, and they'll stop at nothing to win. We think they're covertly backing Sombra regardless of the war."

"Javier Cortez has been cozying up to the Caribbean witch dynasties, looking to build magic enhanced technology," Storm jumped in. "His witch—Ramon Escarra—is from one of those families. We also know Sombra has been running conventional guns for the Spanish and giving cover to arms dealers and blockade runners."

"Lovely," Nicki grumbled.

"Go back to the witch part," Elian said. "I have heard of the Escarra family. Hispaniola, correct?"

Drangosavich nodded. "Yes. One of the major dynasties. What we aren't sure about is whether Ramon's involvement with Cortez is sanctioned by the family. He's the hot-headed youngest son, and he has a history of striking out on his own to make a name for himself."

"As one of the witch dynasties from Spanish lineage, the Escarras might see a way to increase their power in the region by throwing in with the empire's interests in the war," Storm added. "Or 'junior' might be making a mess of their neutrality and dragging them into a conflict they had no intention of entering."

"Interesting," Elian mused. "As I understand it, each of the dynasties favors particular types of magic. The Escarras, I believe, were sea witches. I have some ability with the ocean, but not on the scale of a true aquamancer."

Kovach's eyes narrowed as he thought. "Adam's examining the occult objects. It is going to take some time. He said he wants to go through the not-witchy stuff first. Maybe that will provide an idea of what Escarra thinks is worth going out on a limb for."

Nicki looked from Storm to his partner. "Did you really get in a bar fight, or did you run into Cortez's ruffians somewhere else?"

"We followed up on your lead on a 'secret lab' last night, and we went in thinking it could belong to Cortez," Drangosavich said. "It *was* a laboratory, and I can't imagine who it would have belonged to except Cortez, but the facility was abandoned. Didn't look like it had been used in several days at least. So if that's where they were holding your brother, they've moved him." He looked to Liliana with compassion.

"We got jumped by ruffians when we went outside. They were just hired muscle, but it was a hell of a fight," Storm said, with a grin that said he relished the altercation. Drangosavich heaved a forbearing sigh, just short of rolling his eyes.

"Luis was definitely there." Everyone turned to Liliana. "I sent out

Spark of Destiny

'ghost spies' to canvas for us. They brought back reports of a man who looked like Luis being held against his will in an old warehouse with scientific tools."

"Do I want to know about 'ghost spies'?" Storm asked.

"It's sort of like the telephone game with spirits," Nicki said, which got a confused look from the two newcomers.

Liliana explained the experiment, which earned an appreciative smirk from Storm and a thoughtful frown from Drangosavich.

"That's actually…innovative," Drangosavich said.

The phone rang, and Conroy excused himself to answer. He returned seconds later.

"It's for you, Miss LeClercq. Your friend says she has broken the code."

Nicki let out a squeal of glee. She turned to the two agents. "You've got to hear this—it might be the breakthrough we need to find Luis—and Rick."

It was a tight fit to cram everyone into the office. Nicki took the phone receiver. "Cady—we've got an audience, so speak loudly. What did you find?" The others leaned forward to catch Cady's reply.

"We're lucky. That code is the one my friend's brother let slip," Cady said. "It's directions to move men, weapons, supplies, and equipment to Fort Harrell and make it a fortified base and lab. There's a list of what they wanted—Gatling guns, assorted weapons, building supplies, and laboratory equipment. It very clearly mentions the fort, but there aren't any directions or a location."

"That's brilliant," Nicki told her. "You're amazing."

"Not really," Cady demurred. "But here's the thing—I can't find any mention of a Fort Harrell in other sources. Maybe it's a secret location, and your agent friends will know."

"I'll ask them," Nicki promised with a look at Storm and Drangosavich. "You're a lifesaver!"

"I'm glad it helped. And be sure to say hello for me to Jake and the others," Cady replied before hanging up.

Nicki led them to the library and pulled out the note Hernandez had slipped into the crate.

Drangosavich reached out to take the letter and showed it to Storm, who pinched his nose and closed his eyes.

"The Navy likes to think this code is secret, so let's not tell anyone," Drangosavich said. "Is your friend military?"

"No. She just does the puzzles in the *Pall Mall* Gentleman's magazine," Nicki told him, clearly proud.

"Did you say Fort Harrell?" Storm asked. "I've heard of that. It was from the Seminole conflict. They didn't use it long, and afterward no one needed it, so the fort was abandoned. But that might give us a clue where to look because Fort Harrell was in the Everglades."

Nicki and Liliana looked at each other wide-eyed. "Swamp magic!" they said in unison.

Jake chuckled at the perplexed agents. "My cousin thinks in mysterious ways, but I promise you that this will make sense."

In the days since Jake and the others left for the salvage run, Nicki and Liliana had transformed the library into something out of Sherlock Holmes. Maps, paintings, and papers from the Havana crates were tacked to the walls, interspersed with notes where the two women listed theories and possible links.

Spread out on the table were more items from the cargo, and at one end lay the box of carved soapstone figures from the *HMS Centurion*.

"Lili and I have been studying these things since you left," Nicki told them. "We couldn't quite put it all together until the code got translated, but look at this—Hernandez was trying to point us toward the Lost City in the swamp."

"Now that we know what we're looking for, it all makes sense," Liliana said.

Nicki and Liliana walked the men around the room, letting the secrets unfold as they narrated the links between the pieces they had uncovered.

"I admit this is all persuasive," Storm said, "but no one knows for certain where Fort Harrell is located. It hasn't been used in almost sixty years, and the records have disappeared."

"That's okay." Nicki triumphantly pointed to her main map. "Because we've figured it out."

Jake and Drangosavich went back to the beginning and made a slow tour of the documents while Kovach and Storm gravitated toward the map. Elian edged toward the box of carved soapstone.

"What about this? Why did he send it?" Elian directed his question to Liliana.

Liliana smiled like a cat with a canary. "These are connected to the ghosts who want another shot at the Spaniards who took their lives. *Los Ahogados*—the drowned ones. They want revenge—and they're willing to help us to get it."

"The Boyers from Calusa Key are also ready to put a flotilla together and come help," Jake said. "One of their crew was shot and those Sombra bastards tried to blow up their ship. It's personal for them. And not just the crew of the *Diligence*—I think we'd get the whole wrecker clan, cousins and all."

"Good." They all turned to see Adam standing in the doorway with Ben a few steps behind. "Because I've played around with the Sombra prototype and did a little retooling of my own with the techno turtles and some of my experimental designs. Combined with regular weapons and a good plan, I think they'd give us a definite edge in a fight."

Jake turned to Elian. "Do you have a better idea about the occult items in the *Vincente's* cargo?"

Elian nodded. "From the symbols and what I know of aquamancy, the relics and ritual pieces would help a water witch summon and control the ghosts of dead sea monsters to use as weapons against their enemies. I'd like Liliana to take a look to make sure."

Jake's eyebrows rose. "The ghosts of monsters? Not the monsters themselves?"

Liliana looked thoughtful. "Controlling a large, sentient living being is difficult, especially to keep the hold for very long and force it to fight against its instincts. A witch with sea magic and perhaps a touch of mediumship could use such relics and rituals to summon the creatures' spirits and use them against their enemies. That would be dark magic, forbidden, but possible."

Drangosavich looked from Adam to Storm and sighed. "This is going to involve explosions, isn't it?"

Adam's eyes sparkled. "I hope so."

"They're the best part," Nicki added with enthusiasm.

"You're all barking mad," Drangosavich murmured.

Conroy knocked on the doorframe to get their attention. "Excuse me—the *Allegheny Princess* has arrived. Captain Adair is tethering the airship and radioed to let me know he'd be here soon."

"We've got an airship, a flotilla, a ghost squad, a submersible, an automaton, armed metal turtles, and experimental weapons," Jake said. "If that's not enough to mount a rescue, I don't know what is."

Chapter Twelve

Enough with your games! When will you be finished with something I can actually use?" Boss shouted so loudly that Luis flinched. Only the armed guards kept Rick from swinging a punch as the pirates' leader bullied the inventor.

Despite it all, Luis squared his shoulders and raised his head. "I have bits and pieces and no instructions, no diagrams. We don't even know if these pieces go together. First I have to figure out what they might be, then whether they are part of the same thing and how it works, and then see if they can be put together. I'm doing the best I can."

Boss pulled his pistol and pressed it against Luis's temple. Luis closed his eyes and held his breath. "You lied before. The spell showed it. Are you lying now?" He cocked the gun.

"It's my fault." Rick jumped in to protect Luis. "I'm trying to help but he's lost time showing me what to do. Please, don't blame him. I'm up to speed now, so we'll be able to make more progress." Rick's palms sweated and his heart thudded double-time.

Boss turned to level the gun at Rick, and gave him a dead-eyed, lizard glare. "Cortez says I can't shoot you—now. But in three days you're excess baggage. You'd better hope your friends want you back bad enough to give us the cargo, or it'll be *bam*." He pantomimed taking the shot point-blank at Rick's forehead.

"The gators and the monster don't care if there's a little lead in their meat. Maybe we'll toss your body over the fence and take bets on what drags your carcass away first," Boss continued.

The monster, Boss had said. What was the creature in the swamp? A huge gator? Rick's heart was in his throat, but he was determined not to show fear to their captor. Luis kept his head down, but Rick could see him trembling.

"Now get back to work," Boss ordered. "I'll be by at the end of the day to see if you've made enough progress to earn your dinner and drink rations. If you're stalling, you'll be on half rations and half sleep until the goddamn work is done!" His voice rose through the tirade until he was shouting loud enough to echo from the cement walls.

Boss kicked a metal chair on his way out, sending it clattering across the floor. Luis winced at the noise. The door slammed behind him, leaving two armed guards to oversee their work.

"Show me what to do." Rick stepped up beside Luis and laid a hand on his. "At least one of us can get out of here alive."

Luis turned and his large, dark eyes were filled with fear, anger, and determination. "Don't say that. We are both going home," he said fiercely. "Don't give up."

"I'm not," Rick assured him. "I know my friends will look for us. I'm just not sure they'll be quick enough."

"Then we'll have to be faster." Luis moved back to the work table. Rick could see that Luis's hands no longer shook.

"Keep assembling the piece you were working on," Luis told him. "I'm fairly certain I can get it to do something by tomorrow. I'll keep working on my project."

That "project" Rick knew was the little flying contraption Luis planned to use to blow up the ammunition storehouse and buy them time to escape.

"If the pieces originally belonged to Sombra, why can't Cortez get

Spark of Destiny

the schematics from them for us to put the stuff back together?" Rick asked in a hushed tone as he tried to put odds and ends together that he felt fairly certain were never meant to be a whole.

"Sombra might have had the items on their ship, but my bet is that the technology was stolen from someone else," Luis replied. "Even if it were experimental, there should have been drawings back in Spain, inventors who know what's going on."

"Or Sombra bought a pig in a poke that was never functional, and this is a fool's errand."

"Maybe," Luis allowed. "If Cortez forces your friends to make the trade, I'm afraid of what is in the other crates. Either this really is 'alien' technology or the inventor was miles ahead of anyone else. Maybe there are several unrelated devices, or Sombra got conned and it's fake. But if it's real and they could make engines that went so much faster than what we have now—it would change everything."

"I imagine a lot of people would like to get their hands on that." Rick never stopped his work as they talked. "Railroads, armies, shipping companies."

"I think there's another piece to this," Luis said. "I heard Blue and Cortez arguing about the *Vincente* cargo before they brought you here. Cortez said 'engines like that would be worth millions' and Blue said 'if you're going to call the monsters, you have to outrun them.'"

"Monsters?" Rick spared a side glance to his partner.

"I'm making a big leap here, but what if the magic items in the cargo helped someone summon sea monsters? Giant squid, Kraken. Leviathans. Sea dragons."

"Those are children's tales," Rick scoffed, hoping he wasn't wrong.

"Maybe. But sailors have told the same stories for centuries. What if they're real? Suppose a powerful witch could summon those monsters and force them to do his will? They'd want a boat that could move faster than the creatures and their target."

"Is Blue powerful enough to do that?" Rick's impression from the fight aboard the *Diligence* was that Blue wasn't as skilled a witch as Elian.

"Maybe Blue isn't, but if he's from one of the witch dynasties, then someone in his family probably is—and they would love to get hold of something that gives them more power than their rivals," Luis replied.

Hours later, Gatling gunfire broke the silence, staccato bursts that continued for several minutes.

Monsters on land are real. Jake and I have fought some. Why couldn't there be monsters under the water? We saw what happened in New Pittsburgh when dark witches tried to coerce creatures from the deep mines to do their bidding. What if they could summon and control sea monsters or their ghosts?

Whoever controlled the monsters would control the trade routes. They could blockade countries to get what they wanted, throw the world economy into turmoil, blackmail governments. And if they had the only ships fast enough to outrun the creatures, they would rule the seas.

Rick tried to keep his thoughts focused on the pieces he assembled. Without instructions, he could only guess at its purpose or configuration, but by the time Boss returned, the strange object lit up and made a whirring noise.

"What does it do?" Boss demanded.

"I have no idea." Rick earned himself a slap across the face for his honesty.

"I think it's a regulator." Luis pulled Boss's attention away from Rick. "Part of an engine assembly. As I said before, there were no instructions. But when you have the other cargo, we'll be able to see where these pieces fit."

Rick held his breath, afraid Boss would turn his temper on Luis.

"And what did you build?" Boss raked his gaze over Luis's side of the worktable. The flying disk was well-hidden, but Rick feared that working on it might leave Luis with little to show for his time.

"Components." Luis gestured toward a spread of very small elements. "I've been testing them to make sure they connect and trying to figure out what they do in a larger assembly."

He held up one piece that covered half the palm of his hand. "This is part of the control panel. It helps adjust the electrical flow to the motor." Luis picked up another odd-shaped item. "Part of the pressure gauge."

Spark of Destiny

"Keep at it," Boss snapped. "We'll have the other cargo soon, one way or the other." He turned to Rick with a malicious smile. "Make use of your 'assistant' while you have him. Because he'll be gone—one way or the other."

Both Rick and Luis sighed in relief when Boss left. Luis gripped Rick's shoulder hard enough to bruise. "Don't listen to him," Luis hissed. "We're both getting out of here—alive."

"I know," Rick agreed, but he doubted more with each passing hour.

The deadline was impossibly short for his friends to figure out where he had been taken, even with their specialized skills and resources. He appreciated Luis's support and his attempts to remain optimistic, but Rick turned his focus on helping Luis keep Boss distracted until he could work the escape plan.

At least one of us will get home.

Rick couldn't read Boss's mood, but getting full rations and being returned to their cells on time told him that they had met the threshold of expectations. Luis waited in front of the cell next to Rick's this time when they were taken back, and the guards didn't object.

"I hope you don't mind," Luis said when the lights were off and the guards were gone. "It feels safer to be close together."

"I don't mind," Rick replied. Another burst of gunfire startled them. Rick pulled his bedding over to the common wall, and Luis did the same. The one dim security light barely glowed enough to make out each other's features, but it was better than being alone. He was still surprised the guards had allowed Luis to move into the adjacent cell but wasn't going to question it and test their luck.

Luis reached through the bars and took Rick's hand, squeezing tight. Even in the half-light, Rick saw a fierce glint in the other man's eyes. "I'll have the disk ready tomorrow night. We leave together—or not at all," Luis whispered. "Promise me."

"I promise," Rick replied. He wasn't entirely sure just what that promise entailed, but he appreciated Luis's defiant confidence. "Together," he murmured, still holding on as he fell into a fitful sleep.

Chapter Thirteen

"It's hard to see anything." Nicki trained the high-powered binoculars on the swamp as the *Allegheny Princess* flew in ever-broadening concentric circles.

"That's because it's difficult to be stealthy during the day in an airship, which is why we're flying in the dark," Cullan Adair pointed out. "Besides—you're not looking for buildings right now. You're looking for light that shouldn't be in the middle of nowhere."

Nicki muttered curses in French under her breath, but she adjusted the focus on the lenses. She and Cullan both had special binoculars Adam had "tweaked," adding night-vision enhancements. Even with the extra help, she felt like she was staring into an abyss.

Nearby, Liliana sat in one of the airship's comfortable chairs, eyes closed, face taut with concentration as she listened for the ghosts. She hadn't called on the spirits of the *Centurion* yet, saving them for a last resort if things went bad. Instead, she reached out to the drowned ones, the souls who had lost their lives in the black water amid the cypress trees, asking for their help and offering to guide them to the light in return.

On the table next to Liliana lay an odd metal box with a large dial, Adam's Maxwell Box. Nicki had seen the invention used and could vouch that it worked. The quirky inventor had figured out that ghosts were attracted to certain energy frequencies and repelled by others. While Liliana didn't need help summoning spirits, in a pinch the Maxwell Box could amplify her connection to good spirits or drive away malicious ghosts.

So far they hadn't needed it, but Nicki felt better knowing they had it. Other than the *Princess's* Gatling guns, the rest of Adam's unconventional technology was with Jake and Kovach, where she hoped it would provide an edge against the pirates.

"I never realized how big a swamp the Everglades is," Nicki said as she and Cullan kept up their vigil. "This is worse than looking for a needle in a haystack."

"Patience," Cullan urged. She knew his first mate was guiding the airship and that Cullan had come to personally help the search because he counted Rick as a friend.

"Everything we could find about this area says it's not normally inhabited. There aren't towns or camps. If there are a few hermits with fishing cabins, a lantern or two isn't going to show up. But if you're right about them taking over an old fort and making a secret base, they need enough light to see what they're doing," Cullan added.

"I hope Rick's okay." Nicki had tried to stay busy to avoid worrying, but now that they were gathering information to make an assault on the hidden base, she couldn't avoid thinking about what had happened. "And Luis, too. Of course."

"You said Luis is an engineer. Cortez needs him to copy the experimental technology and put it together," Cullan pointed out. "Rick helps Adam in his lab a lot. He could fake it enough to make them think he could lend a hand. And if they plan to use Rick as a hostage to try to get Jake to give up the *Vincente*'s cargo, they need to keep him alive. Don't worry—we'll get them back."

Nicki took solace in Cullan's assurance, but inside she fretted. She had been close to Jake and Rick all her life, and both men held a special place in her heart. Nicki knew she'd be inconsolable if

Spark of Destiny

anything happened to either of them, and that Jake would be devastated without his best friend.

So we simply must not fail.

Once they realized the link to Fort Harrell, Drangosavich had contacted a friend in the military history archive in Washington, D.C. Fort Harrell might be forgotten by everyone else, but historians had long memories. The official information had been scarce, but they'd ended up with approximate coordinates to narrow their search in the middle of a trackless swamp.

Even with that clue to guide them, the old fort remained hard to locate.

"Go east." Liliana's unexpected comment made both Nicki and Cullan startle.

"What?" Nicki asked.

"Go east," Liliana repeated in the dreamy voice that told Nicki her friend was still channeling ghostly input. "Slightly north. Strange people in the old ruins. Noisy. Disturbing the peace."

Cullan stepped over to the speaker tube that connected the observation deck to the bridge. "Circle us around to go a bit more northeast. Keep a sharp eye out—we know the people who took Rick have an airship of their own with a black balloon."

"Once we find the base, I can run the gunnery mount again," Nicki volunteered. "Like the last time at the mines."

"Let's hope it doesn't come to that," Cullan replied, paling a little.

Nicki knew that down below, in the dark, silent water, an unlikely flotilla waited. Harry and his boys had brought the rest of the Boyer clan, half a dozen tug boats capable of navigating the shallow waters or blockading the most direct exits.

They also carried smaller, flat-bottomed punts that could be launched soundlessly and maneuvered through channels to reach the fort. The *Diligence* carried Adam and the *Oceanus,* ready to move unnoticed beneath the surface to spy for lookouts, hidden underwater traps, or other dangers.

"There!" Nicki pointed, and Cullan shifted to follow her directions with his binoculars. The *Princess* flew as low as they dared, going in for a closer look.

"That's got to be it. It's just a hair off the coordinates Jacob gave us, and there are too many lights to be a single cabin." Cullan returned to the speaking tube. "We have visual confirmation. Give them the coordinates, and let's get this show on the road."

Nicki turned to Liliana, whose serene expression made clear she was still communing with the spirits. "What are they telling you?"

Liliana's soft humming suggested that she was listening to voices only she could hear. "They don't like the new people…interlopers… don't belong. Old ghosts…slumbered for a long time…disturbances woke them."

"Yes, yes—Cortez's people are very rude," Nicki replied. "Can the ghosts tell us anything about what's going on?"

"More than a squad…less than a platoon," Liliana conveyed in a singsong tone. Nicki figured this ghost must have been a soldier. "Boxes in one bunker, people in the other. Using some other buildings too. Rough men, bad people. Trespassers."

"So anywhere from eight to forty people, if ghosts can count," Cullan said. "What he's calling a 'bunker' is probably a concrete building—they can't go underground here because of the high water table."

"There's got to be a tower to tether their zeppelin, and it's doubtful that they've got any boats bigger than some punts," he mused. "Water's too shallow, and there are too many cypress trees. But there has to be a fairly easy way in and out because Cortez and his crew have to come and go without too much trouble—probably take a small boat and rendezvous with a larger one in open water."

"So our folks should be able to follow that route inside." Nicki felt hope rise.

"The tugboats can't and neither can the submersible, but that's why they've got the small craft. If Cortez's men are on the upper end of that estimate, our folks are way outnumbered because they won't bring everyone in from the bigger ships," Cullan worried.

Spark of Destiny

"They'll just have to be sneaky. Jake is good at that," Nicki confirmed.

"It's up to them. Now, we wait and keep watch," Cullan replied.

The *Princess* flew large circles around the old fort's location. Liliana didn't return to a full trance, but her distracted look suggested to Nicki that the medium was keeping her senses open should the ghosts return with news. Nicki and Cullan took turns with the binoculars, eyeing the camp's lights in case any change might suggest that Cortez's people realized they were under attack.

"I wish we could have used Adam's flying saucers. They came in handy before." Nicki stared into the darkness as if she could force the resolution to their mission by sheer will.

Adam Farber had created flying versions of his techno turtles, metal disks that could zip and hover and fire bullets. They had turned the tide of an air battle over the Atlantic for the *Allegheny Princess* not long ago, one of the scariest and most exhilarating moments of Nicki's life.

"We talked about using them for surveillance, but Adam still hasn't gotten the cameras to work well in low light," Cullan reminded her. "I'm not sure they could orient themselves when it's this dark, and I've got no desire to lose his experimental technology in the bottom of a swamp."

"We need him to fix that. This sort of thing happens way too often," Nicki noted.

An hour passed, and Nicki tapped her foot impatiently. "They should be inside by now. Something should be happening." She pressed the binocular lenses against the bulletproof observation deck's large window for a better view.

"They're probably staying quiet as long as possible to plant charges and figure out where Rick and Luis are being held. After all, they don't want to blow up the hostages by mistake," Cullan cautioned.

"*Mon Dieu*! Of course not. Still, it would be nice to have a sign that something's going on."

Nicki frowned as the lights disappeared. "I take it back! Something happened—the lights are gone!" A second later, she swore under her

223

breath. "No, wait. The lights aren't gone—that's a black airship. We've got trouble!"

"Shit," Cullan muttered, followed by an apology. "Strap in—this is going to get bumpy."

Eric Mueller, Cullan's first mate, had already turned the *Allegheny Princess* away from the black airship, a sharp maneuver that had Nicki grabbing for the railing and Liliana holding onto the arms of her bolted-down chair.

"Lili—can your ghosts fly? I mean, are they stuck on the ground?" Nicki barely kept herself from tumbling across the deck as the *Princess* made another fast maneuver.

"I don't know."

"Can you send them into that other airship and frighten the crew? We don't know if the people in the camp know about Jake and the others yet. Much as I'd like to blast these blighters out of the sky, it'll make too much noise," Nicki admitted.

"I don't command the spirits," Liliana demurred. "I speak with them and ask for favors."

"Now would be a good time to ask for a big favor," Nicki said as the ship veered again and nearly tore her grip from the railing. "I've got no desire to see the swamp close up."

Once again, Liliana closed her eyes and concentrated. Her lips moved silently, and Nicki couldn't help being curious about how her friend might phrase the request to the ghosts.

See that airship? Can you temporarily haunt it, please? Nicki imagined Lili's unspoken conversation. *Want to have some fun with those bad guys in the other airship? Could you please jump out and yell "boo"?*

Moments later, the black airship made a sudden descent, followed by an erratic change of course and sharp ascent that took it away from the *Allegheny Princess* and deeper into the swamp. It zigged and zagged, rising and falling, until Nicki lost sight of it in the darkness.

"You did it! Please tell your ghosts they're amazing," Nicki told Liliana when the medium finally opened her eyes.

Cullan came down from the bridge. "What in the…Sam Houston…

Spark of Destiny

was that?" Likely adjustimg his language since there were women present.

"Liliana sent the swamp ghosts after the airship," Nicki crowed, grinning widely. "She put the fear of God—or ghosts—into them."

Cullan glanced at the soapstone carvings. "You didn't use those spirits?"

Liliana shook her head. "They're willing. But that's the problem—they'd love a good fight a little too much. I'll enable them if the tide goes against us, but once I do that, I'm not sure I can rein them in."

"I think I'd sleep better if I didn't know that." Cullan sighed. "But Jake and the others are on the move. Keep an eye peeled—they won't have easy access to a transmitter if they need help, so they'll have to signal another way."

Just then, the sound of an explosion made Nicki's ears ring. She ran to the large window and watched a plume of fire streak upward against the night sky from the spot where the base's lights had been. It burned too bright to look at for a few seconds, then shrank to an orange fireball on the ground, illuminating everything around it.

"What was that?" Nicki gasped.

"I don't think it's something our side did," Cullan replied. "I'd better get back to the bridge and find out."

Nicki turned to Liliana. "Any ideas?"

She shook her head. "The ghosts say they don't know—but they see 'invaders' coming against the bad men and that new people are outnumbered."

"That's Jake and the others. Lili, if it's going badly for them, you've got to send in the *Centurion* spirits," Nicki urged.

They both looked at the crate with the soapstone carvings. Nicki didn't have Liliana's gift, but she felt a restive energy coming off the box, raising the hairs on her neck.

"You wanted one last chance to defeat the Spanish," Liliana said to the ghosts. This time she didn't close her eyes, but Nicki could see her friend marshaling herself to bargain with the spirits. "Harm no one but the pirates, and do not hurt Elian or Luis because they're prisoners, and they're on our side. Help our side defeat the pirates, and I will do my best to send you on to your rest if that is what you desire."

Nicki caught her breath. The temperature in the observation deck plummeted, growing so cold that frost formed on the windows. The air stirred, fluttering Nicki's skirts and hair. She felt a powerful *presence* coalesce between one heartbeat and the next, and then it was gone.

"I think they heard you." Nicki held a hand over her thumping heart.

"I know they did," Liliana replied with a wolfish smile.

"Do you think they'll protect Jake and the others?" Nicki couldn't help worrying that the ghosts might not be able to tell one side of the conflict from the other.

Liliana nodded. "Elian is there. He'll see them and know I sent reinforcements. But I fear that's all we can do now except trust the others to find Rick and Luis—and bring them back safely."

Nicki had never been the praying type, except when the situation proved dire. Now, she asked the fates to protect her friends and loved ones and crossed her fingers, hoping that they heard.

"Nicki—if you still want to run the Gatling gun, now's the time. We're not sneaking up on anyone anymore, and the folks on the ground might need our backup," Cullan called from the stairs.

"Finally!" she said with a mischievous glance at Liliana. "Now it's my turn to help. Wish me luck." She headed for the gunnery mount beneath the airship, hoping it wasn't too late to make a difference.

Chapter Fourteen

Everglades, that same evening.

"We should have heard something by now!" Jake paced the deck of the *Diligence*.

"Looking for a needle in a haystack is easy compared to finding a 'lost' fort in the swamp after dark." Kovach leaned with his back against the railing.

"Have I mentioned that I've never really liked boats?" Storm stood by the stairs to the bridge, doing his best to avoid looking at the ocean.

"You like boats better than airships," Drangosavich pointed out.

"I prefer to keep my feet on the ground," Storm clarified.

"Cullan just confirmed the coordinates," Harry shouted from the bridge. "It's a go!"

Jake and Kovach sealed the hatch on Adam's *Oceanus*, where Adam had been waiting for the signal. They lowered the submersible as Ben and the techno turtles plopped off the side of the tugboat and into the water. While the swamp was too shallow for the submersible, Adam meant to check the mouths of the channels to look for underwater barriers or explosives.

Silhouettes of other boats bobbed in the faint moonlight, a small flotilla of wrecker ships belonging to Harry's family and friends. They would blockade the channels so that none of Cortez's people could escape, even if they managed to elude the teams heading for Fort Harrell.

"Go get Rick—but come back alive, you hear?" Harry told Albert and Ralph as they headed down the stairs to meet up with the others.

Jake saluted the tugboat's captain. "That's our goal. See you on the other side."

In addition to the *Oceanus*, the *Diligence* carried three flat-bottomed punts. Wally and Cook lowered them over the side, then Jake and the others climbed down rope ladders to get in.

Jake, Elian, and Albert took the lead boat, relying on Albert's locator magic to hone in on the lost fort and fine-tune the coordinates. Kovach and Ralph took the second, while Storm and Drangosavich took the third boat—with room to bring Rick and Luis back with them.

The punts moved silently over the dark water, barely registering the dip and swirl of the long pole oars. The water grew blacker and shallower as they navigated toward the interior of the great swamp. Jake felt certain he wasn't imagining the glow of eyes in the shadows, just like he wasn't hallucinating the biting insects that swarmed despite the preparations they had used to coat their skin.

"Still heading the right way?" he murmured. Albert nodded.

"The energy of this swamp is potent," Elian said. "Largely untapped. That could work in our favor if Cortez's witch is as untrained as I believe our interactions suggest."

Ralph tracked their movement with a sextant, keeping them fixed on the coordinates, while Albert used his magic. They paddled and then poled deeper into the Everglades, and the cypress trees seemed to close around them, shutting them off from the outside world. Despite the warm night, Jake shivered.

They came prepared for battle, although Jake hoped it didn't come

Spark of Destiny

to that. Kovach had several conventional guns as well as one of Adam's experimental force pistols that shot a blast of energy instead of a bullet. Jake had his Colt and other weapons, but he also had Adam's disruptor gun that could blast a hole in a solid object without firing a projectile.

He didn't doubt that Albert and Ralph carried guns and knives of their own. Elian's magic was all the weapon he required. Jake felt sure the two agents were also well-armed.

Somewhere ahead of them in the black cypress water was Ben with the techno turtles. All three punts carried lanterns to light their way, shuttered in an attempt to hide their position. Moonlight filtered down through the trees, shifting when the wind moved the leaves.

They moved through the darkness for nearly two hours. Jake slapped at mosquitos and tried to avoid the gaze of the reflective yellow eyes of the alligators.

"Up there." Albert pointed toward a place ahead where Jake glimpsed the dim glow of electric lights and heard the hum of generators, a foreign sound so deep in the swamp.

"The trick is to find the dry parts you can stand on," Jake replied.

"It's rather cocky of them not to have guards," Albert said.

Elian closed his eyes and concentrated, stretching out with his magic. "There are sentries, but much closer toward the camp. I don't think they like this place."

"Or they lost the first few to the alligators," Jake replied. "And they probably figure no one is crazy enough to come looking for them here." *If they hadn't taken Rick and Luis, we would have left them alone. Now, all bets are off.*

Albert nudged Jake. "Look." He pointed toward the bank, and Jake strained to make out what he was supposed to see. Then he noticed movement and saw something dark emerge from the water and crawl onto the wet bank. At first he thought it was some sort of swamp creature, only to realize that Adam's techno turtles were taking up their positions.

Ahead of them, Ben pulled himself up onto the spongy ground as if walking along the swamp bottom was completely normal. Adam remained in the submersible back at the mouth of the channel, where he could monitor the input from Ben and the turtles as well as emergency signals from the *Allegheny Princess*.

"Here's where we get off." Jake pulled their punt over to the side where the land looked firm, and they could hide their boat in the trees. Storm and Kovach did the same close behind them.

They climbed out, careful not to land in the water. The ground squished beneath his feet, and Jake was glad for his boots.

Their plan was simple—perhaps foolhardily so, Jake thought. Sneak in, try to avoid a confrontation, get Rick—and Luis if he was also here—grab the stolen crates if they could, and get out without dying.

Jake and Storm crept forward to see the layout of the camp while the others watched for guards. They kept low, sticking to the shadows, cautious with every step to ensure that the ground remained solid beneath their boots.

Frogs and night birds filled the darkness with their songs. The smell of salt water and wet vegetation, with an undertone of sulfur, hung in the humid air. A strange howl made Jake shiver despite the heat.

Jake couldn't shake the feeling that they were being watched. He signaled for Storm to stop and made a slow circle with Adam's night-vision binoculars. For a second he thought he saw a figure in the darkness, vaguely man-shaped but too tall to be human, with legs and arms too long for its body. When he tried to focus on the form, it melted into the night.

Storm cocked his head in a wordless question. Jake shook his head and gestured for them to keep moving. *I swear I saw something. But it wasn't a person, and it was wrong for a* werkman.

Maybe Ralph and the others were right about creatures in the swamp. Let's hope we don't meet any.

They slunk closer until they could make out the details of the camp. Two concrete buildings were prominent, along with a couple of ramshackle wooden buildings and the tall metal docking tower for the black airship.

He and Storm traded a pair of Adam's special night-vision binoculars back and forth. One glance and Storm muttered an expletive.

Shit. Two caisson-mounted Gatling guns faced them. Jake couldn't see the entire perimeter but figured more guns were likely. A sniper's roost in the scaffolding of the tower added another danger. The airship wasn't tethered, and Jake worried that meant trouble for Nicki and the others in the *Allegheny Princess*.

A soft rustle in the brush startled Jake. One of the techno turtles crawled where it had a clear shot into the camp. If all went according to plan, the rest of the dozen mechanical creatures would quietly ring the base, and thanks to some quick adjustments by Adam and Kovach, all were now armed.

One of the bunkers had guards posted outside, while the other did not. Jake guessed that the one with the guards might hold prisoners, and the other housed the stolen cargo.

Jake counted fifteen pirates and figured that if Cortez and his witch were present, they were likely in a bunker. That meant their rescue team was outnumbered at least two-to-one, but they also had Adam's technology. Jake hoped it would be enough of an advantage to get them out alive.

They crept back to the others and whispered their news. While they were gone, Ralph and Elian used their magic for reconnaissance as well.

"Luis and Rick and the crates from the *Vincente* are in the guarded bunker," Ralph told them, reporting on his astral travel. "There were cells and a lab. Maybe a few other rooms. Two guards inside. The other building has more boxes—smuggled weapons. No guard. There are a total of eight Gatling guns. Do you think they were expecting us?"

Jake shrugged. "Maybe. Or they don't like what lives in the swamp."

"Escarra is in the first wooden building," Elian added. "He put down some wardings, but they're sloppy and badly constructed. When we're ready to reveal ourselves, I can break them easily."

"Can you sense any *creatures* out there?" Jake asked, remembering what he had seen and heard. "Ones that aren't normal?"

"I'm sure there are," Elian replied. "This is their home. We're the intruders."

Jake wasn't sure he agreed, but he didn't argue. "Can you use magic to gum up those Gatlings? They could stop us before we even get started."

Elian nodded. "I can break the ones I can see. And I'm certain I can manage some distractions to divert attention if you want to send Ben to take care of the rest."

"That works," Storm said.

"If we stay out from in front of them, we should be able to use the force gun and the disruptor to damage them if Ben can't get to them all." Jake hoped he was right.

"Let's move. The longer we stand here, the more likely someone takes a shot at us." Storm practically vibrated with energy, ready to move.

"Good luck, everyone," Ralph told them.

Storm, Drangosavich, and Ben circled to the left to destroy the camp's defenses on that side and silence the guards, while Jake, Kovach, and Elian headed to the closest bunker to bust the prisoners loose. Ralph stayed with the boats, where he could use his astral projection to keep tabs on the situation.

Jake glanced skyward, looking for the *Allegheny Princess*, but couldn't see much through the trees. He hoped their part of the mission had gone smoothly, and that Nicki wouldn't need to reprise her exciting—but extremely destructive—turn in the gunnery pod.

He saw a faint green glow around the mechanism of the two closest Gatling guns and heard a metallic crunch. *Nice job, Elian.*

Once they were inside the perimeter, they headed for the bunker with the prisoners. The base offered little shelter, and Jake knew there was no way to remain concealed.

"Stop!" one of the guards shouted, repeating the command in Spanish.

Elian gave a twist of his hand, and the guard dropped to the ground, neck snapped. A rifle shot struck dangerously close. Elian made the same motion, and the sniper fell from his perch, landing with a wet thud.

"Keep going," Elian told the others. "I'll keep them busy."

Sigils that Jake hadn't seen before flared on the ground and sides of the bunker. They burned away and left nothing but ash. Jake and Kovach kept running. When the second Gatling gun nest came into view, Kovach shot the force pistol, unleashing a blast of power that tore the guns from their caissons and left them lying in a heap.

"Damn, Adam makes good stuff," Kovach muttered.

By now, shouts alerted the camp. Jake heard gunfire and hoped that Storm and the others were holding their own. A volley of shots came from the treeline, and Jake guessed that Ben's cameras had shown the situation and Adam had activated his armed techno turtles in response. The attack forced the guards back, clearing a path for Jake and his team.

Odd lights flared from Elian's direction, and Jake wondered if the witch had created another "bubble" to protect them like he had for the ship on the night of the attack. Whatever magic he was doing, it wouldn't last forever.

Jake used the disruptor gun to blow the bunker's steel back door off its hinges. An answering hail of bullets forced them to stay to one side. Jake holstered the disruptor and fired back with his Peacemaker, as Kovach did the same. Neither of them wanted to risk bringing down the whole bunker if they fired Adam's experimental guns inside.

More shots rang out, cutting off their entrance to the main room. Jake and Kovach flattened themselves against the walls.

"Cover me," Kovach hissed.

Jake returned fire while Kovach peered around the corner and dove back out of range.

"Four guards and Cortez. Looks like a lab. There might have been cells on the other side," Kovach reported.

"I'll go high—you go low," Jake said, and Kovach nodded.

They swung out, guns blazing. A bullet narrowly missed Jake's head, and another whizzed past Kovach's ear. Jake and Kovach fired back, dropping two of the guards in the first volley. After the next exchange of fire, the room went quiet.

"Was that all of them?" Jake mouthed.

Kovach held up four fingers and nodded and made their way inside, only to freeze in their tracks.

"One more step and he dies." Cortez stood next to the cells at the back of the room, with his gun pointed at Rick. At that distance he couldn't miss.

"I want the rest of the cargo," Cortez told them. "That was the deal."

"Put down the gun," Jake said. "The feds are with us. You can't win. It's over."

Cortez's features twisted in fury and madness glinted in his eyes. "My witch will stop all of you."

"Not if our witch stops him first." Jake glanced at Rick, who was on his knees, eyes wide with fear.

Jake caught a glimpse of a dark figure moving in the other cell behind Cortez, whose attention was focused on Jake and Kovach. A loop of cloth dropped over Cortez's head and tightened against his throat, yanking him hard against the cell bars. He fired blindly, sending Jake, Kovach, and Rick scrambling for cover.

"Drop the gun," the dark-haired man shouted at Cortez, pulling the make-shift garrote tighter. "Do it or I'll crush your throat. I wouldn't mind."

Cortez's gun fell to the floor.

"Toss the keys out to the center," the man ordered. "Try to pull something, and I'll strangle you and search your pockets myself." For good measure, he tightened his grip until Cortez made a panicked noise as his hands flailed to reach his pockets. Three iron keys on a ring hit the cement floor with a *clank*.

"I've got him," the prisoner shouted. "Hurry up and let us out."

"Took you long enough," Rick quipped as he rose to his feet. He looked pale and shaken in contrast to his cocky humor. "Nice move, Luis."

Jake looked to the other man who still held Cortez tight against the bars. "Luis—Liliana's brother?"

"That's me. Want to take this piece of trash off my hands?"

"With pleasure." Kovach slammed a fist into Cortez's chin and the man dropped like a stone when Luis released his grip.

Jake hurried to unlock the cell doors and pulled Rick into a bear hug. "Thanks for not dying." He tried to lighten the mood, even though his heart was still pounding.

"Thanks for finding us." Rick stepped back. "I told Luis you'd come."

Kovach knelt on Cortez's back and used the man's belt to tie his wrists, then secured his ankles with the shirt Luis had used to strangle the pirate.

"Come on, We need to get out of here." Jake led them out of the cells and back through the lab.

Luis moved toward the lab tables and swept the odds and ends into an empty duffel. "We shouldn't leave this stuff behind—it's the *Vincente's* cargo they stole." Rick helped lift the other end of the heavy bag.

The inventor grabbed something that reminded Jake of one of Adam's flying contraptions. "There's nothing but weapons in the other bunker. We should be able to blow it up with this."

"Not until we're sure Storm and the others aren't nearby," Jake said. "Then you can blow up whatever the hell you want."

Gunfire sounded outside the bunker as they headed out. Jake peered cautiously out of the doorway, wary of stepping out into a firefight.

Elian stood with his hands outstretched. A shimmering curtain of energy shielded the building as they emerged. Bullets hit the iridescent scrim and dropped to the ground. Beyond the magical barrier, Jake glimpsed Storm and the others exchanging shots with the pirates, who were holed up in one of the wooden buildings.

Jake turned to Rick and Luis and nodded toward the metal contraption Luis held. "Let 'er rip."

"How did you get here?" Rick asked as Luis fiddled with his invention.

"Long story," Jake said. "Why?"

"Luis built a boat, in case we need it. Probably shouldn't leave it with the bad guys," Rick replied.

"Remind me once we're done shooting," Jake said.

"I can't hold the shielding much longer," Elian warned. "We're going to have to fight our way out."

"Have you spotted Cortez's witch yet?" Rick asked.

"No, but I can sense that Escarra is still nearby. He's biding his time," Elian answered.

Jake edged toward the front, using the bunker for cover as much as possible. Storm, Albert, and Drangosavich were pinned down at the side of one of the wooden buildings. Half a dozen of the pirate guards lay dead or injured in the open space between structures. The remaining pirates had fallen back to the other building, shooting from the protection of windows and doorways.

"Fire in the hole!" Rick yelled.

Jake heard a whir and buzz, then a deafening bang as Luis's flying contraption tore a hole into the side of the second bunker on impact but didn't ignite the weapons inside.

"I've got this." Jake fired the disruptor gun, blowing away the side of the cement building and exploding the munitions in a fireball.

From somewhere in the swamp came a roaring howl.

Overhead, Jake glimpsed the *Allegheny Princess*, and moments later, an airship-shaped shadow crossed the moon, telling him that his friends overhead had their hands full outmaneuvering the pirates' craft.

Some of the guards broke from their positions and ran into the swamp. Minutes later, their screams told Jake they had met up with whatever he'd glimpsed, and it had gone badly for the pirates.

"Ramon Escarra—surrender now. This is the Department of Supernatural Investigation, and we have a warrant for your arrest," Storm shouted.

By Jake's count they were still outnumbered, and that didn't include whatever tricks Cortez's witch had up his sleeve.

"What do you know about the witch?" Jake asked Luis.

"I never saw him do anything, but the guards all acted scared of him, and Cortez seemed to think they were invincible together," Luis replied.

Fog rolled in from amongst the trees, and a cloud of mosquitos descended, forcing them to swat the insects away to keep them from their eyes and noses.

"Behind you!" Kovach shouted, and Jake wheeled to see a huge alligator coming right for him from the treeline.

This has got to be Escarra's swamp magic.

Jake's disruptor sent the gator flying, blown apart from the blast. He spotted the glint of more yellow eyes and knew that Escarra was marshaling the swamp to fight them.

A burst of gunfire forced Storm and his team to run for fresh cover. Jake caught a flash of bright light from inside the guarded building and figured Escarra was holed up there, conjuring the magic for his last stand.

Might be our swan song as well. This isn't going the way I'd planned.

Elian had remained still, but now he murmured something under his breath, and his fingers twitched in a complex pattern. The mosquitos vanished as quickly as they came, and the fog thinned. Whatever magic compelled the alligators from their lairs seemed to be broken, and they melted into the darkness.

Jake glimpsed motion near the old house, where several of Adam's techno turtles had drawn closer, ringing the hideout. Overhead, the sound of an airship's engine misfiring made Jake's head snap up, fearing the *Princess* had been hit. Instead, a black shape plummeted to the ground deeper into the swamp, and its hydrogen ignited with a roar.

The pirates fired on them again, and Jake wondered if they had decided to die rather than be captured—and whether Escarra had agreed to that suicide pact.

"Come out unarmed, and we won't kill you," Storm yelled, which sparked another barrage of bullets.

A sudden wave of freezing air descended on the base, sweltering to frigid in seconds. Gray figures dressed in the military uniforms of several centuries past materialized out of nowhere, advancing in a grim line toward where the pirates sheltered.

Jake shivered. Cold permeated his lungs when they passed, and frost made his fingers tingle. Their dead eyes paid him and his team no heed, fixed on the pirates' last refuge.

"What the hell?" Kovach murmured and crossed himself.

Elian laughed, even as he wove complicated counter spells in the air. "My dear Liliana has played her hand. Brilliantly, as usual."

The trapped pirates fired again and again at the ghosts, to no avail. Nothing stopped their relentless progress.

Escarra stepped from the doorway, shouting an incantation. The ghosts paid no heed and marched forward.

Boss, the pirate Jake recognized from the attack on the *Diligence*, broke from cover, hands raised in a gesture of surrender. "Don't shoot! We'll surrender. Call them off!"

Jake glanced at Elian, who shook his head. "That is beyond my ability. Liliana speaks to the ghosts, not me."

Jake stared wide-eyed as the spirits swept forward in an inexorable gray tide. They passed right through Boss, whose eyes bulged and mouth opened in a silent scream before he fell to the ground.

Escarra screeched spells and curses. The ghosts paid no heed. The witch ran inside and slammed the door, but the revenants marched right through the walls.

Inside the house, shots fired, and men screamed in terror.

Seconds later, an eerie silence descended.

One of the ghosts walked through the wall and stood facing them on the porch. By his uniform, Jake guessed he had been the commander of the ghostly raiders. The ghost gave a curt nod as if to indicate the completion of their mission, then faded to nothing.

Storm and Drangosavich rounded the corner of the building and kicked in the door, guns raised. Albert hung back, and Jake saw that

Spark of Destiny

his sleeve was bloodied, and he cradled his arm close to his chest. Jake heard Storm cursing, and then the two agents emerged.

"They're all dead—and not a mark on most of them," Storm told them. "What the hell was that?"

"Liliana sicced the crew of the *HMS Centurion* on the Spaniards, I suspect," Jake told him. "The ghosts have wanted vengeance for four hundred years. I guess they got what they came for."

Luis beamed with pride. "That's my sister."

Rick looked at Luis with concern. "Did Escarra's death break the curse?"

"Curse?" Jake glanced between the two men. Rick gave a quick explanation.

"Elian will know," Luis said with confidence. "But I felt a shift when Escarra died, so I think it broke the spell. Elian is a stronger witch, so he can fix it if there's anything left."

Jake turned to Luis and Rick. "Is there anything important to retrieve from the bunker—besides Cortez?"

Luis shook his head. "No. Anything that came from the *Vincente* is in the bag. Apologies, but I made a point to be sure that everything they gave me I assembled wrong."

Rick clapped him on the back. "I'm sure Adam can help figure it out. You two are going to get along famously."

"Adam, who?" Luis asked.

"A friend of ours, Adam Farber."

"What? You know Adam Farber?" Luis's eyes widened, and his mouth gaped in surprise.

"Guessing that you've heard of him?" Rick laughed.

"What self-respecting inventor doesn't know of Adam Farber?" Luis grumbled before Jake interrupted.

"What happened?" Jake turned to Albert.

"It's a graze," Albert assured him with a rueful glance at his injured arm. "Not too bad."

Jake glanced at Storm for confirmation. "He might need a few stitches, and he ought to clean it well, but he didn't get hit badly."

Jake insisted on using a piece of Albert's torn shirt to bind the

239

wound. "We'll get a poultice on that as soon as we get back to Calusa Key so it doesn't go sour. Don't take chances."

Storm and Drangosavich went through the wooden buildings and checked the remaining bunker to make sure nothing had been overlooked and no stragglers remained. By now the fire in the other cement building had died down to embers. In the distance a golden glow and sparks lit the sky from where the airship had crashed. Ben had thoroughly smashed the Gatling guns, so there was no worry about them falling into the hands of anyone desperate enough to try to use the base again.

"You're sure this 'air boat' of yours works?" Jake asked Luis, skepticism clear as they maneuvered the craft to the water.

"It was my escape plan, so I'm certain of it," Luis assured him.

"Where's Ben?" Kovach looked around for the *werkman*.

"I saw him head back when the ghosts showed up," Elian replied. "I imagine that he and the turtles are on their way to your inventor friend by now."

Luis and Rick explained about Escarra's curse.

Elian checked Luis over thoroughly. "It's gone," he assured them. "No traces left." He cleared his throat. "You might want to put off mentioning that to Liliana until she's over the shock of everything that's happened."

"Take Albert with you," Jake told Luis and Rick. "Albert knows where the rendezvous point is. We'll meet you there." They headed for the boat, carrying the heavy bag with the salvaged parts between them.

Storm and Drangosavich rejoined the others and looked out over the carnage.

"What about the bodies?" Jake asked.

Storm sighed. "We'll take Cortez back for questioning. He's trussed up well enough he won't give anyone trouble—unless he wants to be thrown overboard to the gators."

"No one is going to miss a crew of pirates," Drangosavich said in a matter-of-fact tone. "And since this is supposedly a 'lost' fort, there shouldn't be anyone else coming through here. It was decommissioned, so it's not government property. I suspect the alligators and vultures will take care of the remains even if we don't bother dumping the bodies in the swamp."

Jake couldn't come up with a reason to argue that suggestion. "Guess we're done then. That was…one for the nightmares."

Epilogue

"You're alive!" Nicki shrieked and hurtled toward Rick, clasping him in a hug that knocked the wind out of him, before kissing him on the cheek. "I was never going to forgive you if you got killed."

"Glad I didn't disappoint." Rick hugged her back.

Liliana's exclamations in rapid-fire Spanish greeted Luis, who let his sister smother him in an embrace.

Jake, Adam, Elian, Storm, Drangosavich, and Ben trooped in behind them, hanging back to let Rick and Luis enjoy their welcome.

"We are equally happy to have you back in good shape," Conroy told them, and Edward nodded in agreement.

"And believe me, we're happy to be here," Rick told him.

After the battle at Fort Harrell, they had returned to Calusa Key with the wreckers. Between Elian's magic and the salvage crew doctor, Albert's wound was quickly dealt with, leaving no permanent damage and only a minor scar.

They'd spent the night with the Boyer clan and had been up until dawn celebrating both their win against the pirates and their survival with Cuban rum and cigars as well as an impromptu feast of boiled shrimp, fried conch fritters, and fresh oysters.

A headache suggested Rick might have had more rum than necessary, and while he had enjoyed the cigars at the time, his mouth tasted like ash. He'd kept pace with the others, egged on by Ralph and Albert, but right now he never wanted to see another oyster.

They had slept late and woke to the smell of strong black coffee and a brunch of fresh fruit, guava turnovers, eggs, and cold shrimp. When they took their leave of the wreckers late in the afternoon, it was with plenty of backslaps and promises to work together again.

Rick wouldn't have minded sleeping for the rest of the day, but he knew that after the phone call Jake had made in the wee hours to let everyone at the compound know they were okay, Nicki and Liliana would be fretting over any further delay.

"Sit down, eat, and tell us everything," Liliana said as Conroy ushered them into the reclaimed dining room, where there was a table large enough for everyone. Ben took his place in the corner, sporting a few more dents and scratches from their foray into the swamp, but was otherwise undamaged.

"When we called to let everyone at the house know Luis was safe and the danger was over, our cook made a huge paella and brought it over," Liliana added.

Conroy and Edward provided plates filled with the spicy seafood and a rice dish for everyone. Pitchers were filled with sangria to celebrate, followed by Liliana's Cuban coffee.

Luis told his story about being captured by Cortez and taken first to a place in Key West and then to the base in the Everglades.

Rick filled in his part from the time he'd been kidnapped aboard the *Diligence* until the rescuers arrived.

Nicki and Liliana recounted the action aboard the *Allegheny Princess*, leaving Jake and the two DSI agents to finish with the fight at the swamp base.

"Where's Cortez?" Nicki asked. "You didn't bring that awful man here, did you?"

Storm shook his head. "No. He's under guard in the Key West jail until we can get him on a train back to New Pittsburgh. Elian warded the cell just in case Cortez actually did have a bit of magic on his own, or sympathizers that might try to free him. He'll go to prison for a long time—after we've had a chance to learn more about his connections and customers."

"Are you going to take the *Vincente's* cargo with you?" Adam spoke up, and his expression made his opinion clear.

"Funny thing about that cargo," Drangosavich said. "According to our report, the few damaged pieces that had been reclaimed from the wreck were lost in the swamp during the fight with Cortez, as were any old relics. Total loss. Such a pity." His droll tone was at odds with the wry smile that quirked up at the corner of his mouth.

Adam brightened like a kid at Christmas. "That's fantastic. I mean, what a shame."

Rick shot a quizzical look at Drangosavich. "Why?"

Storm and Drangosavich exchanged a glance. Storm leaned forward. "I don't trust the Spanish—or the Americans—not to misuse the technology or the magic. It's not safe until we actually know what the pieces do—and maybe not even then. In the wrong hands, it could escalate and prolong this war. Not to mention what summoning sea monsters would do to international trade. Without the advantages of the *Vincente's* cargo, our sources suspect the fight with Spain will be over before the end of the year anyway, with a fizzle instead of a bang. That's reason enough not to fuel the fire."

"We've told you about all the major players who are dogging Sombra's heels to get experimental technology," Drangosavich picked up the story. "Drogo Veles and plenty of others would love to snatch the relics. I suspect that includes most if not all of the witch dynasties since they're always looking to one-up each other."

"It's not possible to keep someone from recreating what Sombra lost—but that will take time. It will slow down how quickly the technology gets distributed. And it gives our side a head start figuring out how to stay a jump ahead," Drangosavich added with a pointed look at Adam. "Since the 'lost' technology is being shipped here—along with the occult items—for safekeeping."

"Hey, Luis. I've got some time before I'm due back at Tesla-Westinghouse," Adam said with a mischievous grin. "Want to set up in the warehouse here and work on the salvage tech together?"

"I'd love to," Luis responded immediately. "What Edison-Bell doesn't know won't hurt them."

"Let me know if you need an extra set of hands." Rick bit back the laugh at Adam's expression. It didn't take keen observation to see that the two inventors were quite enamored of each other.

"The more, the merrier." Adam's delivery was deadpan, but the scowl said volumes.

"What about the crew of the *HMS Centurion*?" Rick remembered the ghosts that had saved their asses in the swamp.

"They are avenged," Liliana replied. "The spirits were pleased to discover that stopping the pirates would severely damage Spain's prospects in the war. The ghosts have moved on."

"I had a conversation with Harry Boyer during the celebration at the wrecker compound," Elian said. "There may be other opportunities for Liliana and me to work with their salvage crew on ships with haunted or magical objects. I'm intrigued by the possibilities."

"And we hope your involvement with Brand and Desmet also continues," Jake hurried to add.

"We would be honored," Liliana replied.

Rick frowned. "Hey, where's Cullan and the *Princess*?"

"Probably back in New Pittsburgh by now," Nicki replied. "The ship didn't get damaged in the fight—thanks to Liliana and her ghosts. They're what caused the pirate airship to wreck, although I was ready in the gun turret, just in case. Cullan headed back right after he dropped Lili and me off."

"Was Ramon Escarra really from the Hispaniola witch dynasty?" Jake asked. "And is that going to open a new can of worms?"

Storm leaned back in his chair. "From the call I got this morning, the patriarch of the Escarra family disavows Ramon and his actions. He claims Ramon disobeyed his father to throw in his lot with Cortez and had been disinherited." He smiled. "Interestingly enough, while the head warlock washed his hands of Ramon, he didn't deny an interest in relics that would summon powered-up sea monsters."

After the meal, they all headed into the parlor for a round of scotch and a chance to let the food settle.

Rick thought Jake looked deep in thought. "What's on your mind? We're supposed to be celebrating, in case you missed that."

"The *thing* we heard at the fort, the one that killed the pirates who ran into the swamp—do you think it really was a swamp ape?" Jake asked. He and Albert had debated that question late into the night, with the wreckers contributing what they knew from legend and old stories.

"Why not?" Rick replied. "The Everglades are huge and mostly empty of people, just like the big forests where people think Bigfoot lives. There's plenty of room for creatures to roam around and not be seen."

"When I was in the bunker, I'd hear the big guns fire now and then, usually late at night. The guards said there were monsters in the swamp and that they carried off anyone who went too far from the base," Luis volunteered.

"I figured that was what Boss told them to keep them under control, but the guard swore he'd seen someone get dragged away by something that looked like a tall, skinny gray ape with arms and legs that were too long for its body," Luis added. "That doesn't prove anything, but the guard certainly believed."

"We've seen more than our share of cryptids and creatures, even back in the city," Rick said. "What's one more?"

Jake groaned. "I just remembered the cursed doll and the other bad mojo stuff that got slipped aboard the airlift. I guess we need to figure out what to do with all that now that the shooting part is done. We can't just leave it locked up forever."

Rick sipped his scotch and enjoyed the burn. "Andreas and Renate Thalberg could sort all that out in a trice, I'm sure. Even faster if we can persuade Elian to help."

"Happy to do so," Elian replied. "Although having a few days to catch my breath after all this would be much appreciated."

"See? That was easy," Rick joked.

Jake smiled, but it didn't quite reach his eyes.

Relaxed by the sangria and scotch, filled with good food and unwinding after their recent near-death experiences, the gathering in the parlor segued into recounting past adventures. Rick glanced around and realized that Jake had left the room. He followed and found his friend on the house's wide front porch, glass in hand, leaning against the railing and staring up at the night sky.

"Not in the mood for a party?" Rick asked, standing close enough to bump shoulders.

Jake shrugged, a sure sign he wasn't quite ready to share what was on his mind.

"We won—and this time we didn't blow up nearly as much stuff," Rick said. "Didn't have as many casualties, either. That's worth celebrating right there."

"When the pirates grabbed you and took you away in that airship, I didn't think we'd ever see you again," Jake finally admitted, keeping his gaze trained on the horizon. "I've known you all my life, and then you were gone, and I didn't know what to do."

"You did exactly what you needed to do," Rick affirmed. "And it worked. I'm back, safe and sound, and so is Luis."

"It could have gone wrong in so many ways."

"That's always true," Rick pointed out.

"Nothing bothers me when we're fighting together," Jake said. "I can be ridiculously brave when I know you've got my back. And it isn't that I didn't trust Miska or Mitch or Jacob, because I do, with my life. Obviously. But none of them are you. It's just—different."

Rick placed a hand on Jake's shoulder. "I understand. Honestly—it's the same for me. I knew I could trust Luis, and we were coming up with a plan to escape. But deep down, I knew that you wouldn't stop until you found us, so I didn't panic. We just had to stay alive until you got there. I never doubted that you'd come for us."

"There wouldn't be a Brand and Desmet without you," Jake said, voice rough with emotion.

"It would be inconvenient having to change the name on everything," Rick replied, intentionally misunderstanding.

Jake gave him a light punch in the arm. "You completely missed the point."

"I get it. Truly, I do," Rick answered, jostling Jake's arm. "But the truth is, the risk goes with the job. Given what we do, the kinds of things we trade in, our type of clients, there's always going to be danger. Unless you're ready to quit—and we're a bit young to retire."

Jake chuckled and shook his head. "Not planning to retire just yet. Your dad would kick my ass. And I know all of that. Tomorrow, I'll be fine. Tonight, all the possibilities, everything that happened…it's just too close."

They clinked glasses. "Then give yourself time to let it go," Rick said. "In the morning, we'll be business as usual. I'm going to have another glass of scotch and watch Luis try to teach Mitch how to play dominoes. Jacob is taking bets."

With that, Rick left his friend at the railing and headed back inside. A lifetime's experience told him that Jake would sift through the fears and battle exhaustion in due time, rebounding to his usual self.

Rick admitted to himself that he was also hiding in the alcohol and company. Later, when everyone else had gone, and the house was quiet, he'd revisit the worst moments in his dreams. They all would, even Mitch and Jacob, he felt sure. *Maybe especially Mitch and Jacob.*

Nicki rose to meet him before he reached the main gathering and slipped her arm through his. "Everything all right?"

Rick gave her a smile that he knew she could see right through. "Of course."

"Fibber."

Rick shrugged. "It didn't happen if you don't talk about it." He hadn't been lying about believing that Jake would mount a rescue. Rick just hadn't been certain that they'd be in time. Locked up in his cell in the swamp base, Rick had envisioned plenty of possibilities, from being spirited off to somewhere in Spain to getting fed to the alligators—or the creatures that lurked in the darkness.

Nicki squeezed his arm. "We're all outrunning the memories, at least for tonight. Come back to the party. Jake will be along in a bit. We can watch Adam and Luis try to out-compliment each other, and maybe if you're lucky, Kovach will lecture you about being careful again." Nicky winked. "Cady will be expecting Jake to call tomorrow and let her know he's not dead."

The thought of Kovach had Rick rubbing his arm. He could still feel where the man had punched him the first minute they'd had alone. Right before he berated him for being careless and worrying everyone, followed by a warning never to do it again because who would Kovach have to annoy if it weren't for Rick. Odd, but Kovach's veiled concern made him feel warm inside.

Rick rejoined the others, enjoying the good-natured teasing and conversation of new friends and seasoned comrades-in-arms like the warmth of a fire to drive away the chill.

He looked around the circle of close friends and found family, the people who had proven their loyalty and shown their bravery, and realized that there was nowhere else he'd rather be.

Tonight we celebrate cheating the ferryman. Tomorrow will take care of itself.

Afterword

Spark of Destiny picks up several months after the action in *Iron & Blood*, where we first meet Jake, Rick, Nicki, and many of the other characters. Mitch and Jacob have plenty of additional adventures in the Storm & Fury collection of short stories and novellas that are "extra episodes" about their cases. You'll also see Mitch, Jacob, Renate, and other characters in the Sharps & Springfield series by Gail's alter ego, Morgan Brice, beginning with *Peacemaker*.

Watch for more Jake Desmet Adventures!

Acknowledgments

Thank you so much to our editor, Jean Rabe, and our wonderful cover artist, Lou Harper. Thanks also to the Shadow Alliance street team for their support and encouragement, our fantastic beta readers and the ever-growing legion of ARC readers who help spread the word. And, of course, to our "convention gang" of fellow authors for making road trips, panels, and the writing life fun.

About the Authors

Gail Z. Martin writes urban fantasy, epic fantasy, and steampunk for Orbit Books, Falstaff Books, SOL Publishing, and Darkwind Press. Urban fantasy series include *Deadly Curiosities* and the *Night Vigil*. Epic fantasy series include *Darkhurst, The Chronicles of The Necromancer, The Fallen Kings Cycle, The Ascendant Kingdoms Saga,* and *The Assassins of Landria*. Under her urban fantasy MM paranormal romance pen name of Morgan Brice, she has six series (*Witchbane, Badlands, Kings of the Mountain, Fox Hollow, Treasure Trail,* and *Sharps and Springfield*) with more books and series to come.

Larry N. Martin is the author of the sci-fi adventure novel *Salvage Rat,* and the portal fantasy series, *The Splintered Crown, A Tankards and Heroes novel*. He is the co-author (with Gail Z. Martin) of the *Spells, Salt, & Steel: New Templar Knights* series; the Steampunk series *Iron & Blood;* and a collection of short stories and novellas: *The Storm & Fury Adventures* set in the Iron & Blood universe. He is also the co-author (with Gail) of the *Wasteland Marshals* series and the *Joe Mack - Shadow Council* series from Falstaff Books.

Find them online at www.GailZMartin.com, on Facebook.com/WinterKingdoms, at www.DisquietingVisions.com blog, on www.Pinterest.com/Gzmartin on Goodreads https://www.goodreads.com/GailZMartin and BookBub https://www.bookbub.com/profile/gail-z-martin. Never miss out on the news and new releases—sign up for our newsletter: http://eepurl.com/dd5XLj

Join our Shadow Alliance street team so you never miss a new release! Get the scoop first + giveaways + fun stuff! Also where we get our beta readers and Launch Team! https://www.facebook.com/groups/435812789942761

Support Indie Authors

When you support independent authors, you help influence what kind of books you'll see more of and what types of stories will be available because the authors themselves decide which books to write, not a big publishing conglomerate. Independent authors are local creators, supporting their families with the books they produce. Thank you for supporting independent authors and small press fiction!

Also by Gail Z. Martin & Larry N. Martin

Jake Desmet Adventures
Iron & Blood

Spark of Destiny

Storm & Fury: Collection

Spells, Salt, & Steel: New Templars
Spells, Salt, & Steel: Season One

Spells, Salt, & Steel: Season Two

Wasteland Marshals
Wasteland Marshals Volume One

Joe Mack: Shadow Council Archives
Forged: Joe Mack Adventures Volume One

More by Gail Z. Martin

Darkhurst
Scourge

Vengeance

Reckoning

Ascendant Kingdoms
Ice Forged

Reign of Ash

War of Shadows

Shadow and Flame

Convicts and Exiles: Collection

Chronicles of the Necromancer / Fallen Kings Cycle

The Shadowed Path: Jonmarc Vahanian Collection

The Dark Road: Jonmarc Vahanian Collection

The Summoner

The Blood King

Dark Haven

Dark Lady's Chosen

The Sworn

The Dread

Deadly Curiosities

Deadly Curiosities

Vendetta

Tangled Web

Inheritance

Legacy

Trifles and Folly: Collection

Trifles and Folly 2: Collection

Trifles and Folly 3: Collection

Assassins of Landria

Assassin's Honor

Sellsword's Oath

Fugitive's Vow

Exile's Quest

Outlaw's Vengeance

Night Vigil

Sons of Darkness

C.H.A.R.O.N.

More by Larry N. Martin

Salvage Rat

The Splintered Crown

Printed in Great Britain
by Amazon